# CADAVER & QUEEN

***Cadaver & Queen***
is Alisa Kwitney's first title
with Harlequin TEEN

# ALISA KWITNEY

# CADAVER & QUEEN

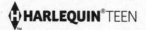

ISBN-13: 978-1-335-47046-1

Cadaver & Queen

For Matthew, Matan and Matt, child, youth and man.
We are all constantly reinventing ourselves
by stitching together the old and the new.

And in memory of my friends Suzanne Levine and John Gould.

# PROLOGUE

THE ROOM SLOWLY CAME INTO FOCUS: WHITE tiled walls, a white enamel bowl on a small table covered by a sterile white cotton cloth and set with gleaming steel and brass surgical instruments. The only splash of color was a bottle of scarlet blood hanging upside down from a hook. A nurse in a starched white cap checked the bottle's rubber tubing and then walked away, her ankle-length skirts rustling as she passed.

Where was he? Victor tried to rouse himself, but he still felt thickheaded and vague, and even though his eyes were open, he was utterly disoriented. Why was he lying flat on his back, almost naked, in this white room? There was nothing but a thin sheet covering him below the waist. After a moment, he realized that the room was an operating theater, designed with a high ceiling, low-hanging lights and tiered seats so that students could observe surgeons at work without getting in their way.

His mouth felt dry, and there was a metallic taste in the

back of his throat. Copper or blood. Something bad had happened to him, but what?

His mind flashed on disjointed images—a bedraggled dollymop, pale cheeks rouged and neck striped with dirt, singing off-key as she swigged from a bottle of cheap gin; an old woman's swollen and arthritic hand sparkling with jeweled rings as she stroked a Pomeranian lapdog. None of it made any sense, yet his skin prickled with unease. And cold. The room was chilly, and his bare chest was pebbled with gooseflesh.

There was a squeak of wheels behind him, accompanied by the murmuring of male voices from above. "By Jove," said one, "she's a looker." The nurse must have returned, wheeling in some more equipment. He recognized the approving voices as belonging to his fellow medical students, who must be watching from the gallery, just out of his line of sight. *They must be here to watch my surgery.* He felt lightheaded; for a vertiginous moment, the room seemed to tilt and spin around him.

He heard a woman's light footsteps behind him, then smelled the vinegar odor of Lister's disinfectant.

*Help me.*

He tried to raise his hand, but nothing happened. Alarm surged through him as he tried again. What was wrong with his arms? Lying prone, he couldn't see his right arm, but out of the corner of his eye he caught a glimpse of his left, which had been positioned at an angle away from his body and secured with a restraint. He didn't feel any pain in either limb, though. He didn't feel anything at all. An instant later, he realized that he couldn't feel his legs, either.

He could not turn his head.

He tried to call out, but no sound came from his mouth. His heart set up a wild gallop, but no other part of him moved.

His brain filled with the animal impulse to search for an escape route, but his gaze remained fixed on the same section of the white room.

*I can't move my eyes.*

His mind flashed to his teachings. Cranial nerves III, IV and VI—oculomotor, trochlear and abducens—all completely paralyzed. He was as immobile as a corpse.

"Good afternoon, gentlemen." Dr. Grimbald, the head of surgery and Victor's adviser, nodded to the students in the gallery as he entered the room. As usual, he had waxed the tips of his mustache so they curled up, but his thin mouth was compressed into a tight line.

Victor's pulse slowed and steadied. If he needed surgery, there was no one better than Grimbald in England, possibly in the world. But what sort of operation did he require? Any cervical injury that left him unable to move his head and neck should also affect his diaphragm, but he was still breathing on his own. So there was reason to hope: he didn't have a spinal cord injury. He might not be permanently damaged. Could he have ingested some sort of poison? Curare was sometimes used as an anesthetic, and it could cause temporary paralysis.

He racked his brain, trying to remember if he had been handling curare, but the last thing he could recall was studying in the library. Henry had tried to tempt him to go back to their room for a whiskey, saying, "What's the use of swotting? You know you'll end up with top marks, you always do. Bloody prize pupil. I think you should slack it for one exam and give the rest of us a chance."

But…maybe there was something else that had happened after that. *Damn it.* Why couldn't he remember?

"Nurse," said Grimbald. "Do you mind telling me what

this is doing here?" He held up the rubber face mask for Clover's portable regulating ether inhaler.

The nurse looked confused. "It's for the anesthesia, sir."

The waxed tips of Grimbald's mustache seemed to twitch with annoyance. "Why on earth would I need anesthesia? You were told to prepare for a Bio-Mechanical procedure."

For a moment Victor was certain that he had misheard. After all, living people weren't turned into Bio-Mechanicals. That procedure was reserved for the deceased.

"I… I must have made a mistake, Doctor," said the nurse, giving Victor a startled look. "I didn't read the chart carefully enough. I'm terribly sorry."

"I don't want apologies, I want action. Where is the Galvanic Reanimator?"

The nurse hung her head. "It's still in Professor Makepiece's laboratory."

"Go and fetch it immediately."

*They think I'm dead!* Victor couldn't breathe; the room darkened around the edges of his vision. *Stop it*, he told himself. *Breathe.*

If he wanted to save himself from becoming a science experiment, he had to gather his wits, and fast. After a moment, his head cleared, and he saw the nurse bobbing her head and walking away as quickly as her long skirts permitted. Grimbald muttered something about incompetence.

*Please*, thought Victor, staring up at the man who had been his academic adviser for three years. *Look at me.* Grimbald had always said to observe everything and assume nothing. "Too often," he told his students, "we see only what we expect to see." *Can't you see that I'm breathing? The ulnar pulse at my wrist may be too faint to detect, but try my carotid. My heart is beating. My pupils would react to light.* He tried to blink as a signal that he was conscious, but even that small movement was beyond him.

Then something wonderful happened. Grimbald frowned and leaned over him. "Victor?" For a glorious instant he thought he was saved, and then Grimbald went on speaking and extinguished all hope. "My boy, I don't know if there really is any such thing as a soul, but if you can hear me, I hope you know that I am so sorry. But a surgeon cannot afford to be a sentimentalist." So there was to be no last-minute reprieve. The sharp sting of terror was turning into something deeper, an ache of anguished sadness for all he was leaving behind, and for all the possible futures he might have had.

Stepping back, Grimbald raised his voice so it would carry to the gallery. "Gentlemen, I know some of you knew the deceased. He may have sat next to you in class, or shared your table at dinner, or locked shoulders with you in a scrum out on the rugby field. Some of you may have qualms about seeing one of your own cut up like so much meat. But you are here to learn, and I do not want to see a single one of you avert his eyes."

He couldn't see the students in the gallery, but he wondered if Henry was among them. Victor hoped he was. It was comforting to think that his friend was here, by his side, right till the end.

"Now, most of the time, the cadavers we receive are not in optimal condition, and it may take up to five bodies to create one working Bio-Mechanical. This is an unusually fresh specimen, and in remarkably good shape. The only unusable part is the left forearm." Grimbald pulled back the sheet, and although Victor couldn't see anything, he felt a prickle of sensation where his skin was exposed to the cool air. "I'm not sure how much you gentlemen can see from the gallery,"

Grimbald went on, "but I'm looking at several deep lacerations and extensive nerve damage."

*Lacerations? Damage?* The words summoned a flash of
memory: a scalpel, slicing down at him while he grappled
with someone, and his left arm coming up instinctively to
deflect the blow.

Before he could remember anything more, Grimbald was
speaking again. "Rather than lose any more time waiting for
the correct equipment to arrive, I might as well demonstrate
the correct limb grafting technique." Grimbald raised the
bone saw in his bare hand. "Now, remember, this is not the
way to perform an amputation on a living patient." There was
a ripple of laughter from the gallery, and then the saw came
down, and oh, *dear God.* Whatever had made him numb was
wearing off. Inside his head, Victor screamed as the blade's
sharp teeth sliced through the layers of skin and muscle and
bit into the bone of his forearm.

The room faded to gray and then to black. His last conscious thought was that he would rather stay with the light
and the pain, as long as it came with an explanation.

*What happened to me?*

# 1

STANDING ON TIPTOE, LIZZIE TRIED TO SEE over the barricade of dark suits. At five foot four, she had never considered herself short, but the thirty or so other students were all men, and even the smallest of them had a few inches on her. On the bright side, at least they were indoors, so they weren't all wearing top hats with their formal dark cutaway morning coats.

"What do you think is taking so long?"

Lizzie turned, but the boyishly slender young man standing beside her was speaking to his companion, a handsome fellow with olive skin and dark curly hair.

"It's a display of power," said the handsome one, sounding amused as he leaned casually against a marble side table. "We're meant to understand just how low first years rank on the totem pole."

That made sense. The room itself was big and imposing—vaulted ceilings, stained-glass windows and an enormous scrolled-iron chandelier. Even though the sun was shining outside, the air inside was cool and dry and slightly scented with sweet candle wax. In other parts of the school, the flickering gaslight from wall sconces had been replaced by Edison's modern incandescent lamps, but this room had never been converted to gas, let alone to electricity. It gave the impression that this was a place of ancient rituals and arcane secrets, rather than an institution dedicated to the pursuit of science and medicine.

The grandfather clock in the corner of the room chimed, and the hum of excited conversation died down. Lizzie could hear footsteps, but no matter how she craned her neck, she couldn't see who had entered the room.

After a moment, conversation picked back up again; whoever it was, it wasn't the head of medicine.

"False alarm," said the slender young man. He caught her glance for a moment before quickly looking away. *Oh, for crying out loud*, she thought. *I may not be a raving beauty, but I'm not a monster, either.* She had left her room feeling professional yet attractive in a crisp, high-collared white shirtwaist blouse with a little navy bow in front, and a neatly tailored navy wool skirt that showed a daring amount of her buff leather lace-up ankle boots. Her brown hair was naturally thick and wavy, so all she had to do was pile it into a high bun to achieve a fashionable Gibson-girl effect. If this had been the lobby of a theater or a museum, she felt certain that each and every one of these gentlemen would have at least acknowledged her presence. Yet here in this bastion of male power and privilege, she was invisible.

"Pardon me, miss." The boyish young man turned to her and smiled. So, she wasn't invisible after all. "I know we haven't been properly introduced, but I wonder if I may be of some assistance. Are you in the nursing school? I'm afraid it's located in a different wing."

Lizzie stifled a sigh. "Thank you, but I'm not a nursing student." That made three times this morning. Perhaps it had been a mistake, choosing Ingold over the London School of Medicine for Women. The women's school had offered a full scholarship as well as the chance to live in one of the world's great cities, but no, she had elected to strand herself just north of nowhere. Wild, windswept moors might sound romantic in *Wuthering Heights*, but the reality was rather bleak, especially when you were isolated socially as well as geographically.

Still, Ingold held all the other cards—prestige, academic excellence, the chance to follow in her late father's footsteps. On the other hand, here she was, apparently doomed to repeat the same conversation for the next four years. That was the problem with choosing a college; by the time you discovered the school's true face, you were already married to it.

"So...are you visiting one of these lucky chaps, then?" He gave her a smile that must have melted teachers' hearts back in grammar school.

"No," Lizzie said firmly. "I'm here because I'm a medical student. Like you."

"A medical student! Are you really?" Then, looking a bit flustered, he amended, "I mean, how remarkable. And your accent—American?"

She nodded, trying to decide whether this was genuine interest or some sly form of English mockery.

"Sorry, how tedious. Everyone must be pestering you with the same two questions. I'll refrain from asking you which part of the colonies you're from, how's that? I'm William Frankenstein, by the way."

Not mockery, she decided, or at least not aimed at her.

"Elizabeth Lavenza." She held out her gloved hand, the way a boy would have done. Will shook it without hesitation.

"Very pleased to meet you, Miss Lavenza."

"Stop flirting with the nurse, Will."

Will looked back at the young man leaning nonchalantly against the marble side table. "She's not a nurse, Byram."

"Oh?" Byram seemed amused by this. "What are you, then? You look too healthy to be a patient." His smile made Lizzie wish she'd worn a jacket over her blouse.

Will punched his friend in the arm. "She's a medical student, you cretin."

The cretin raised his eyebrows. "In that case, perhaps *I* can be the patient."

Lizzie felt her face flushing with embarrassment. Despite being a brunette, she blushed like a redhead, in great big scarlet splotches. "Something tells me you're incurable." As she turned, she heard a snort of laughter behind her, which made her muscles seize up. She had to concentrate very hard on making her legs move.

*Maybe I'm not up to this.* It was the insidious little voice that kept whispering in her ear. Not the work; she knew she was more than capable of handling *that*. She was less certain she could cope with all the people here. Ever since she had walked through Ingold's front gate forty-eight hours earlier, she had been constantly surrounded by people, and she had never felt more alone.

There were two sharp raps from a gavel, as startling as gunshots, and the room fell silent.

"Good morning, gentlemen."

Lizzie couldn't see who was speaking, but his full baritone carried like an opera singer's to where she stood.

"I am Ambrose Moulsdale, head of medicine, and it gives

me great pleasure to welcome you all to the Ingold Academy of Medicine and Bio-Mechanical Science."

The last word, proclaimed in that ringing, orotund voice, echoed from the paneled walls.

"You are now officially members of a very select group," Moulsdale continued. "For while there are many fine medical schools in England, there is no place that compares to Ingold. You will receive opportunities here that are available nowhere else."

The select group all pressed more tightly together and leaned in, anxious not to miss a single word.

*All right*, thought Lizzie. *Time to speak up for yourself, my girl.*

"I beg your pardon." She tapped a medical student on the shoulder. "Could you move over a little, so I can see?"

"Sorry," said the student, without bothering to turn around. "There really isn't room."

"You could *make* room."

"Hush!"

Lizzie had no idea where Americans had gotten the idea that the English were polite. Certainly not from the English. At the other side of the room, she spotted a small opening in the wall of masculine backs and moved to claim it.

Now she could see that Moulsdale was a tall, stout, middle-aged man with doughy cheeks, small, dark eyes and a trim, salt-and-pepper beard. Tucking his thumbs into his waistcoat pockets, he beamed out at his audience.

"Everything you have ever done in your lives has led you here, to this moment. Take a minute to savor it."

And just like that, Lizzie felt all her anger and upset drain away. She took a deep breath and realized that she hadn't really permitted herself to enjoy any of this experience. Admittedly, she had read her acceptance letter so many times that she had memorized it, but she had never stopped worrying that something would go wrong. She had pictured herself finally arriving at the school, just to be told that it was all a clerical error and she would have to go back home.

No one had told her to pack her bags yet, but she hadn't had one carefree moment since her ship had steamed away from New York harbor.

Moulsdale had changed all that with a single sentence. *Savor it.* She found herself smiling at her fellow classmates, barely registering the bemused glances they gave her in return. What did she care if they thought her presence here peculiar? Lizzie just wished her father could have lived long enough to learn that all his years of teaching her biology and chemistry and physics had paid off. Most people thought her desire to study medicine was bizarre enough. The fact that she was interested in designing prosthetic limbs put her in a category reserved for the truly freakish. If she couldn't find work after graduation, she could probably join a circus and display herself alongside the bearded lady and the world's smallest man. Her father had been the only person who thought she was wonderful instead of odd.

But here was Moulsdale, conjuring a future in which she and her fellow classmates would accomplish marvelous things. They would transform the way wars were fought with new and improved Bio-Mechanical soldiers. They would save countless lives. They would, by God's own grace, conquer death itself.

It was then, with a showman's talent for manipulating an audience, that Moulsdale's tone turned somber. "*Some* of you, that is. Not all of you. I know, I know, each of you is used to being top of his class at school. But what's considered exceptional at other institutions is merely a passing grade at Ingold.

Look to your right and to your left." On her right, there was a short, plump boy who looked too young to shave; on her left, a lantern-jawed fellow whose mouth seemed too small for his face. "One of you will either drop out or be dropped before graduation." Suddenly the air seemed to crackle with invisible currents of ambition and fear.

"Guess *I'm* safe," said the fellow with the heavy jaw, looking right at Lizzie. Before she could even think of a suitable retort, Moulsdale was speaking again.

"You have chosen a very demanding program. In addition to lectures, you will be expected to observe patients from the very beginning of your education, and every student must do some laboratory research before selecting his specialty. And whether you ultimately choose the School of Medicine, the School of Surgery or the School of Biological Engineering, Ingold will test you as you have never been tested before. If at any time anything seems to come easily, you may rest assured that you are doing it wrong." Moulsdale clapped his hands. "Right then. Everyone ready? Follow me."

**Z**

THERE WAS A FRANTIC JOSTLING FOR POSITION
as the students stampeded after Moulsdale, stepping out into
a cloistered hallway that protected them from the rain but
not the chill of a Yorkshire morning. Somehow, Lizzie found
herself at the end of the line, and as the last boy to enter the
surgical building didn't bother to hold the heavy door for her,
she had to pull it open with all her body weight and then dart
through the gap before the door slammed shut.

The new students were already crowding eagerly into the
rows between patients' beds, and Lizzie hurried to join them,
earning a disapproving look from a nurse in a starched white
cap.

"Mind your elbow, you great lummox. You made me spill
the patient's dose!"

"Sorry," said Lizzie, hurrying to catch up to the others,
who were congregating around one of the patients' beds.

Like the others in this sick ward, he was a young man,
probably no older than the medical students who surrounded

him. Ingold, Moulsdale explained, had a history of caring for soldiers who had undergone battlefield amputations, like this brave boy who was just one of the many unsung heroes of the Second Boer War. Lizzie nodded and hoped no one was going to ask her anything specific about the conflict. Back in New York, she hadn't even registered that the British were at war, and she had only learned that "the Boer" referred to South Africa when she was on the ocean liner carrying her to England. Even now, she had only the vaguest sense of what the war was about—independence or gold mines or a batch of unruly barbarians rebelling against the queen, depending on whom you asked.

"Now," said Moulsdale, picking up a chart, "this is a particularly interesting case. Private Holden here lost his right arm in the battle of Blood River Poort."

"Royal Rifle Corps," Private Holden said cheerily. "I'd salute, but as you can see I'm missing a bit of equipment." It was difficult to envision the small, wiry man in striped hospital pajamas wearing the dark green uniform of the rifle corps, let alone to picture him on the far side of the world in the South African Republic, fighting Botha's Boer commandos. "The limb was almost completely severed and badly mangled, and our surgeons amputated and closed the wound with a skin flap." Moulsdale pointed to the man's right sleeve, which had been pinned back to reveal a bandaged arm that ended just above the elbow.

"Amputation is such an insufferably *ordinary* injury," whispered Byram. "I was rather hoping we were going to see a Bio-Mechanical."

Moulsdale, apparently not one of those teachers with bat-like hearing, kept right on talking. "Private Holden is well aware that he is no longer in possession of his right hand. In addition, he has the evidence of his own eyes to confirm the fact that he is now an amputee."

"I knows what I am," said Holden, sounding defensive. "A useless cripple."

Moulsdale did not correct him. "Yet Private Holden persists in telling us that he suffers from severe pain in his right hand, even though it is no longer attached to his person."

*Phantom limb pain*, thought Lizzie with excitement. Phantom limb pain fascinated her. She had been studying up on it for the past two years.

"I ain't claimin' nuffink," said Holden. "It's true."

There was a low buzz of speculation from the assembled students.

"And there you have it," said Moulsdale. "What, then, would you suggest as a treatment for Private Holden?"

One boy raised his hand. "Perhaps the wound requires cauterization?"

Moulsdale shook his head. "A sound treatment for infection, but there is no sign of sepsis in or around the wound site. Anyone else?" He turned to Will, who was not raising his hand. "How about you? No ideas at all?"

"Er," said Will.

"Yes?"

Everyone looked at Will, who was watching Moulsdale the way a rabbit watches a cat. "Um. P-perhaps…"

"Go on."

Will took a deep breath. "Perhaps a resectioning of the arm? The scar tissue might be causing pressure on the nerves."

"Ah." Moulsdale put his thumbs in the pockets of his waistcoat. "An interesting suggestion. Yet a more observant person might notice the presence of a bandage, which implies recent surgery. Recent surgery, of course, implies an absence of scar tissue." Moulsdale shook his head. "I must say, I expected a bit more from a Frankenstein."

Will looked as though he'd been slapped.

"Your brother was a fine young man, and an outstanding student. A loss to us all, my boy. A tragic loss." Moulsdale's supple voice grew hoarse with suppressed emotion, but his small, dark eyes did not reflect much feeling. "Let us hope that you can live up to his example." Moulsdale turned back to the group. "Any other suggestions? Come on, lads, this is your chance to impress me."

No one volunteered. *They don't know the answer*, she realized, *but I do—recalibrate the electromagnetic fields*. Stuck in the back, Lizzie raised her hand, but of course Moulsdale couldn't see her.

"No one at all? Ah, yes, you, young man. What is your name?"

"Outhwaite, sir," said Lantern-jaw. "Why not take some of those special photographs that see through the body and show the bones?"

"Not a bad idea at all. In fact, we have already taken an image using Röntgen rays. The film showed nothing amiss." Moulsdale looked around. "Anyone else?"

"Pardon me, Professor Moulsdale." Lizzie's voice seemed to echo in the big room, too loud, too American, too female.

Moulsdale raised his eyebrows. "I'm afraid that we do not solicit the opinions of our nursing students."

"I'm not a nursing student, Professor." Her heart was pounding too quickly, making it difficult to speak. "I'm a medical student."

Moulsdale frowned at her. "Are you indeed?"

"Yes, sir. And I have an idea. First, may I inquire as to the current whereabouts of Mr. Holden's missing arm?"

"It has been disposed of," said Moulsdale. "Why, what do you suggest? It cannot be reattached. The nerve endings were completely severed."

Her pulse steadied; she was on familiar ground here. "Yes, I understand that the *physical* connections were broken. But there is also the etheric body, composed of subtle, vital and electromagnetic energies. In Private Holden's case, his physical arm was amputated, but his etheric arm was not."

Moulsdale stroked his beard and then nodded. "That is correct, Miss…"

"Lavenza. Elizabeth Lavenza."

Moulsdale raised his eyebrows; clearly, he recognized her name. "As Miss Lavenza explained, the patient's pain arises from electromagnetic currents, invisible to the eye, impervious to the scalpel and to all our modern medicines. In such cases, all a physician can do is alleviate discomfort with the use of opiates." Turning to the rest of the students, he added, "The lesson here, you see, is that we must know our limitations."

"Begging your pardon," said Lizzie, amazed at her own audacity, "but my father believed there was a treatment for phantom limb pain."

"My father believed in garden fairies," quipped Byram. "Particularly when he'd been nipping at the gin."

"Your father, however, was not one of the most brilliant scientists of his generation," said Moulsdale, who appeared to only enjoy jokes when he was the one making them. "He was in my class at school, you know. Always tinkering, even then. I was very sad to hear about his passing. Great man, Lavenza. Never got the appreciation he deserved."

All eyes turned to Lizzie again, but she could feel the change in attitude as if it were a wind blowing from a new direction. Her new classmates might not like her any better, but now they couldn't just dismiss her.

"Sorry, Professor," said Byram, not sounding in the least repentant. With his curly dark hair and arched eyebrows, he looked a bit like the naughty, nymph-fondling satyr she had seen in an oil painting at the Hoffman House hotel in New York City.

Moulsdale looked smug rather than irritated as he addressed the group. "Let this be a lesson, gentlemen. Do not make assumptions. Now, as for you, young lady—just what would the estimable Dr. Lavenza have suggested?"

"Well, the problem is that the etheric body and the physical body are not in alignment. The answer is to recalibrate the electromagnetic fields. It would be easier to do if we still had the severed limb, but it's still possible."

"You mean, galvanize the man with electrical current?" Moulsdale stroked his double chins.

"In essence," said Lizzie, "yes."

"Sir?" It was Outhwaite, of course, ready with an objection. "Wouldn't there be a risk of electrocuting the patient?"

"A fair objection," said Moulsdale. "Though perhaps, if Professor Makepiece set the Galvanic Reanimator to its lowest setting, and concentrated the galvanic current in the area of the missing limb…"

The Galvanic Reanimator was the device used to create Bio-Mechanicals. The school's literature proclaimed it "the newest, most powerful and scientifically advanced model in the world!" From what Lizzie had read, its lowest setting would probably reduce Private Holden's stump to a knob of broiled flesh.

"I don't really think—" she began, but Private Holden's shout of "Oi!" drowned her out.

"'Ang on a sec!" Holden sat up straighter in his bed. "Don't I get a say in this? I don't fancy bein' done like a Sunday roast."

"Begging your pardon," Lizzie said, "but the levels of electricity required are extremely mild. There would be no need to use the Galvanic Reanimator. My father invented a device he called an etheric magnetometer, which can deliver a very mild voltage along with a pure violet light, that helps destroy harmful bacterial growth." She didn't bat an eyelash as she lied. Someday, she hoped, she would be able to take credit for her own work, but she was a realist. If people knew the invention was hers, they would dismiss it out of hand.

"An' it really don't 'urt none?" It was hard to believe the man was a wounded veteran. He sounded more like a nervous child.

"I have it in my room, if you'd like to test it out," she said without thinking.

"*Miss* Lavenza." No tolerant amusement in Moulsdale's voice now. "I asked for suggestions. I did *not* hand over the case to a first year student on her first day. We have our own equipment, and thus far, it has proved extremely effective."

The back of her neck went cold. "Sorry, sir."

"Well, I likes the li'l lady's plan." Holden gave Lizzie a wink. "I wants to try the ether whatnotemer. If you give us your word it don't 'urt none, that is." He looked at her inquiringly.

"It doesn't hurt." She looked at Moulsdale apologetically. "I'll stop speaking now."

Moulsdale regarded her for a moment. It struck Lizzie, too late, that the head of medicine hadn't really wanted the first years to impress him. He had wanted to set them up to realize their own vast ignorance, so that he could dazzle them with his great expertise.

She had gotten this first lesson wrong. Totally, horribly wrong.

There were murmurs from the other students. Lizzie took a deep breath and waited for Moulsdale to tell her to pack her bags.

"Very well, then." To Lizzie's astonishment, Moulsdale pulled a gold pocket watch out of his vest and examined it. "You may go fetch the magnetometer from your room. We'll continue on rounds and meet you back here at ten o'clock."

"Yes, sir. Thank you, sir."

"Frankenstein, Byram, you two may accompany Miss Lavenza and render her any assistance she requires." Before Lizzie could say anything, he added, "I know you two won't mind missing out on rounds, since we're only going to look at more insufferably ordinary cases." It seemed that Moulsdale did, in fact, possess bat-like hearing. With a brusque nod, he moved briskly toward the next patient, while the rest of the group scrambled to follow.

How clever, and how cruel. In punishing them, Moulsdale had found a way to punish her as well, by turning Byram and Will against her. "I don't actually require your assistance," she said. "The magnetometer is quite manageable."

"I'll stick around, if it's all the same to you," said Byram, with a little shrug. "I'm sure this will be a sight more diverting than traipsing around after old Moulsdale."

"I was actually going to offer to come along," Will said quickly.

"And why would you have done that?"

"Wouldn't want you to think I was as rude as *Oaf*waite the Dim."

"Who?"

"Outhwaite," said Byram. "The inbred fellow with the long chin and the pronounced under bite."

"Ah, you mean Lantern-jaw."

"Horrible fellow," said Will. "We knew him at Eton. Stole my favorite pen nib when we were thirteen, and kept short-sheeting my bed." He paused. "It's all right to smile, you know."

She smiled at him cautiously.

"Come along, you two. Moulsdale's sure to kick up a fuss if we show up even five minutes past the hour." Byram began walking down the hall, and Lizzie saw that he had a slight limp. "Well? What are you waiting for?"

Lizzie hesitated. She didn't really trust Byram. Will seemed genuinely kind, though. *Perhaps they're just being friendly.* It wasn't entirely out of the question, although it would be a first.

In the end, she let her feet decide for her and followed Byram out of the sick ward and onto the cloistered walkway that led to her room.

# 3

HE WOKE TO THE SOUND OF HIS OWN BREATH-
ing, rapid and shallow. He did not know where he was; the
room was pitch black. More frightening still, he did not instantly know who he was. He felt the icy rush of panic cours-
ing through his veins, and then forced himself to take a deep
breath and assess what he did know. He had been dreaming,
he recalled. He tried to recapture the details. He had been
standing in his room, arguing with a round-faced young man
with receding ginger hair and wire-framed spectacles.

"Don't be an imbecile," the young man was saying as he
poured a shot of whiskey into a glass. "Grimbald will never
condone murder."

"Perhaps not. But Grimbald's not the one in charge," he replied in the dream. "Moulsdale is the one pulling the strings."

"That fat lushington?" The young man handed him the
whiskey, then poured another for himself. "He's too busy guz-
zling Madeira to hatch some mad plot to replace the queen.

Besides, even if Queen Victoria's health has been deteriorating, she's not dead yet."

"That's what I'm trying to tell you, Henry. She *is* dead. From the state of the body, I'd say she's been that way for at least a day." He threw back the whiskey in one quick swallow, but the brief warm burn of alcohol didn't make him feel any better. "Can you think of a reason why the heads of school would be keeping Her Majesty's death a secret? Because I can."

"Come on, man. Listen to yourself. What you're saying is preposterous!"

"I know it's hard to take in, but we have to face it. They intend to transform her."

"Calm down, Victor. Here, you look like you need another drink to steady you." His back turned, Henry poured the whiskey. "Bottoms up." His smile seemed a bit forced as he handed Victor the glass. Perhaps he was beginning to realize the full danger of their situation.

"Thanks. I realize you might not want to believe it because he's your mentor, but Moulsdale's the ambitious one." He tossed back the second shot, which left a medicinal aftertaste in his mouth. "Listen, you don't need to take my word for this. You're the top medical resident. They approached me first because I'm surgery, but they'll need *your* skills to keep her functioning. Moulsdale will go to you next."

Behind the spectacles, his friend's eyes flickered with a strange look, part triumph, part guilt. "He already has."

In the dream, Victor recalled trying to respond to the spectacled man, only to discover that he could not speak, or even swallow. As he clutched his throat, the room began to spin around him. Henry, who had been his friend since the age of thirteen, said, "I'm sorry, old sport, but you're on the wrong side of history." He did not look sorry; he looked terrified and triumphant. Then Henry's face and the room both began to fade to gray. Victor felt himself falling, and without thinking, he grabbed on to Henry's lapels.

"What are you—get off!" With a wild look of panic, Henry grabbed something from the instrument tray and slashed it down toward Victor's face. Instinctively, Victor raised one arm to protect his eyes and felt the sharp cut of the blade a moment before the pain registered.

*This can't be happening.*

Feeling as though he were moving in slow motion, he reached for his friend's wrists, trying to immobilize him. Henry brought the scalpel down again, and then again, slicing into Victor's forearm. On the last cut, Henry hit bone and the blade bounced off. There was metallic clatter as it fell to the floor.

*I've been stabbed.* Stabbed and poisoned.

He stared at his oldest friend, who looked as stunned as Victor felt. How could this be happening? They had climbed trees together, fought imaginary pirates, stolen sweet rolls from the kitchen and eaten them with fingers salty with sweat and dirt. Henry knew all his secrets. Victor had thought he knew all of Henry's secrets, too.

*Take it back*, he wanted to say, as if this were just another quarrel.

But there was no going back this time. Victor felt the arterial throb that signaled rapid blood loss, a stinging rush of cold and then nothing.

That was the end of the dream.

He lay on his back, staring wide-eyed into the darkness, trying to make sense of things. *Victor*, he thought, his eyes finally adjusting to the gloom. *My name is Victor, and I was poisoned by a man I thought was my best friend.* He tried to move and discovered that he was bound, hand and foot. He tried to call for help, and all that came from his mouth was a low, guttural noise that sounded more animal than human.

Then he heard the sound of footsteps. *Thank God*, he thought. *Help.* He turned his head to the sound of heavy locks being slid back, and then there was a creak and Victor had to close his eyes against the sudden bright light. When he could open his eyes again, he saw that his room had an arched roof and stone walls and resembled a windowless medieval dungeon. A young woman dressed in a nurse's starched white linen cap and apron was carrying a small gas lantern. Standing just behind her was the man from his dream, stocky and pale, with receding reddish-blond hair and protuberant eyes magnified by round spectacles.

Henry Clerval.

"'E's awake!" The nurse, a buxom redhead, took only an instant to compose herself. "I mean, he's awake, Doctor."

"Yes, I can see that, Probationer. Turn on the light, if you please, so I can read his notes."

Probationer? That meant the girl was only a student nurse. *How do I know this, when I don't even know where I am?*

Victor's eyes followed the probationary nurse as she turned on a table lamp, and the doctor examined the chart that hung over the back of the bed.

"It's just—I didn't expect him to be awake." She frowned. "Is he really a Bio-Mechanical? He looks so human!"

"Don't be such a ninny," Henry said, not looking up from the chart.

*He's nervous*, thought Victor, *and trying to cover it up.*

"Of course he's a Bio-Mechanical. The newer models don't have the greenish pallor or the heavy stitching, that's all."

"Poor thing. He must have been quite young when he died. And good-looking."

*When he died.* The words were chilling but made no sense. He was sick, certainly, but hardly dead. Did she mean that he was dying now?

The nurse tilted her head to one side. "Why, just look at him watching me! As if he understands every word I say."

Henry sighed as he looked up from the chart. "Don't they teach you anything? He may be listening to your voice, but that doesn't mean he comprehends your meaning." He replaced the chart. "Bio-Mechanicals can be trained to follow simple commands and perform basic tasks, but that is all. That thing may look like a man, but he has no memories, no emotions, and no more intellect than an ape."

Victor lifted his head, and his left hand gave an involuntary twitch. *That's not true*, he tried to say, but all that emerged from his mouth was a strangled mess of vowels.

"There! I think he did understand you, Doctor!"

"Because he grunted? Don't be absurd."

"But what if he just can't form the words? There was a young fella in my village that hit his head and folks called him an idiot, but he knew what they were saying. He could still write, you see, he just couldn't speak."

"Fine." Henry extended his pencil to Victor, then, flustered, recalled that the patient was bound. "Undo his right wrist."

The nurse loosened the binding. Victor tried to clench and unclench his hand, but found he could only move two of his fingers. The rest felt numb and unresponsive. He tried to ask what had happened to him, but the sound that emerged was a long moan.

"Right, then. Shall we hand him the pencil and paper and

see if he can write us a message?" Henry placed the pencil into Victor's right hand, and it slipped out instantly. "There," said Henry. "Satisfied?" Victor's left hand, still bound, contracted in a spasm.

"But look, he's trying!"

"It's a reflex action. Until they are trained, Bio-Mechanicals are only capable of rudimentary reflexes. They can't sit up and feed themselves, let alone write or converse."

"But, Doctor—"

"Look. I'll show you." He reached out a finger, placing it in the center of Victor's right palm. Victor attempted to close his hand around it, but could not quite bring his fingers to touch. "There? See? Simply an autonomic response of the—" He broke off as, with shocking suddenness, Victor's left hand shot up, breaking through its restraint and closing around the other man's finger like a vise.

"Doctor, what's happening?"

"I don't know. Try to pry his fingers open." Victor stared at his own hand, appalled. The hand was half-covered by a brass gauntlet that reached from his elbow to the middle joint of his fingers. *Dear God,* thought Victor, *what have they done to me?*

"He won't let go," said Henry through gritted teeth. "Give him the sedative, and be quick about it."

"I haven't given any injections yet! How much morphine do I need?"

"Depress the plunger to the first marking. Inject him at an angle, into a vein."

As the nurse fumbled with the syringe and vial on the tray behind her, Victor tried to unclench his fist. It refused to obey him, but now he could feel sensation in that hand—a warm rush of blood, and something more. A memory flashed behind Victor's eyes: some man's neck, the bones cracking beneath the pressure of his hands. *That's not my memory.* But how could he know what belonged to him and what did not, when he scarcely remembered who he was?

"Hurry, I think he's going to break my finger!" There was a sickening crack, and Henry cried out in agony.

Victor watched in horror as his left hand began to crush the man's already broken finger. Victor turned to the nurse, begging her in his mind to prepare the sedative already.

"Got it, Doctor!" Wide-eyed, the nurse approached him with the metal and glass syringe in hand. Victor grunted, trying to tell her to tap the syringe to remove any air bubbles.

"For the love of Christ, woman, inject him!" Henry's face was white with pain, and his eyes were beginning to roll back.

Before she could bring the needle any closer, Victor's left hand lashed out, slapping the hypodermic from her hands. The nurse screamed, and Victor gave a hoarse shout. *You will not touch her,* he thought, and the hand turned, as if contemplating him. *I can make it listen,* thought Victor. *I can make it obey me.*

"I've got another needle, Doctor!"

There was a blur of motion in the corner of Victor's eye, a quick jab in his right arm, and then the darkness began to settle back over him. His last thought before succumbing was that he hoped the hand fell asleep at the same time he did, and would not wake before him.

# 4

INGOLD WAS TUCKED INSIDE A WOODED VALLEY and surrounded by hills, and had, at various times in its past, been a Cistercian monastery, a noble home and a ruin. The monk who established the order in the early twelfth century had described this corner of Yorkshire's North Riding as "a place of horror and dreary solitude." The school preferred to describe its location as "a stunning bucolic haven," but clearly, some of the students disagreed. On the day Lizzie arrived, some pranksters had hung a banner across the entryway that read Believe the Monk.

On the steamship journey from New York City to York, Lizzie had read up on the school's history. Ingold was not the first medical school to produce Bio-Mechanicals: Nikolay Pirogov, the brilliant Russian field surgeon and scientist, came home from the Crimean War and founded the surgical department of The Academy of Military Medicine at St. Petersburg, where he announced his intention of creating a new kind of soldier to spare young men the horrors of war. Lord Sidney

Herbert followed suit in London, as did Johannes Friedrich von Esmarch in Germany, but it was Pirogov who succeeded in 1869, with the creation of the first Bio-Mechanical. Nearly a decade later, a second generation of Bio-Mechanicals was tested by Pirogov during the Russo-Turkish war. Slow-moving and unable to fire a rifle, these Bio-Mechanicals were famous for shuffling forward even after sustaining severe chest and head wounds. They did succeed in deterring Turkish troops, however, mainly because the Turks thought they were demons.

It was about this time that Great Britain began producing its own Bio-Mechanicals at Ingold, while its sister school in Germany rolled out its own models. According to Lizzie's book, *Ingold Abbey: Parting the Mists of Myth*, the school's design was widely considered the most advanced. The book's author, Letitia Broadbelt, provided no proof of this, although she did include side-by-side illustrations so a reader could compare British and German Bio-Mechanicals. The German model appeared to be both larger and bulkier than its British counterpart, and the top of its skull seemed flatter. Lizzie looked for an explanation, but alas, there was no text accompanying the images.

Instead, Miss Broadbelt had gone into great detail about the history of Ingold Abbey, noting that the place had been looted and rebuilt so many times that it seemed at odds with itself. When Lizzie had arrived earlier in the day, she had learned that there were four main buildings—the School of Surgery, the School of Medicine, the School of Engineering and the School of Nursing—all designed in a Gothic ecclesiastical style that made Lizzie think of austere hooded monks chanting dirges and arranged around an open central courtyard. Each school building had its own student living quarters, which were located in separate buildings arranged in a loose outer quadrangle. After some discussion among the staff about the propriety of allowing a young woman loose among the male medical students, Lizzie had been placed in Nightingale House, with the nursing students. The head of nursing, Ursula Shiercliffe, had explained this in a way that implied that it was the young men's virtue, and not Lizzie's, that was in need of protection. Perhaps Shiercliffe thought that a female unnatural enough to become a medical student might be unnatural enough to seduce unwary men.

The problem was, she wasn't completely sure how to get from the medical building to the nursing school and then out into Nightingale House. No one had given her a map and, as far as she could tell, corridors led to staircases that led to other corridors without apparent rhyme or reason, and even the remarkable electric lanterns that lined the hallways could not dispel the medieval gloom. She wouldn't have wanted to admit it out loud, but she was glad that Byram and Will had offered to keep her company as she walked back to her room to fetch the magnometer.

"I can't imagine how the monks managed to find their way around with nothing but the odd candle," she said over her shoulder.

"If you think this is dark, you wouldn't like the tunnels," said Byram.

"Tunnels?"

"See that?" Will pointed to a grate in the stone floor and then to a small door tucked into an alcove. "There are subterranean passageways, built by the monks to escape King Henry VIII's soldiers," said Will. "The Bio-Mechanicals use them to get around the school without getting in the way."

"They say a servant girl got lost down there, back when

this place was still a private home," Byram added. "Rumor has it the poor girl's ghost still roams the ancient tunnels."

Lizzie snorted. "Do you actually think you can scare me with that story?"

"Not at all," said Byram. "You don't seem the superstitious type. Still—" he dropped his voice "—you can't deny that the old stone hallways have a cool, dusty, sepulchral odor...as if the presence of the living cannot entirely dispel the echoes of the dead."

She glanced back, eyebrows raised. "What was that? A quote from one of Mr. Poe's horror stories?"

Byram put his hand on his heart. "You wound me. I write my own material, thank you very much."

She had to laugh. "You are a complete idiot."

"And you are completely lost," said Byram, stopping abruptly in front of a tapestry as faded and frayed as an old tea towel. "Admit it."

"I'm not lost. I'm just not entirely sure which building we're in."

"Here," said Will, opening a door for her. "I think it's easier to get our bearings on the outside." Even though the walkway was covered, the flagstones under her feet were slick from the constant mist of rain, and she was aware of Byram walking with deliberate care behind her, no doubt mindful of his bad leg.

She paused, squinting up at the white limestone facade of the Gothic tower on their right. "I think this might be the place."

"Not unless your room is in Percival House, with Will and me." Byram limped over to the door and pointed to a small brass plaque.

"So Nightingale must be over there." Will stepped over the

low cloister wall and crossed the grassy square that formed the center of the quadrangle. Then he turned back, frowning. "Can you manage that in your skirts? If not—"

"I can manage it." She straddled the wall, trying not to think how inelegant she must look. Will had offered her a hand; she refused it. She turned back to see Byram twist his ankle as he stepped over the wall.

"Are you all right?"

Byram lifted his chin. "I could ask the same of you. Really, what would you have done if we hadn't come along? *Women.* No sense of direction whatsoever."

Lizzie bristled. "While men strike out with false certainty, praying that they'll figure it out along the way."

"Ah, but women are so much wiser than men," said Will, smiling back at her over his shoulder. "They know that acknowledging weakness is not in itself a weakness."

She hated those kinds of compliments. They put women in the same category as dogs—nobler and *simpler* beings than men. "And what does it get them? A lifetime of planning dinner menus and cornstarching gravy stains out of linen tablecloths."

Byram stopped in front of Nightingale House, holding the door open for her. "I take it, then, that you do not agree with the theory that women are most suited to the occupation of wife and mother?"

"Are you trying to annoy me?"

"It's in my nature, I'm afraid."

"Try to overcome it." She stepped inside the dimly lit building, willing her eyes to adjust quickly to the gloom so she could find her room without wasting too much time.

"Come on. We don't have all day," said Byram.

"Fine, follow me," she said, and promptly walked into a

firmly corseted human body. "Oh! I am so sorry, I didn't see you standing there…"

"Obviously," said a commanding female voice. "What is less obvious to me is what you three are doing near the nurse's quarters during lessons?" Now that Lizzie's eyes had adjusted, she could see that the person she had the misfortune to walk into was none other than Ursula Shiercliffe, head of nursing. In her black, high-necked gown and jet earrings, Shiercliffe looked more like a headmistress than a nurse, but Lizzie had been told that her white lace cap with its long trailing veil was a sign of her rank.

"Dr. Moulsdale sent us to go back to my room to fetch my magnetometer."

"Did he indeed? Perhaps he was not aware, then, that no male students are allowed in this wing."

"Begging your pardon, ma'am," said Will quickly. "We had no idea that Miss Lavenza roomed with the nurses."

Lizzie, embarrassed, bit the inside of her cheek.

"It is 'Matron,' not 'ma'am.' And Miss Lavenza was aware, or should have been." Shiercliffe gave her a piercing look. "I do recall giving you a rather thorough explanation of what would and would *not* be permitted, given your rather unusual circumstances." Shiercliffe raised her eyebrows, making it clear what she thought of these circumstances.

"I had thought, once we were close enough, to go into my room on my own," said Lizzie, refusing to be cowed. She was not a nursing student. Shiercliffe had no authority over her.

"Your room is right over here." The matron stopped in front of a door that looked like all the others in the hall. "Be quick about your business. I have too much to do as it is, without having to tarry here keeping an eye on these two."

"I will," Lizzie promised.

Her room, which had once been a monk's cell, was long and narrow and sparsely furnished with a single bed, an old, scratched desk and chair, a rag rug and a lopsided wardrobe that was too large for the space and covered part of the window. That didn't matter much, as there wasn't much of a view: the window opened onto the courtyard where the hospital sheets hung out on lines in good weather.

Lizzie walked over to her bed. Her mother had designed and sewn the pink and red patchwork quilt, along with the embroidered pillow that gave the room its only feminine touches. Lizzie should have been taught to stitch her own trousseau, but her mother had died when Lizzie was only eight. As much as she had missed her mother while growing up, it was hard to imagine trading all those years in her father's laboratory for a collection of embroidered linens.

Kneeling on the floor, she pulled her trunk from under the bed. She had packed the magnetometer wrapped in clothes to protect it, so now she had to rummage through a jumble of wool winter skirts, everyday shawls, spare underdrawers and—there they were—the underarm dress shields she'd been looking for that morning.

Outside the door, which she hadn't bothered to close completely, she heard Byram say, "Surely you don't think we're a bad influence on Miss Lavenza, Matron?"

Shiercliffe's response was unintelligible.

"I've never been a bad influence before." That was Will.

"I'm rubbing off on you," replied Byram.

"Just see that you don't rub off on Miss Lavenza," said Shiercliffe, so sharply that Lizzie stifled a laugh.

"You don't have to worry too much about that one," said Byram. "She's nobody's fool."

On the other side of the door, Lizzie forgot what she was

doing for a moment. There was an old adage that eaves-droppers seldom heard any good of themselves, but unless she had misheard him, that sulky, cynical boy had just paid her a compliment.

"Miss Lavenza?" Shiercliffe poked her head around the door. "Whatever is taking so long?"

"I'm sorry, I packed it away a bit too well." Lizzie frantically felt around in her trunk until her hand hit something hard. "Found it." She held up the box.

"About time, too." Shiercliffe held the door open, her cool gaze taking in the disordered state of Lizzie's trunk. "You might want to brush the dust off your skirt. And I take it that you will not make a habit of these group excursions?"

"I won't," said Lizzie, trying not to look as flustered as she felt.

"And that goes for you two, as well," Shiercliffe said, addressing the boys.

"Our word on it, Matron," Will said, but Shiercliffe's slender form was already heading down the hall away from them, her white lace veil trailing behind her like a nun's.

"Well," said Byram, "I guess we know what she needs."

"Byram! There's a lady present."

"You mean Lavenza? Nonsense, man. She's just a lowly soldier in the great war against disease, same as we are."

*He gets it*, she thought. Perhaps having a bad foot wasn't so different from being the only female. "Thank you," she said, meaning it.

"Well, I thought I should probably be kind, since you're probably about to make a complete fool of yourself in front of Moulsdale and the entire class."

She was still trying to think of a suitable rejoinder when they arrived back at the sick ward.

# 5

MOULSDALE WAS CHECKING HIS POCKET WATCH
while the other first year students were debating, so it was the
patient, Private Holden, who first noticed Lizzie's approach.

"Cor, blimey, that took you long enough," he said. "What
did you do, stop off at the local for a pint?"

"She got lost a few times," said Byram.

Lizzie shot him a dirty look, and thought how unfair it was
that she couldn't say that it was his bad foot that had slowed
them down.

"Well, now that you are finally here," said Moulsdale, "perhaps you can get on with it?"

She moved forward, feeling terribly self-conscious as she
pulled off her gloves so that she could untie the velvet bag.

Moulsdale sniffed. "Is that all the bits and pieces? Looks
rather small."

Lizzie pulled out the polished wooden box and set it on
the patient's bedside table. A brass plate was engraved with
the words Lavenza's Patented Etheric Magnetometer, but the

truth was, her father had never received a patent, which he would have put in her name. He was never good about doing paperwork, and Nikola Tesla beat him to it by a matter of days, calling the device by another name. It was why her father had been forced to see patients, and why he had caught the infection that took his life.

*Don't think about that now. Concentrate.*

Lizzie opened the lid, revealing an assortment of glass and metal attachments of various shapes and sizes. She selected a medium-size glass wand that widened into a bulb at the end.

Holden sat up straighter. "'Ere now, where you plan on puttin' that?"

"These are applied externally," she reassured him as she attached the glass tube into the black celluloid handle. "We simply turn this dial," she said, "and the machine begins oscillating at a high frequency." There was a buzzing sound as a violet light appeared inside the glass wand. "Are you ready?"

"You sure it's safe?" He looked rather dubious.

"Yes, you should feel nothing more than a mild tingling sensation. See?" She passed the wand over her own hand, so that everyone could see the small arcs of light flickering like violet tongues over her palm. "It doesn't hurt." She moved the glass wand over the bandaged stump.

"I can feel it!" Holden gave a little whoop of excitement. "There's a tingling!" The other medical students moved in closer, crowding around her.

"Careful not to knock the table with the control box," she warned Outhwaite as she moved the wand, which crackled with electricity. She thought about telling the students to back off, but Moulsdale was standing next to the box, as well. She didn't want to order him to move. "All right, I'm going to make the current a little stronger. Excuse me, sir."

Moulsdale moved aside so she could reach the box, and she turned the dial slightly, just a fraction higher than the lowest setting. "Ready?" Turning back to the patient, she placed the wand on his stump.

"Ow! That stings a bit."

"You're probably not used to the sensation. Try to bear with it a little. We want to give the fields time to align." She ran the wand over the stump again as the man grimaced and twitched as if he had palsy. She glanced at Moulsdale, who was standing beside Outhwaite and looking singularly unimpressed.

"Crikey. I can't take much more o' this."

The wand sizzled as it passed over his stump, but Lizzie knew that the sound was misleading. At this setting, the wand gave only a very mild charge.

"Surely you can't be more delicate than I am? I used it on myself a moment ago, remember?"

"Aargh!" There was a popping sound as the glass wand shattered, and the patient sat up, using his good arm to fling the magnetometer away from him. There was a crack as the celluloid handle slammed against the floor, and then a thud and the box, connected by the electrical wire, fell after it. "She tried to cook me! Doesn't 'urt, she says. In a pig's eye it don't 'urt." Holden wasn't lying. A singed, burned smell filled the air. "Stupid cow! Whatcher tryin' ter do, finish what the Boer started? Why don't you go back to America and burn some of your own sort?"

Heart pounding, Lizzie couldn't stop staring at the broken magnetometer. "I don't understand! It shouldn't have hurt you at all."

"Yeah, well, it did."

As Outhwaite and a few of the others smirked at her, Will bent down to pick up the box.

"Leave that for Miss Lavenza," said Moulsdale, waving him away. "And now we can see why 'do no harm' is the first tenet of good medicine. When no cause can be determined, it is sometimes all a doctor can do to treat a patient's symptoms and make him as comfortable as possible. To this end, the correct treatment for Private Holden is a prescription of laudanum, to soothe his troubled nerves."

"Oi," said Holden, "laudanum! 'Ow am I goin' to afford laudanum? I'm a cripple now, remember?"

"Questions of finance are not in my purview." Moulsdale checked his watch. "Time to move on, gentlemen? Miss Lavenza, perhaps you can tend to the man's burns. There are salves in the medicine cabinet."

He led the medical students away, laughing and chatting about women and contraptions. Will glanced over his shoulder, and Byram shrugged as if to say, *What can we do?*

"Women," said Private Holden, presumably to himself, since the patients on either side of him were both fast asleep or unconscious and Lizzie was the only person left standing in the ward. "Why don't you stick with the things you're good at? Ow!" he exclaimed, as she pressed the cool compress to his stump. "Not so hard. Don't you know anythin' about nursin'?"

She sighed, spreading the salve on his stump as gently as she could. "I'm not a nurse."

"Oi...'ang on." Private Holden was grasping his stump and staring at it. "Now that the burnin's stopped...I don't feel any pain anymore!" His face split into a wide grin. "I take it all back, darlin'. You're a marvel."

"That's wonderful." She smiled a little wanly. Two min-

---

utes earlier, and this revelation might have redeemed her. "I don't suppose you could mention that to Dr. Moulsdale when you see him again?"

"'Course I will, you ministerin' angel. 'Course I will."

Perhaps something could be salvaged from this disaster after all.

Taking a deep breath to steel herself, Lizzie looked at the magnetometer, which was lying on the floor, four of the five glass tubes broken and the celluloid handle cracked. No telling how badly the coils inside were damaged. She picked up the remaining tube and wrapped it as gently as though it were a small corpse. It was only as she began packing up the box that she saw that someone had turned the dial to its maximum strength.

# 6

THE MEDICAL STUDENTS AND NURSES DINED together in the refectory, a hall where medieval monks had once broken their bread, but Lizzie was too preoccupied to appreciate the high, curved, wood-beamed ceiling and arched windows. It was hard to concentrate on anything when her head was throbbing, and the constant hum and clatter of the other students wasn't helping matters.

"Still fretting? You're going to get frown lines," said Byram, waiting for her to slide into the low bench before seating himself.

"Someone changed the setting on my machine and destroyed my reputation. That's a perfectly good reason to be in a blue funk."

"For a female, sure." Byram poked at his stew. "But *doctors* can't afford to get the dismals from every little setback."

"This isn't about feelings. This is about fairness." She nudged him with her elbow. "Let me out. I need to explain what happened to Professor Moulsdale."

Byram continued investigating the contents of his stew. "Don't be such a sawney-headed chunk. Who do you think set you up in the first place?"

"What are you talking about? Outhwaite was standing right there, smirking at me."

"He wasn't the only one."

"What possible reason would Moulsdale have for changing the setting?"

Byram regarded her from underneath heavily lidded eyes. "Our head of medicine doesn't cotton to students who are *too* clever."

For a moment, she was speechless. "But what about the patient who got burned? That goes against the Hippocratic Oath."

"You mean, 'first, do no harm'? Not actually part of the oath, as a matter of fact. Besides, Moulsdale follows the Hypocritical Oath—*first, do no harm to one's career.*" Byram forked a piece of potato. "You made the mistake of showing up Moulsdale." He popped the morsel into his mouth with a flourish, then made a face. "Gad, that's awful."

"Oh, Lord, what do I do if you're right? If Moulsdale has it in for me, I'm doomed."

"Must you constantly sound as though you're rehearsing lines for a melodrama?" Byram flung his hand back onto his forehead. "Doomed, I tell you, doomed!"

Lizzie was glaring at Byram when Will set his tray down with a clatter of cutlery.

"Why is Lizzie looking like she wants to throw her bowl at you? What have I missed?"

"Just some gloom and doom."

Mouth too full to speak, Will raised his eyebrows. "Mm?"

"Oh, please, don't. I can't bear to watch the way you shovel that swill into your mouth."

Will swallowed and then took another bite of his food. "So don't watch."

"Unbelievable. Do we even know what kind of meat is in the stew?"

Will examined one piece. "Geriatric mutton, by the look of it."

As the two argued whether the food at Ingold was more or less disgusting than the food at Eton, Lizzie caught fragments of other people's conversations.

"...and then he stuck his thumb straight into the wound, as if it were a plum pudding, and brought out the bullet."

"...the entire bottle of absinthe, completely empty..."

"...didn't even realize the poor blighter was dead until the nurse came in and asked me what I thought I was doing to the corpse!"

"Faculty, of course, gets to dine on steak pie," said Byram. "No wonder Moulsdale looks like a well-tailored pachyderm."

The faculty sat on a raised dais, underneath a faded tapestry of a greyhound, a rabbit and a sly-looking unicorn next to a sullen maiden with a receding hairline. Moulsdale's plate held a heaping slice of pie, while Grimbald, the tall, thin, head of surgery, had taken a much more modest portion.

"Aren't you going to eat anything, Lizzie?"

She realized that Will had been watching her. "I'm too busy worrying whether I'm going to be expelled."

"For one little mistake?"

"Will, I'm female. I don't get to make mistakes." She slumped on her seat. "Maybe they'll transfer me to nursing."

Byram dabbed at his mouth with a napkin. "Do you always vacillate between brashness and abject despair?"

"Not always, but frequently."

"Well, then. Once you swing back to boldness, you can try out your whatsit again. There must be any number of patients around you can practice on."

"I can't, even if I wanted to. The device is broken." And without a laboratory, she would have no way to attempt to repair it.

"At least you had the nerve to try," said Will.

"It would have been smarter to keep my mouth shut."

Will shrugged. "If you were the type to do that, you wouldn't be here, would you? My brother was always the first to raise his hand. He had the right answer, and he wasn't going to waste time pretending to be modest."

"What happened to him?"

Byram shot her a warning look. "He died last year."

"Oh, Lord, I am so sorry… I had no idea." Except that now she recalled Moulsdale offering Will his condolences, so she *should* have had an idea. "And now I sound exactly like all the people who told me they were sorry when my father passed away. I never knew what to say, so I just smiled and looked embarrassed. Which is what you're doing now." Lizzie buried her head in her hands. "Never mind me. I want to sink through the floor now."

"Well, you can't, so sit up straight," Byram said, setting aside his plate with a sigh. "Now, laugh as though I've just said something amusing."

"Why should I?" Lizzie's voice was muffled by her arms.

"We have an audience."

Lizzie sat up, just in time to see Outhwaite and another first year pass by their table. Outhwaite knocked into the table, causing some of Will's stew to spill onto his jacket.

"Miss Lavenza, I do apologize for my clumsiness." Outh-

waite's smile seemed too small for his long face. "I don't suppose you could whip out that little box of yours and set me
to rights? But oh, no, wait…the thingammy broke, didn't
it?" Outhwaite shook his head. "What a pity. I suppose it was
rather a flimsy design, though."

Lizzie half rose from her seat. "It wasn't flimsy, it was delicate, and if you hadn't—"

"Hadn't what? Are you *accusing* me of something?"

"Easy, Tiger." Byram put his hand on her arm, pulling her
back down. "In another moment, you'll require either Will or
myself to defend your honor, and while it would be lovely to
smash my knuckles into Outhwaite's chin, we might want to
put off the fisticuffs until our second day of medical school."

Outhwaite gave a nasty laugh. "What he means is he doesn't
want me to mess up his pretty face. *Again.*"

"Outhwaite *always* had a thing about my looks," said Byram,
apparently unperturbed. "Don't worry, old man, some girls
actually like fellows with arse-shaped chins."

Outhwaite made a move toward Byram, but his companion held him back. "They're not worth it," he said. "Besides,
we don't want to start something here."

"True. I'll find a better opportunity to break you into little
pieces. Rather like Miss Lavenza's little toy."

"So it *was* you! You turned up the dial!"

"That would have been cheating," said Outhwaite, a sneer
in his voice. "I don't need to cheat against a *female.*"

The realization hit her: *So it wasn't him, which meant it was
Moulsdale, just as Byram had implied.*

This time it was Will who touched her arm. "Doesn't sig-
nify, one way or another. Makepiece will set it to rights."

"Makepiece?" Outhwaite gave a snort of laughter. "The

head of engineering won't even talk to first years. He only ever sees the second years when they've chosen their specialty."

"He'll see us." Byram twirled a spoon between his fingers. "He's particularly keen on seeing the etherometer."

"Etheric magnetometer," Lizzie corrected automatically.

"It's all bosh," Outhwaite told his companion. "Makepiece would never see them, and they don't even have the bottle to try."

Byram smiled as if this were a pleasantry. "Care to place a wager?"

"Five pounds says you don't so much as knock on his door."

"Ten pounds says you're a bally jackass."

"Byram!" Will stifled a laugh, but he looked as nervous as Lizzie felt. It was a fine idea, going to Makepiece—as long as they didn't get in more trouble for doing it.

Outhwaite glared down at Byram. "I'll need proof, of course."

"You'll have it." He held out his hand and gave Outhwaite a challenging look. "It's a wager?"

Outhwaite shook his hand. "Don't forget, I want proof." He walked off with his friend, laughing as though he'd already won the bet.

"I say, old chap," said Will, once Outhwaite was out of earshot. "Was that really wise?"

Byram shrugged. "It was satisfying…which is seldom the same thing."

# 7

AFTER DINNER, LIZZIE, BYRAM AND WILL MADE their way through the misty September evening to the School of Engineering. Through the open cloister windows, drifts of gray fog slipped past the tumbled stones of some ruined abbey wing like wandering wraiths.

"Charming," said Will, hunching his shoulders against the dank night air. "You have to admire how the school has preserved the atmosphere of utter desolation."

"Oh, I quite like it," said Byram, pausing to consider the tumbled stone walls. "It makes me want to write a Gothic novel about the ghost of a mad monk. Lizzie here can be the poor maiden who wanders off in the night."

"And why am I wandering around? Insomnia? Indigestion?"

"A poor sense of direction." Byram glanced sideways at her and then back down at the uneven stones. His limp was more pronounced now.

"You heard a mysterious noise and saw a ghostly shape,"

said Will. "And came out here, where you stumbled upon a catafalque inscribed with an ancient Latin curse."

"Ah," said Lizzie, trying to recall if a catafalque was the same thing as a coffin. "And the curse says?"

*"Sapere Aude,"* whispered Will.

"Dare to know," Lizzie translated automatically. "Isn't that the Ingold school motto?"

"Indeed," said Byram. "And who can refuse a dare?" He paused for a moment at the door to a grim, gray-stoned laboratory building, contemplating the eerie green light visible from the narrow arched windows. Something about the quality of that light—its cold, unnatural absinthe luminescence—made the back of Lizzie's neck prickle with unease.

Will cleared his throat. "Remind me why we're doing this?"

Byram lifted the big brass knocker and let it fall with a hollow clang. "To help our friend Lavenza here. And because Outhwaite got up my nose."

"A fine reason to get suspended for skipping study hall on our first day of school," said Will. "Well, guess no one's home. Shall we head back?"

"Are you really that easily discouraged?" Lizzie put her hand on the doorknob and turned. The door was heavy, but not locked. "Come on, maybe Makepiece is inside and just didn't hear us."

Inside, the strange, green tint of the lighting made the room appear like some unearthly realm, and gave a slightly sinister aspect to copper pipes that snaked and coiled around the walls. The room had a faintly chemical odor that made it feel unhealthy to breathe too deeply. In one corner, there was a large metal spiral encased in glass. This was a Tesla coil, and when turned on, it could conduct an enormous amount of voltage. Lizzie had used a smaller version in her father's laboratory, and it had generated enough electricity to shock a man senseless. This large-scale model could easily kill a careless student.

Of course, she had no intention of being careless.

"Ugh," said Will, standing in front of a large vat that contained a dismembered male arm floating in a luminous green liquid. "What is this?"

"They're specimens," said Byram, investigating a series of smaller vats. When Lizzie stepped closer to him, she saw that each vat had an organ floating inside—a heart, a brain, a kidney. "Human, I believe."

There was a glint of gold on top of one of the vats, and Lizzie picked it up. "I think someone's lost something."

Will made a face. "Is that meant to be an autopsy joke?"

"No, look." She showed him the small gold locket, which had been engraved with the initials *JTM*. She opened the catch, revealing a small photograph of a pretty little blonde girl.

"That must be Makepiece's daughter," said Will. "Rumor has it she's an invalid of some sort."

"They say she lives at the school somewhere," added Byram, idly passing his finger back and forth through the blue flame of a Bunsen burner. "But for some reason, no one ever sees her."

Will shook his head. "I can't believe you're actually playing with fire." He snapped the locket shut and handed it back to Lizzie. "I'm guessing the girl's a bit of a sore subject with Makepiece, so I wouldn't go asking him any questions if you want to get on his good side."

"I may be American, but I do know better than to go digging into a professor's personal life." She replaced the locket on top of the vat. "Now you can stop looking so nervous."

"We're standing in a room with a bunch of pickled organs—I

think I have a right to look nervous." Will threw up his hands. "Why am I even here? I should be at Cambridge, reading classics."

"I will remind you that the *Iliad* is filled with blood and gore," said Byram, bending to examine the severed arm more closely.

"It sounds less grisly in Classical Greek." Will looked sideways at Lizzie. "Suppose this is old hat to you."

"It's a bit different from my father's laboratory." The Tesla Coil, she knew, was used to generate high-frequency alternating current electricity. Her father had used electrostatic generators, which produced a lower voltage direct current. "This must be the Galvanic Reanimator," she said, picking up a brass helmet and examining the various leather straps and attachments. "Do they just use it once, to bring the Bio-Mechanical back to life, or do they have to keep shocking them?"

Will, about to sit down in the chair, jumped back. "Are you insane? Put that down!"

"It's not going to bite you," said Byram, with an evil grin. "Unless… Want to test it out?"

"Imbecile." Will turned away from Byram and then gave a startled shout.

A man in a coarse-spun jacket stood nearby, broom in his hand. Underneath his cap, his face had a greenish pallor that was accentuated by the reflected light from the glowing vats. Where had he come from?

"Somebody tell me that's not Makepiece."

"Don't be absurd, Will." Byram walked up to the man, his limp carefully controlled. "This is a Bio-Mechanical. I thought you visited your brother here. Didn't he show you any corpse walkers?"

"You forget, I was fifteen then. My parents were antiquated embarrassments and my brother was an insensitive science Morlock. I spent the whole day sulking out on the hill with a dog-eared copy of Elizabeth Barrett Browning's poems while Victor showed our parents around the school."

Byram smiled. "I recall that time. You wore nothing but black for a year."

"I was in mourning for the lost innocence of childhood."

"Well, now that *you're* the insensitive science Morlock, here's your chance to inspect a Bio-Mechanical." Byram made a dramatic flourish with his arm, like the ringmaster at a circus directing the audience's attention to a new performance. The Bio-Mechanical ducked its head. On closer gaze, Lizzie saw that the creature was misshapen as well as ugly, his back twisted so that his left shoulder was perceptibly higher than the right.

"Poor devil," said Will.

"Really, Will, that's not a very scientific reaction." Byram reached out a hand, and the creature recoiled. "No, don't worry, I won't harm you." He took the broom away, then pushed off the Bio-Mechanical's cap, revealing matted black hair and a face crisscrossed by scars. The creature started making odd little grunting squeals. Byram turned its head to the side, exposing the short metal rods on the side of its neck. "See? Electrodes. One on each side. They use those to galvanize the corpses."

Will stared at the Bio-Mechanical, his expression one of mingled fascination and disgust. "Is that all that makes them mechanical? The electrodes?"

"Some of them have other enhancements—mechanically augmented arms or legs, mostly, or reinforced chests. Don't think this one has had anything special done to him, though."

Byram pulled at the creature's shirt, presumably to determine if it did, indeed, possess any enhancements. It bleated in alarm, like a sheep before shearing.

"Let go of him, Byram," said Lizzie. "He's frightened."

"Don't be daft," said Byram, releasing him all the same. The creature shuffled into a corner, then stopped, as if unsure what to do next. "Bio-Mechs can't feel fear." Byram pulled out his pocket handkerchief and wiped his hands, a faint look of disgust on his handsome face. "Wonder what he's doing here, anyway?"

Lizzie picked up the creature's cap from the floor and handed it to him. "He must do small jobs for the professor. Although he seems so…limited. It's difficult to imagine him as a soldier."

"Don't underestimate Igor."

They all turned to see a biblical prophet of a man who had emerged from a side door. He was white-bearded and gaunt, with bushy eyebrows that flicked up at the ends like angry wings. Only his spectacles and his threadbare gray suit proclaimed him a citizen of this new twentieth century. They needed no introduction to be told that this was Edmund Makepiece, as his photograph hung on the wall in Mouls-dale's study alongside Grimbald's.

He must have come on through the same back entrance as the Bio-Mechanical, thought Lizzie.

"Igor is a good deal more intelligent than he appears," Makepiece went on. "Unlike most people, who advertise their stupidity the moment they open their mouths." The scientist folded his arms and raised his eyebrows. "This is, I believe, the moment when the bravest of you opens his mouth to explain what you are doing in my laboratory."

# 8

IGOR IS A GOOD DEAL MORE INTELLIGENT THAN
*he appears.* Professor Makepiece was glowering at Lizzie,
Byram and Will over his half-moon spectacles, and she knew
she had to speak before he got even angrier, but all she could
think about was the Bio-Mechanical hunched beside her,
pathetically holding his cap in his hands.

"Igor," she said, taking the cap and placing it back on his
misshapen head, "I'm sorry if we were bothering you before."

He stared up at her for a moment with something like surprise, then dropped his gaze.

Byram shot her an irritated look. "Professor Makepiece,"
he said smoothly, "we apologize for this unauthorized visit."

"I did not ask for an apology. I asked for an explanation,
and I am all agog to hear it." Makepiece picked up the broom
and handed it to the Bio-Mechanical. "Go on, Igor. Sweep
up." With his fierce eyebrows and his shaggy white beard,
he still looked like a biblical prophet, but his voice sounded
dryly amused rather than offended.

With an anxious look over his twisted shoulder, Igor shuffled off and began to push the broom ineffectually across the
floor, never pausing to look up.

"Now," said Makepiece. "Without unnecessary embellish-
ment or circumlocution, please explain what you three are
doing here." He glanced at the jar of eyes, which was still sitting on a low table instead of on the shelf where it belonged,
and then back at Byram. "Besides rearranging my stock, that
is." Again, there was that droll note in his voice that belied
his stern expression.

"Well," said Byram, a hint of mischief in his overly polite
expression, "Miss Lavenza is really the cause of our visit, so
perhaps she should explain."

Makepiece lowered his spectacles and regarded her with
interest. "Indeed?"

*All right*, she thought, *here goes nothing.* "Yes, sir. You see, I
have a device with me...something my late father invented.
And it needs fixing."

"A device? What sort of device?"

Squaring her shoulders, she described the way the etheric
magnetometer operated at much lower frequencies than the
Galvanic Reanimator, and how this resulted in far less damage
to living tissue. Makepiece stroked his beard and made a little
humming sound of encouragement, so she went on, talking
about the experiments her father had done using violet light.

"Wait," Makepiece said, and for a moment she thought he
was angry with her. "Are you saying that the violet light can
actually destroy harmful bacteria with its tithonic waves?"

Lizzie nodded cautiously, and then Makepiece shocked her
by clapping his hands and breaking into a full grin. "You
clever girl," he said, his eyes bright with excitement. "So
much to show you, and where to begin?" Before she could

respond, he turned and took a jar from the shelf. "Here," he said, handing it to her. "Take this." The jar was filled with dozens of squirming live earthworms.

"Sir?"

"Give them one each." At her befuddled look he added, "The salamanders, of course," and pointed to a low table filled with glass aquariums. Each aquarium contained a different species of salamander, some small and orange, others large and dark, their glistening bodies patterned with bold splotches of yellow or blue. There was even an aquatic specimen, corpse white, with frilled appendages coming out of its head.

"Ah, yes, bacterial growth," Makepiece muttered, stroking his beard. "That's always been the fly in the ichor."

She exchanged wordless glances with Will and Byram, who shrugged. Makepiece didn't seem to be paying her any attention, but maybe this was a test of her character, to see if she was squeamish about the earthier aspects of lab work. If so, it was an easy test to pass; she had never minded touching worms.

As she walked around the room, dropping worms into cages, she watched Makepiece out of the corner of her eye. Standing with his hands clasped behind his back, he made a little sound as he noticed the gold locket. Picking it up, he opened the catch and stared down at the photograph as if he had forgotten there was anyone else in the room with him. "All right," he said abruptly, snapping the locket closed and stuffing it into the pocket of his jacket. "Ask me a question."

Byram was the first to speak. "Are you thinking of using Lizzie's device to make a Bio-Mechanical?"

"No, no, don't ask the obvious, my boy. That only impresses fools. Look around the lab. Ask an evidence-based question."

So it was a test, but not the one she had been expecting. While Byram sulked and Will looked terrified that Makepiece might call on him, she looked around the laboratory, at all the coils of electrical wiring and the jars and test tubes, and tried to think of a truly impressive question that would reveal both her keen powers of observation and the subtlety of her mind. *Nothing.* Finally, out of desperation, she blurted out a completely inane question, because it was the only one she had. "Is there a reason for all the amphibians, sir? I thought most labs kept mice and rats."

Makepiece nodded at her approvingly. "Most do. But you see, salamanders have a rather exceptional ability." He pulled one, wiggling and scrabbling against his hand, out of its aquarium.

Lizzie peered at the squirming amphibian, which was nearly eight inches long and as thick as a man's wrist.

"Hold it right there."

Lizzie put her hand on the salamander's slick skin as Will and Byram drew closer. In one quick motion, Makepiece brought a scalpel down on the creature's thick tail, severing it. Will gave a strangled scream and stumbled back as the salamander's tail snapped back and forth a few times.

"Now, now, nothing to worry about." Makepiece held the salamander's tail as it continued to writhe. "The tail is a decoy… In the wild, it would snap off in a predator's jaws, giving Sally here a chance to get away."

"So she's going to be all right, Professor Makepiece?" Lizzie was trying to keep the poor creature from escaping without hurting it as it attempted to scrabble out of her grasp. Her heart was still pounding in her chest, but unlike Will, she knew she had to appear unaffected by Makepiece's actions. Anything less, and they would probably kick her out of school.

"Oh, yes, she's as right as rain. As a matter of fact," Makepiece went on, "Sally here will regrow this appendage in a
matter of days."

"Will she really?" Byram limped forward, looking at the
tail. "I've never heard of such a thing."

"Oh, yes," said Makepiece, returning the salamander to
its cage. "And what's even more remarkable, she can regrow
a severed limb. Some of her relatives can even regrow hearts
and spinal cords."

"Incredible," said Byram, for once without a trace of irony
in his voice. "And so you are looking to understand why these
creatures are capable of these feats while we are not?"

"But we *are* capable," said Makepiece, his dark eyes glit-
tering with excitement. "Up until the age of eleven, a child
can regrow the tip of his finger, if the cut is clean enough.
And the liver is capable of regeneration, as well." There was
a plaintive meow, and Makepiece bent down to pet a small
black cat that was winding in and out of his trouser legs.
"The question is, why do we lose this ability? Why can't we
regenerate lost limbs…weak lungs…the nerves of the spinal
cord?" Makepiece picked up the cat, which began to purr. "I
believe the answer lies in the electromagnetic charge of the
affected area."

"That sounds like my father's research," said Lizzie.

"Your father was working on the electromagnetic field generated by the living body. I am speaking of the vital spark of
animal electricity that circulates *within* the body."

"Wait…you knew my father?"

"Knew him? Why, we worked together, my dear. And we
were friends."

"You were?"

"Yes, he and I were both intrigued by the possibility of

using electricity to stimulate cell regrowth, but then we had a bit of a falling-out. I'm afraid your father became concerned about the ethical considerations of reanimating corpses. He seemed to feel we should establish the legal status of Bio-Mechanicals before proceeding with the experiments."

"He never spoke of it to me," said Lizzie, biting her lip. Perhaps her father would not have approved of her coming to Ingold.

"Well, to be honest, I think we both mellowed a bit, as one does with age. Always meant to write your father about my more recent experiments...ah, but I suppose pride kept me from making the first move." The cat jumped down from his arms, and Makepiece sighed. "That's the thing about getting older. You think you have all the time in the world, and then one day you look up and you don't have any more time at all."

Byram caught Lizzie's eye and made a hurrying along motion.

"Professor Makepiece," she said, and then was distracted by the cat, which had jumped up on a high shelf, peered down into an open vat and started lapping up the glowing green liquid inside. She gave a little squeak of distress. "Sir, your cat..."

Will, looking pale, scooped the cat into his arms. "What is that? Will it hurt her?"

"Of course not." Makepiece picked up a small vial and dipped it into the vat. "This," he said proudly, "is ichor. Ichor and electricity—the two keys to reanimating the dead," said Makepiece, putting the vial down and scowling at it as if it had personally disappointed him. "The problem is, the ichor degrades, and then the whole creatures just starts to break down, and you can keep injecting more ichor and giving more shocks, but it doesn't really help. If we could trick the body into regenerating its cells..." Makepiece touched the gold locket inside his waistcoat pocket as if it were a talisman. He did not finish his sentence.

"Begging your pardon, Professor, but isn't it a bit of a stretch from salamanders to humans?" Will stroked the cat's head as he looked at the blackboard, where someone had drawn up a blueprint for a mechanical arm that looked both beautiful and terrifying. "After all, we're a lot more complicated than lizards."

"Amphibians, my boy. And when you break it down into a mathematical equation, the underlying principle remains the same."

"If you say so, sir. But it strikes me that the essential spark of self is the soul, not the brain."

"I didn't know you believed in that kind of religious claptrap," Byram said with a laugh.

"Don't you believe in souls, Byram?" Lizzie wasn't sure that she did, either, but she'd never heard anyone say so openly before.

"I believe that if there were such a thing as a soul, a scientist would have found some proof of it by now. What I'm interested in is what you said about limb regeneration." He took a step closer to Makepiece, too absorbed to disguise his limp. "Have you attempted this on a human subject yet?"

Just as Makepiece was about to reply, Will made a choking noise. Lizzie turned to see that he was staring down at the cat in his arms with something like horror in his eyes. "The cat. I was rubbing her behind her ears and…are those *electrodes* coming out of her neck?"

"Yes," said Makepiece, with obvious pride. "I discovered Aldini after she was run over by a carriage. Quite a lot of damage, but as you can see, she's doing just fine now. You might say she's on her tenth life."

"So she's a Bio-Mechanical *cat*?" Will dropped her onto the floor, where she promptly sat, licked her paw and commenced cleaning her face.

"I will never understand the antipathy some people have toward felines." Makepiece scooped up Aldini. "Come on, girl, let's get you some dinner."

"Lizzie," Will whispered, once Makepiece was out of earshot. "I hate to interrupt, but it is getting late. We should get back to the main building before study hall is over."

"But I haven't had a chance to show Professor Makepiece the magnetometer!"

Byram sighed. "Show it to him when he gets back, then, but hurry."

She unwrapped the broken pieces and laid them on a table just as Makepiece reappeared from the back room, chewing on what appeared to be a piece of stale bread. "My condolences on your father's passing, by the way. Meant to write you, but it slipped my mind. Very sad thing, but of course, he would insist on still seeing sick patients." Pausing at the magnetometer, he stroked his beard. "What's this?"

"It's my father's etheric magnetometer. I can fix it, but I just need some glass tubes, some wire and a hollow rubber tube."

"Your father's invention, you say? Interesting. I've never known him to work on such a small scale."

Lizzie swallowed, wondering if he had guessed that it was she who had invented it. "He thought that the small size would make it easier to transport."

"Did he now? How practical." Makepiece looked at her. "Always thought your father could have used a few more pragmatic considerations in his work. Never did seem to consider how things would work in the real world."

Lizzie, who had thought the same thing, felt it would be

disloyal to agree. "I don't suppose you'd consider letting me attempt a repair here?"

Makepiece picked up a broken tube, examining it. "Go right ahead. I have all the materials you require."

Lizzie let out the breath she hadn't realized she was holding. "Oh, thank you, sir! I've been quite anxious. I think Professor Moulsdale's already considering my expulsion."

Makepiece raised his eyebrows. "My dear girl, don't worry about Moulsdale. I've already taken care of him and Grimbald."

"You have?"

"Oh, yes, Grimbald's a simple sort of man—he just didn't want to admit a female to the school. Moulsdale's the one for whispers and plots, always thinking everyone else is as devious as he is. He was concerned that you might share your father's position on granting Bio-Mechanicals legal status and work behind the scenes to undermine us. But I swayed them. You are my student, you see." He beamed at her.

Well, she thought, that certainly explained why Moulsdale tried to set her up to fail on her first day. "But...I thought we aren't assigned schools until second year—"

"I let the paper pushers worry about those details," Makepiece interrupted. "As far as I'm concerned, you're part of the engineering school. Assuming you want to be?"

"Yes, absolutely! Thank you!"

In the distance, a bell began to toll.

"That's it, we're cooked," Will said.

"Nonsense," said Byram. "We're all right if we make it back before last bell." He moved toward the door. "Coming, Lizzie?"

She looked from Makepiece to her friends, torn.

"Go on with you, then," said Makepiece, sensing her distress. "Come back here tomorrow right after breakfast and we'll see what needs doing to your magnetometer."

"We have rounds after breakfast," Lizzie explained.

"Then come after that. Come whenever you like. I'm here all day. Bring me a roll, if you think of it. And perhaps a bit of cheese."

In the last moment before she followed Byram and Will out the door, Lizzie looked over her shoulder. Makepiece seemed to have forgotten all about his visitors. He had taken out the gold locket and was looking at the pictures again. In the vat beside him, there was a ripple of bubbles in the green liquid around the arm.

"Come on, Lizzie, we have to hurry!"

"Wait," she said, but Will was already tugging at her elbow, pulling her away, and she couldn't say for certain whether she had really seen the fingers of the dismembered hand wriggling like the severed salamander tail.

# 9

SOMETIMES HE THOUGHT HE WAS BACK IN prison. Or perhaps in the workhouse, which was worse. Whatever this place was, at least he wasn't breaking stones here. In his more lucid moments, he thought he must be in hospital. Until, one day, a doctor brought him out of his bedchamber and into a larger, windowless room set with wooden school desks on one side, and rowing machines, stationary bicycles and free weights on the other. The room was oppressively hot, and the floor was warm underneath his bare feet, which meant there was probably a furnace below. The dry heat brought out the distinctive smell of chalk on a slate blackboard, undercut with the stale odor of masculine sweat and wood varnish. Someone had hung a single amateurish landscape painting of a ruined castle on one wall, in a rather futile attempt to make the room seem less like a dungeon.

"Look," said a skinny young doctor with heavy-lidded eyes and an air of profound ennui. "Do this." He lifted one of the smaller barbells in two hands and heaved it up to his chest. "I don't even know why I bother," the young man muttered to himself as he handed over the weight with a grunt. "Not one of you has the mental acuity of a walnut, and yet day after day I have to repeat the same...huh." His mouth dropped open as he watched Victor carefully set the twenty-pound barbell back in its slot in the rack along the wall. The young doctor's expression remained comically surprised as Victor selected a forty-pound weight and executed a set of ten bicep curls.

After that, Victor was brought there each morning for a regimen of daily physical exercises.

The physical training came easily to him. Within a week, he was shimmying up the rope to the ceiling while the doctor timing him smiled and shook his head in disbelief. None of the other patients could even manage to get halfway up the rope. The other patients were all big, hulking brutes with scarred faces, and their mouths hung open as they pedaled laboriously on the stationary bikes, their feet tangling in the pedals, or sat awkwardly on the rowing machines, unable to coordinate their arms and legs. As his strength continued to return, he began doing chin-ups and running up and down the stairs that led down to the furnace. He felt infinitely superior to his inept, dead-eyed companions, but it occasionally occurred to him that he might just be the star pupil at a lunatic asylum. Not much to boast about there.

Yet he did feel pride when the men in the white coats moved him over to the side of the room set up as a classroom and gave him a series of wood puzzles to assemble. He fit together the shapes so rapidly that a new white coat was brought in to observe. This one was older, a gaunt man with a long white beard and fierce eyebrows. After this man left, the children's puzzles were replaced by more challenging games. Right now, he was working on a set of interlocking metal rings, which he was clearly expected to disentangle. *Piece of cake*, he thought as he manipulated the rings so that he could slide them free of each other. *Just like jimmying a lock.* He looked up at the doctor who was timing him with his pocket watch. Was the sawbones impressed? He ought to be. Victor had challenged himself by mainly using his left hand to work the puzzle.

*His left hand.* Victor stared down at the brass gauntlet that began just above the elbow and, fused with screws at the ulna and radius, terminated in a fingerless metal glove that ended just above the proximal interphalangeal joints. He tried to flex his fingers. They did not respond.

Why had he received a Bio-Mechanical graft? What had happened to his own arm? Those memories of prison…he had never been to prison. Perhaps he was thinking of some serialized story he had read in the paper? Victor looked over at the doctor and remembered that it was Henry, his old friend. He tried to speak his name, but the garbled sound that came out sounded like the bellow of a wounded beast.

Henry wheeled around, his eyes round behind his spectacles, and clutched his right arm to his chest. His hand was in a cast.

*I did that*, Victor thought. *With my bad hand.*

"I said do it now," Henry was shouting at an orderly, and Victor felt something sharp jab him in the arm. "He needs to be recalibrated," Henry said. "Take him up to the Galvanic Reanimator."

Victor felt a chill of fear—he felt that he had seen bodies galvanized, but he could not seem to remember how or when—and then, abruptly, he felt nothing at all.

For a long time after that, Victor had only scattered moments of awareness. Waking up in the dark. An orderly helping him to a chamber pot, as though he were an invalid. Someone spooning gruel into his mouth. Sometimes he was shuffling in a long line of men. Sometimes he was running. It was difficult to tell what was a dream and what was not. He knew, though, that Henry dropped by from time to time, inspecting Victor from a safe distance, his hand still in a cast.

One night, after the orderly had nearly choked Victor by spooning down the gruel faster than Victor could swallow it, he dreamed that Henry arrived without a cast and sat on the edge of Victor's bed as though they were still roommates.

"Funny old world," he said, offering Victor a glass of Madeira. "Who would've guessed you would want to be a surgeon? One step above a butcher, really."

"Just what my father believes," said Victor, taking the glass. "But it's not just the surgery. I like working with the engineering department. I like tinkering with things."

"Well, here's to tinkering," said Henry, clinking his wine glass to Victor's. They drank in companionable silence, and then Henry raised the bottle again. "Top you up?"

Victor shook his head. "We'd best get to bed now, or we'll never get to the lecture on time tomorrow."

"Killjoy." Henry went over to his own bed. There was a rustle of sheets, the sound of shoes dropping to the floor, and then a massive belch.

"Scalawag."

"Puritan."

"I'm turning out the light, Henry." He turned the knob on the lamp, casting the room into darkness.

"Henry?"

Victor listened for the sound of his friend's familiar snoring, but he was alone.

Sometimes his dreams felt more real than his waking life.

★ ★ ★

At some point, Victor became aware that he was being drugged. At least, that was Victor's working hypothesis, but he needed to test it. It could be sheer exhaustion that was keeping his thoughts vague and muddled. Now that they were allowing him out for training, Victor realized how weak he had become, and the thin workhouse gruel they served him for breakfast, lunch and dinner left him perpetually light-headed from hunger, and ravenous.

On the other hand, thought Victor, perhaps it was simply malnutrition that was robbing him of his ability to concentrate. In the past, he had never been terribly fussed about what food he put in his mouth, but now he found himself fantasizing about favorite meals: rare roast beef garlanded by crispy potatoes with gooseberry preserve, and a bit of bread to soak up the drippings, a rasher of bacon, a shepherd's pie, even a slice of sharp cheese and a sour pickle.

Despite the narrow cot, too short for his six-foot-three frame, he fell straight to sleep each night as though plummeting down a dark well.

One night, trying to fight unconsciousness, Victor remembered that there was a children's book that began with a girl falling down a well or a hole of some sort. It had been an odd and charming book, with talking rabbits and mad tea parties. He had read it to Will on his last night in the nursery, right before he'd been sent away to school. How Will had carried on the next day, wailing that he would never hear the end of the story now.

*Will*, thought Victor. He hadn't remembered his brother till now. How could he have forgotten his younger brother? The two had been…

But then he was asleep, and whatever they had been went away for a while.

The next time Victor was conscious, he found himself shuffling in a long line of men, all of them chained together at the wrist and ankle like convicts.

"Keep it moving," said a short, muscular man with a wizened, monkey face and beard without a mustache. He wore a navy greatcoat and cap, like a workhouse guard.

A second guard jabbed Victor with a long stick. He had thick ginger sideburns that ended at his chin.

"Come on, lads," said the monkey-faced guard. "Step lively, now."

"Lads, is it? Brutes or monsters is more like," said the man with the ginger sideburns. Victor looked at him, amused. Did the man fancy himself Victor's social superior? "'Ey, Pretty Boy, what you lookin' at?" He bared yellowed teeth at Victor. "Look at me and I'll smash in your ugly pie hole."

"Take it easy, Luther. They don't mean no 'arm," said the smaller guard.

"They don't mean no good, neither," said Luther, poking Victor again.

The sharp jab to his kidney made Victor double over, and the men on either side of him lost their footing and began to fall. Victor reached out and righted the man in front of him, and there was a metallic clink of chains as the other man turned, revealing dull, dead eyes set in a hideously scarred face, his nose flattened like that of a boxer. The man did not seem to register Victor at all, and then Victor saw the electrodes on the man's neck that marked him as a Bio-Mechanical.

*But if he's a Bio-Mechanical,* thought Victor, *and I'm chained to him…what does that make me?*

It was impossible, unthinkable, and yet as Victor stared down at his manacled hands, he could think of no other explanation. How had this happened? The last thing he remembered was standing in the laboratory with Henry and arguing about something. Whether or not to tell something. No, wait, there had been something else…a more recent memory: waking up in a hospital room, chained to the bed. And the day he had worked the puzzle. Victor looked down at his left arm, and there it was: the alien flesh, tanned and leathery and fused with a metallic gauntlet. *Dear Lord*, thought Victor, *it's true. They've changed me.* As if from another life, he heard the echo of Henry's voice: funny old world.

"Move off, now, move off!" The stick prodded Victor again, and suddenly Victor's left hand shot out and grabbed the stick.

"Oh, Jesus, Gibbons, they're not supposed to do that," moaned Luther, and then something heavy slammed into the back of Victor's head, making the lights dance behind his eyes before everything went dark.

# 18

THE DAY, IT SEEMED, HAD ONE MORE SURPRISE in store for Lizzie: there was someone in her room.

"Oi! Turn off the light!" Lizzie blinked at the redheaded young woman who was lying in bed, squinting at her. "What d'ye mean, barging in here in the middle of the blooming night?" Without waiting for a reply, the angry redhead rolled over and pulled the covers over her head.

"Sorry!" Lizzie was already backing out the door, sure she was in the wrong room, until she recognized her steamer trunk, still open on the floor from when she had ransacked it for the magnetometer. "I'm sorry," said Lizzie, "but I think you must be in the wrong room."

"Turn. Off. The. Light."

While Lizzie had been out, someone had crammed a second bed into the corner where the hulking shape of the wardrobe had been, underneath the window. The wardrobe had been moved closer to Lizzie's bed, like a massive wooden barricade. "I'm sorry, but can you please explain what you're doing in my room?"

"Oh, for crying out loud." The redhead sat up, shielding her eyes with her hand. "What time is it, anyway? Midnight?"

Lizzie checked her fob watch. "It's half-past nine," she said, a little surprised herself that it wasn't later. With one thing and the other, it had been a long day, and she was still reeling from the things she had seen and heard in Makepiece's laboratory.

"Half-past nine? Are you positive?" The girl rubbed her eyes and yawned until her jaw popped. "Sorry, I'm completely shattered. Been up for twenty-four hours straight, all of them on my feet." She pulled back the covers, revealing that she was still wearing her corset and chemise. "Anyway, I'm your roommate, Agatha DeLacey. You can call me Aggie."

"Elizabeth Lavenza," said Lizzie. "Did you just arrive here?"

"No," said Aggie as she loosened the laces at the front of her corset. "I've been here for a couple of days." She yawned again, and for a moment, Lizzie thought she wasn't going to say anything more, but then Aggie began speaking again. "I started out rooming with the second years, because I had some practical training with my ma, but then Matron showed up after dinner and said midwifery doesn't count."

Lizzie tried not to stare as Aggie continued to undress in front of her. She wasn't used to sharing a room with another girl...perhaps this was typical female behavior.

"You're a midwife?"

Aggie glanced up, then resumed untying her corset laces. "Me ma is. Ah. Blessed freedom." She dropped her corset onto the bed beside her and heaved another sigh, revealing an impressive amount of pale bosom rising over her chemise.

*Shiercliffe. Of course.* This was the matron's revenge for Lizzie wandering the halls with boys. "Oh," she said, sitting down on her bed to unlace her shoes. "That explains it." She hadn't appreciated how lucky she was to have a single room until now.

Aggie stood up and replaced her corset in her own trunk. "So, what's your story? How did you rate a single? Is it because you're American and are used to big open spaces?"

"I'd hardly call this room big. It's because I'm a medical student." Lizzie tugged off her right shoe and then paused, struck by a thought. What if she couldn't sleep, like last night, and wanted to read her anatomy textbook in bed? A roommate would insist that she turn off the light, and she would have to lie there in the dark, awake.

This was a nightmare.

"A medical student?" Aggie stopped brushing out her hair and stared at Lizzie. "They let women do that?"

"They let *me* do that," she said, not sure if admitting women was standard policy or not.

"Oh, well, and aren't you the special one."

"I beg your pardon?"

"Never mind. Turn off the light, will you?" Aggie climbed back into her bed and pulled up the covers.

"Of course." Mind racing, Lizzie walked over to the light in her stockinged feet and glanced at the hostile, blanketed lump of roommate in the other bed.

She had to do something to fix this. In her experience, girls made far more dangerous adversaries than boys. Boys might be unkind, but at least they were openly cruel. Girls, on the other hand, waged covert wars.

"Listen, I'm getting the sense that I've upset you."

The hostile lump did not move. "Light."

"It wasn't my intention."

"I'm sure it wasn't."

Lizzie paused. She may not have wanted a roommate, but she certainly did not want an enemy sharing her space. "If you could just tell me what I did or said to annoy you…"

"You're doing it now."

"I probably seemed unwelcoming. Is that it? It's just that I wasn't expecting to find someone in my room. I mean, in *our* room. And since it is going to be our room, and it's so small, I think we should try to get along."

"Right." Aggie flung off the covers, stood up and stalked across the room without looking at Lizzie. Then she flicked off the light switch and stalked back to her bed.

The silence felt uncomfortable, barbed with sharp unsaid truths. Lizzie rolled over and tried to drift off to sleep, but all she could think about was how, as a little girl alone in her dark room, she had conjured imaginary sisters and girlfriends to keep her company.

"Aggie? Are you upset with me because you'd like to be a medical student, too? Because being a nurse may not seem as exciting or challenging, but—"

"Stop. Talking. Now."

"All right," said Lizzie. "It's late, but we can talk about it again in the morning."

There was a groan from the other side of the room.

When Lizzie woke, it was already half-past seven, and her new roommate's bed was neatly made up.

Passing by the first year nursing students' table in the dining hall, Lizzie caught a glimpse of Aggie's red hair. She was sitting a little apart from the others, reading *Notes on Nursing* by Florence Nightingale, and for a moment, Lizzie thought about joining her. But when Aggie glanced up and saw her roommate standing there, she instantly looked away and began chatting to one of the other nursing students.

*Fine.* Lizzie scanned the room, looking for Byram and Will instead. They were either not here yet, or already gone.

Never mind; she could always use the time to catch up on some anatomy reading before class. Unfortunately, the only free seat appeared to be at a table with Outhwaite and his constant companion, the plump, milky-skinned boy named Mothersole. As she stood there holding her tray, Lizzie heard a chorus of feminine giggles behind her. Well, what did she care if they acted like a pack of hyenas? Placing her tray on the side table, she took two quick gulps of tea and headed off to anatomy class. She wasn't really all that hungry, anyway.

The lecture hall had once been the abbey's main chapel, and even though the altar and crucifix had been replaced by a table and blackboard, Lizzie thought there was something hushed and reverent in the air as the students took their places on the benches. On the table, Lizzie saw a plaster model of a human head and neck, with sections of the brain marked and colored like the pieces of a child's jigsaw puzzle. On one side of the table, there was a complete human skeleton hanging from a hook; on the other side, there was a life-size portrait of a man who appeared as though he had been partially flayed, revealing slices of muscle, bone, heart and a serpentine coil of large intestine. Lizzie leaned forward and squinted, trying to get a better look. She could make out the words "White's physiological manikin" and on closer inspection, the image was actually made up of four different sections, but where the sections met at the juncture of legs and hips, the figure's groin was as smooth as a frog's. *How strange.* Common sense told Lizzie that men must be built more along the lines of dogs or horses than fish or frogs, but she had yet to see any proof of this theory.

Lizzie had arrived early, to make sure she got a seat near the front. She was removing her father's pocket watch to check the time when she heard someone whisper something in the row behind her.

"I know," came the response. "Well, who can blame her? It's probably the closest she'll get to a man." This was spoken loud enough for her to hear, and was followed by a snort of derisive laughter. Lizzie glanced over her shoulder to see that Outhwaite was smirking while Mothersole placed his hand over his pursed mouth and tittered.

Lizzie felt herself go cold, then hot. She wanted to say, "And it's the closest you two will get to a woman," but she knew it wasn't true. These idiots would probably have their pick of wives, and the worst part of it was the very medical degree that added to their desirability detracted from hers. Never mind. She would rather have a fascinating career than an overbearing husband. Still, it was so unfair that she had to make the choice at all, when men could satisfy both their hearts and their minds.

Outhwaite leaned closer. "By the way, still waiting for that proof you went to see Makepiece…"

"We described the lab to you. In detail. What more proof do you need?"

"The tangible kind. How about your father's magic whatsit, Lavenza? Fixed that yet?"

"Yes, but Professor Makepiece wants me to leave it there."

"Sure he does." Outhwaite leaned back and crossed his arms over his chest. "I think there ought to be some penalty for welching on a bet, don't you, Mothersole?"

Mothersole's protuberant eyes seemed to bulge even more in excitement. "I do indeed."

It was pointless. Lizzie folded her hands and looked straight in front of her, while Outhwaite and Mothersole whispered about the appropriate punishment for false promises.

"Hello, you," Byram said as he slid onto the bench beside

her. "Sorry we're late, but someone's alarm never went off. Thanks for saving us a seat."

"Do we have to sit so close to the front?" Will, as usual, was carrying a novel in addition to his anatomy text. "Grimbald's sure to call on me if I sit where he can see me."

"Lizzie's a bit shortsighted."

"I am not." Or at least, she never admitted it. Bad enough to be a bluestocking without having to wear spectacles as well.

"My mistake," said Byram. "You must squint all the time to give the professors the impression that you're paying attention. Brilliant ruse, that."

Somehow, when it was Byram teasing her, it didn't bother Lizzie. "You might try it yourself, instead of pretending to be bored all the time."

"But I *am* bored. How long d'you suppose we have to wait to get our hands on a corpse?"

"It can't be long enough for me," Will said. "I can't even abide the smell of a ham sandwich after it's been left out in the sun. How am I supposed to poke around in a dead body?"

The hum of conversation died abruptly as Professor Grimbald strode into the room, his handlebar mustache and military bearing making his white lab coat seem like a uniform. He stood in front of the class, arms clasped behind his back, surveying them from his small, dark eyes, and no one whispered or made a joke under his breath, not even Byram. The class had been excited to begin its studies, but Moulsdale's rambling discussions on materia medica and the therapeutic properties of various tinctures and potions were not exactly scintillating. Grimbald's class was another matter entirely. This was Gross Anatomy. Here, at last, the mysteries of the human body would be revealed and explained. Most exciting of all, there would be actual cadavers for the students to examine and dissect. It might be ghoulish, this desire to peel back the layers of protective skin and see the workings of the machinery inside, but all the medical students shared it. Or, at least, all the medical students besides Will, who was looking pale.

"Welcome, gentlemen, to Gross Anatomy and Physiology. I assume most of you understand the distinction between the two?" He paused. "A show of hands, if you please."

Will tried to slip lower in his seat. "How does he expect us to know anything on the very first day?"

"You, in the third row," said Grimbald. "Aren't you Frankenstein's brother?"

"Yes, sir," said Will, looking miserable.

"Can you enlighten your classmates?"

"Form and function," whispered Lizzie, pretending to pick something off the floor.

"Why, yes, sir. Anatomy refers to the form of the body parts," said Will. "Physiology to the function."

"Very good," said Grimbald. "Now, let me ask another question. How can we distinguish between the living and the dead?"

Byram's hand shot up. "The dead don't make very good conversation," he offered.

Grimbald did not smile. "Too general. Why don't the dead converse? Yes, you, in the fourth row."

"I'm sorry," said Outhwaite. "I wasn't raising my hand. I was scratching my nose."

Lizzie, who had raised her hand, looked back at him, then raised her hand again.

"Hazard a guess, then," said Grimbald.

"Um." Outhwaite's eyes darted to Lizzie, then back. "I'm sorry, sir, I don't quite…"

"Anyone else?" Grimbald paced across the room with his hands clasped behind his back, surveying the students.

Lizzie waved her arm.

Sighing, Grimbald bowed his head. Without turning around, he said, "The answer, of course, is that the dead are unresponsive. They do not move, or breathe, or grow. They do not digest food, their blood does not circulate and they do not carry on the various metabolic functions associated with living creatures." Grimbald turned around and began to pace back across the room. "And yes, in addition to all this, the dead do not converse."

Byram's hand shot up. "But sir, what of Bio-Mechanicals? They move and respond to simple commands."

Grimbald nodded. "Indeed. They also take in air and require nourishment. And as such, what is your diagnosis—alive, or dead?"

"Alive, I suppose."

"Yes," said Grimbald, barking the word out and making the students in the front rows jump. "That is correct. Bio-Mechanicals are living creatures, not, as some would have it, *corpse walkers*." There was a nervous titter of laughter throughout the room. "A bullet to the brain or heart will destroy them, and they cannot survive without air, or water, or food. Bio-Mechanicals may start out as corpses," said Grimbald, "but make no mistake—after reanimation, they *are* alive." He paused, and Lizzie thought he seemed distracted, as if his thoughts were far away, lost in some melancholy memory. Then, clearing his throat and straightening his shoulders, Grimbald collected himself and went on. "For now, however, we will focus on learning the most basic forms and functions of the human body. This class will consist of lectures and labs, and yes, gentlemen, you will get your hands on a cadaver."

"Yes," said Byram and Lizzie, almost in unison.

Grimbald paused, staring straight at Lizzie. "However,

given the delicate nature of one of those present, this element of the course will be restricted to include gentlemen only."

"What!" Lizzie's astonished exclamation echoed in the lecture hall, and every head in the room turned toward her. "Professor Grimbald," she said, "how am I meant to pass this class if I am not allowed to participate fully?"

"Young woman, if you have a question, raise your hand." Lizzie raised her hand.

"However, I am not prepared to stop the entire class to address a question that only pertains to one student. Now, let us move on to more pressing matters."

Taking hold of the skeleton, Grimbald moved it to the center of the stage. "Let us begin with the support structure of the body. The axial skeleton refers to the bones that make up the central axis of the body, as opposed to the appendicular skeleton. All told, there are 206 bones in the human body, and for next class, I expect you to know them all."

"Kill me now," said Will under his breath.

In that moment, she could have slapped him. What right did he have to complain? So what if the course was difficult. Medical school wasn't supposed to be easy, and if you couldn't handle the work or the sight of a dead body, then you had to expect to be weeded out. Only the most tenacious students would be able to make it through to the end, which was fine, because she knew she was stubborn enough to withstand just about anything.

*But it doesn't matter what I know or what I can do or how hard I try.* Grimbald made it clear that he didn't want her in his class. Even if she passed every exam, the head of surgery wasn't going allow her to succeed.

On the bright side, he had made the opening gambit and revealed his game plan. *All I need to do is think of a countermove.*

# 11

THAT EVENING, LIZZIE WENT TO MAKEPIECE'S laboratory carrying a bit of bread and a hunk of cheese wrapped in wax paper for the professor. They had repaired the etheric magnetometer two days earlier, but had not yet had the opportunity to test it. Tonight, Makepiece had promised Lizzie, they would give the device an experimental run. Up until today's anatomy class, Lizzie had been counting down the hours, but now she was so infuriated by Grimbald's decision to exclude her that she could barely think about anything else.

"Professor Makepiece?" She was surprised to find that the laboratory was dark and there was a faint, metallic, burned odor in the room. She flipped the light switch, but nothing happened. A fuse must have blown. Lizzie was turning to leave when she heard a low moan. "Hello? Professor? Is that you?" Lizzie paused, her heart pounding. "Are you injured?" Another moan, and this time Lizzie followed the sound to its source. Even though it was too dark to see clearly, she could make out a bulky form lying on a gurney.

"Ghhnn."

"Professor?" She didn't know why she kept saying that. She knew that the figure on the gurney was not Makepiece. It must be a patient, but something about the size of the shadowy figure made her nervous. "Are you in pain?"

"Ghhnn."

*All right, get a grip on yourself*, she thought. *You want to be a doctor? Act like one.*

"Right, then," she said, and drew closer to the patient. "It sounds as though you might be experiencing a bit of discomfort." There was another soft moan, and Lizzie wished she could see better. In addition to being slightly shortsighted, she had poor night vision, and all she could make out of the patient was that he was a large man, his form mostly covered by a blanket.

Surely Makepiece kept a gas lamp on hand in case of power outages. Feeling around on the table, Lizzie's hand came in contact with a glass lantern. "All right, matches, matches…" Her fingers closed on the box, which she recognized by the strip of sandpaper along its side. "Now the trick is to do this without burning my fingers." Lizzie turned the lamp's knob, waited to hear the low hiss of escaping gas, and struck a match. *Success.* She adjusted the light, then moved the lantern so that it illuminated the patient with its pallid yellow glow.

"Gnnn!" The patient closed his eyes tightly, as if recoiling from the light. That might mean a migraine, thought Lizzie, moving the lamp away.

"Is that better?" The patient took a deep, shuddery breath. "Good," Lizzie said, hoping she sounded more confident than she felt. "Now let's take a look at you." The patient's face was badly bruised, with swelling around his left eye, a cut on his right cheek and a split lower lip. He was also taller and younger than she had expected, with untidy thick, dark hair and the broad shoulders of a manual laborer. She reached out and brushed back his thick hair, which was surprisingly silky to the touch, and pressed the back of her hand to his forehead. "Fever. You *are* in a state." The patient squinted up at her, clearly trying to adjust to the light. "But is it a contagious fever? Are you injured?"

She pulled back the covers to continue her examination. He was not wearing the usual nightshirt, and Lizzie tried not to feel missish about the firmly muscled expanse of bare chest that was revealed, or the metal plate that covered the left side of his chest. It was a dull brass color, and appeared to be fused with the flesh. She had never seen anything like it before. "What is this?"

The patient frowned. Perhaps he didn't speak English. She wished she had paid more attention to her father's French lessons. "Um...*parlez-vous français*?" She moved her hands down one well-developed arm and realized that there were leather restraints on the man's wrists, tying him down to the gurney. His left hand was partially encased in a brass gauntlet, and the fingers appeared quite discolored, at least a shade or two darker than his right hand. She decided to loosen the restraints while she was there, to allow the blood to circulate better. Leaning across him to untie his left arm, she saw that the scars and the metal extended all the way around the forearm. Whoever this poor man was, he had clearly suffered some grievous injuries in the past.

"All right, I need to cleanse your wound." Lizzie paused, wondering if she dared pull the blanket farther down, uncovering the man's torso and abdomen. It would be absurd to waste time treating his upper body if there were other, worse injuries lower down.

*Sapere Aude*, she thought. *Dare to know.*

She folded the blanket back and saw that the man's abdomen was marked with bruises. There was a long friction burn running along his right side, which looked terribly painful, and should have been covered by ointment and a bandage. There were also older scars, making Lizzie wonder if her patient had been a soldier, or a prisoner of war.

She licked her lips. "I am going to touch you. Let me know if this hurts, and I will stop." She reached out one hand to touch the largest bruise, and pressed gently to see if any of the underlying organs might have been injured. She glanced up at his face, to find that the patient was lying back with his eyes closed. He looked exhausted, as if watching her took too much effort. Biting her lower lip, Lizzie hesitated only a moment and then tugged the covers down another inch. A thin line of dark hair bisected his flat stomach, which was ridged with muscle. Lizzie felt a strange twist of nervous excitement in her own belly as she drew the covers down past the patient's hip bones.

The patient grunted, and one of his hands closed over hers. Lizzie gave a startled yelp. The man's eyes opened and his blue gaze held hers, and then, in a low, clear voice, he said, "No."

Victor looked up at the young woman who seemed intent on removing his last claim to modesty. Where was he, precisely? The last thing he recalled was…shuffling. Manacles. The monkey-faced guard. And then the knowledge, slamming into him like another kick: *they've changed me.* On the heels of that thought came another: *I don't want to live like this.*

A memory: Henry, staring into his glass of ale, saying,

"It's easy to think well of yourself when the world keeps telling you how wonderful you are. You don't know what you might become if everyone started to treat you as though you were defective."

"Oh, dear," Victor had replied at the time, "are we getting maudlin? Best stop drinking, old man."

But Henry had been right; Victor hadn't known himself. He wished this young woman would go away and stop looking at him. He wished he could close his eyes and fall back into the dark of unconsciousness. God, his head hurt.

"What's wrong? You must let me examine you." The young American woman twisted her hands, trying to get him to release his grip.

She really was determined to get him naked, thought Victor. Despite the pounding of his head, he was bemused to realize that he was not too far gone to see the humor in the situation. "Muh heh," he said. He had managed that first "no" without even thinking, but now he felt as though he were rediscovering some old path that words could take from mind to mouth.

"Your head hurts?"

She understood him! Victor let go of the nurse's wrists and allowed her to run them over his head. He knew the moment she saw the electrodes jutting from the side of his neck, because she sucked in a sharp breath. When she looked up at him, there was new understanding in her eyes. She had thought him a man. Now, she knew he was a *thing*—a construct of cold metal and dead flesh. Victor waited for the nurse to recoil. In his experience, nurses did not like to attend to Bio-Mechanicals. They treated them with cold efficiency, but they did not speak softly to them, or smile, or offer palliatives to ease their pain. As women, they were more in touch

with feeling and nature than men. They had no elaborate in-
tellectual justifications to blind them to what was right and
what was wrong.

But this young woman was frowning down at him as if
he were a chess problem. Then, very slowly and deliberately,
she touched his neck again, near the metal implants. "Is this
where the pain is coming from?"

Her fingers were cool and comforting on his head, the light
pressure she exerted a relief. "Ehsh," he said, even though he
wasn't completely sure if the stabbing pains were traveling up
to his head or down from it.

"Hmm. I have an idea."

*Laudanum.* Thank God, she would give him laudanum and
he would sleep and perhaps, if she was inexperienced enough,
she might give him too much laudanum, enough to send him
floating off out of this nightmare existence.

The nurse stepped out of the circle of light, and he heard
her stumble once in the dark. Victor was disappointed to see
that she did not carry a little brown bottle in her hands when
she returned. Instead, she held a purple velvet bag, which she
set down on the bed, unnervingly close to sensitive areas. Did
the woman have no concept of male anatomy?

"Here," she said, fiddling with an instrument he couldn't
see. "All right, this is going to make a crackling sound, but
don't worry." She took a deep breath. "It won't hurt."

That didn't sound terribly convincing. Now he could see
that she was holding a glass wand over his chest. He grunted,
making it a question.

"It's a treatment. Too complicated to explain."

Now she sounded like a doctor. Victor watched as she
turned a dial, then stiffened as the glass tube crackled with
violet light. "Wuh." That light. A memory flashed through

him: blue-tinged lightning, machete-sharp pain slicing down his spine.

"Wait? But why? This will make you feel better." She moved her hand, and he grabbed the wrist holding the wand. She looked at him, hazel eyes bright with purpose. "Really. It's all perfectly safe. Trust me." Victor realized what she was trying to do: shock him back into unconsciousness, the way Grimbald did with experimental animals.

He released her wrist. If this nurse couldn't kill him, then perhaps she could turn him into a proper Bio-Mechanical— one with no thoughts or feelings.

"That's better. It will all work this time. You'll see."

Victor waited for the charge of electricity to jolt through him. The first time the nurse waved the wand, small tongues of electricity arced down over his chest. Then she raised the wand closer to his face, and he felt the electrodes in his neck begin to vibrate, setting up a low, unsettling hum inside his head.

She looked down at him, smiling a little. She was quite pretty, he realized, with lovely, thick-lashed hazel eyes. His head felt warm, and the heat traveled down his body. *Hope I don't embarrass myself.* Then, in a shocking surge, he felt a sudden paroxysm of pain that had something of pleasure in it. No time to feel embarrassed now. He convulsed, fists clenching, before the darkness he had been praying for released him at last.

# 12

FOR AN AWFUL MOMENT, LIZZIE THOUGHT THAT she had killed her first patient. She began to check for a heartbeat, then paused, looking down at the strange metal plate covering his heart. After a moment's hesitation, she placed her ear near his mouth instead, and was relieved to hear him draw in a breath.

"Are you all right?" He gave no sign that he heard her. Lizzie touched the electrodes with the tip of one finger, then gasped as a jolt of electricity shot through her. She swallowed, trying to get rid of the odd metallic taste in her mouth. Why had the magnetometer knocked the Bio-Mechanical unconscious? It had never had that effect on any human patient.

She was about to slap the subject's face to bring him around when she heard the sound of voices outside the laboratory. "I still say we ought to wait." Lizzie recognized Grimbald's voice.

"We've waited too long already. The queen is malfunctioning and needs to be regalvanized."

"The last thing we want is to draw attention to ourselves

with a royal visit. I do not want to see the school's name in the broadsheets again."

"I still don't see why you've dragged us all out here, Makepiece." That was Moulsdale, sounding irate. "Couldn't we have met in my study?"

"No," said Makepiece. "I have something to show you."

Lizzie looked down at the Bio-Mechanical and found that his eyes were open and that he was looking in the direction of the voices. He turned back to her, and for the first time, Lizzie saw the clear light of intelligence in his blue eyes.

"Hide," he said.

"But…"

*"Now."* Said without garbling or hesitation.

Lizzie quickly extinguished the lamp and gathered up the pieces of the etheric magnetometer. Where could she conceal herself? Looking around the laboratory, she spotted the small wardrobe where Makepiece kept lab coats and aprons. Lizzie moved clumsily through the dark room, knocking into a salamander tank and nearly upsetting a glass vial before she found the wardrobe. She made it just in time. As she pulled the door shut behind her, she heard the professors' footsteps as they entered the lab.

"Botheration, Makepiece, the fuses have blown."

"No, I did it deliberately, to make sure we had no unwanted visitors." Through the cracks in the wardrobe, Lizzie saw the lights come on.

"Dear Lord, isn't that…?" Moulsdale's voice trailed off.

Grimbald scowled. "What's he doing here?"

"Got into a fight with the guards," said Makepiece mildly. "Could be a promising sign."

Lizzie put her eye up to the crack in the wardrobe door

and saw that the three men were gathered around the Bio-Mechanical.

Moulsdale had his hands tucked into his waistcoat pockets as he considered the Bio-Mechanical. "A display of aggression. Very promising. Was it provoked?"

"The guards say no," Makepiece said in a dry voice. "He also seems to have attacked Henry Clerval."

Moulsdale nodded, taking this in. "And was *that* provoked?"

"Whether it was provoked or not is immaterial," said Grimbald. "It was aggression. This could be the breakthrough we've been searching for, Ambrose."

"Or it could be a setback," said Moulsdale. "We need to be able to control them, Graham."

"We need them to be able to attack an enemy," countered Grimbald. "Right now, all they do is shuffle straight into the line of fire."

All Lizzie could see now were the professors' backs as they bent over the patient.

"He appears to be unconscious."

"His breathing is too rapid for that. He's shamming." There was a loud slap. "There. Now he's awake. Well?" Grimbald's voice was edged with excitement. "Are you aggressive?" Another slap. "Or are you just another dumb beast?"

"Grimbald, his hands...he's not restrained."

"So let him attack me." Another slap.

"Grimbald, stop."

"Why?" Another slap, louder than the other. "He's not a man, remember? He doesn't feel pain."

"Grimbald, that is enough," said Moulsdale. "He's not responding, so can we please go back to discussing the more important issue? We need to know when our esteemed royal visitor should return to us."

"It's not the more important issue," said Grimbald. "It's a bloody distraction from our real work—creating Bio-Mechanical soldiers for the queen."

"Yes…for the *queen*," said Moulsdale. "And that is why we must tend to our most powerful patient."

Grimbald snorted derisively. "You and your political machinations."

"You'll thank me someday. We can send Makepiece to tinker with her, but for a full overhaul, Her Majesty needs the equipment we have here. Makepiece, what do you say?"

"She needs to be brought in, and the sooner the better. And that means we need fresh cadavers."

"What about the locals?" This was Grimbald. "They're always particularly superstitious of us around Christmastime. The last time we had a late delivery, the rumor mill started buzzing about grave robbers."

"It can't be helped. We need to work on her now, and for that, we need cadavers."

"Fine, don't listen to me," said Grimbald. "I don't know why I even bother to come down here." He glanced at the figure on the gurney. "What do you suggest we do about…it?"

"Don't worry, Graham. He's my concern."

"Good."

Lizzie waited as the voices moved away. For the first time in her life, she felt thick and stupid as she tried to make sense of the things she had heard. Why was Grimbald so angry with this Bio-Mechanical? She recalled her father telling her that, in his experience, anger was mostly a disguise for fear or guilt, or the curdled artifact of love gone sour.

Lizzie bit the inside of her cheek. Then there was that business about the queen *malfunctioning*. It seemed a terribly disrespectful way to speak about the eighty-one-year-old sovereign, who had been on the throne for more than six decades. Back in the States, Lizzie had heard that the elderly monarch's health had been failing, but when she arrived in London, the broadsheets ran pictures of the octogenarian performing her royal duties. Then again, if the good doctors at Ingold could fix whatever had been ailing the British monarch, they were probably entitled to speak of her as if she were a rusty train engine in need of refurbishment.

A chill went through her. What had they said? *A full overhaul...our most powerful patient.* Suddenly she had to fight to keep her breathing low and quiet.

Through the crack in the door, Lizzie could see Makepiece moving around the laboratory. He came to stand directly in front of the wardrobe, and she held her breath.

"Miss Lavenza," said Makepiece, opening the door without fanfare, "would you mind telling me what you are doing here?"

Lizzie tried to think of a plausible excuse, but her mind went blank. She could, of course, tell him the truth. This man had been her father's friend and was her only ally among the faculty. Then she glanced at the Bio-Mechanical lying on the gurney, his arms once again bound by restraints. Makepiece must have refastened them.

"I brought you something to eat," she said. Which was true. "We were going to work on the magnetometer."

"I was in my private rooms! You know that you're not supposed to be in the lab when I'm not here." Lizzie hadn't realized that there was a door that led directly to the professor's living quarters. Well, that explained why he seemed to live in his workplace. She hung her head, hoping that she looked sufficiently penitent. "I came in looking for you, and then I saw someone injured and in pain, so I tried to help. I thought he was a patient, but that's no excuse."

He looked marginally less upset. "You didn't realize that he was a Bio-Mechanical?"

"Not right away," said Lizzie. "I just saw that he was in pain, and wanted to render some assistance."

"That's interesting. So he appeared human to you? Sensible?" Makepiece tugged at his beard again. "Then why were you were hiding? How much did you hear?"

A chill went through her. His voice was sharper than she had ever heard it, but Makepiece was not the sort of professor who lost his temper. "I... I didn't hear anything. I just... When you came in with the other professors, I was frightened. I didn't want to get in trouble for being in the laboratory." The patient was watching her, she could feel it, and she knew in her gut that he was wondering whether she would reveal that he could speak. She hesitated. If he had wanted the professors to know that he could understand them, he would have spoken up himself. Without consciously making a decision she said, "What is he doing here, Professor?"

Makepiece stared off into space for a moment, and then dropped his head. "This one has shown certain...*abnormalities* that bear closer investigation." He opened a medicine cabinet and began removing bottles. "I suppose you heard what Grimbald said about Bio-Mechanicals shuffling into the line of fire? And about...other things?"

*She needs to be brought in, and the sooner the better. And that means we need fresh cadavers.* They had been talking about the queen. "The sound was muffled," she said, trying to hold his gaze. She wasn't used to lying; it felt awkward, unpleasant, like trying to talk around a sore tooth. "I could hear that you were all speaking, but I couldn't quite make out the words."

Makepiece seemed relieved. "Yes, well. Not that we were discussing state secrets, but it would be easy to misconstrue some of what was said. We're on the right track, I know we are, but we haven't quite got the formula down yet."

"The formula?"

"For the ichor. Moulsdale hates to admit it, but in some respects, we're still as much alchemists as chemists." Makepiece took a dropper and began extracting liquids from various bottles with Latin labels. "After all, what are we seeking to refine here, if not the elixir of life?" Makepiece shook the test tube, which turned a cloudy gray.

"Professor, I'm afraid I don't quite follow."

"You know about the circulatory system of veins and arteries that brings blood to all the parts of the body? Well, we also have another system of lymphatic vessels that distributes a different substance. The ancients called it *aqua vitae*, the water of life. We call it ichor." Makepiece added a small quantity of a black powder to the test tube, and now it glowed an eerie, fluorescent green. "At the present time, we must constantly replenish the ichor in order to keep the Bio-Mechanicals from breaking down." Makepiece depressed the hypodermic's plunger, and a drop of glowing green liquid hung from the needle's tip. "I keep making adjustments to the formula. Perhaps this batch will prove the winner. If not, then I suppose we'll learn from our mistakes."

Out of the corner of her eye, Lizzie detected a movement; the Bio-Mechanical's left hand was clenched in a fist, the mechanically enhanced muscles clenching so hard that the leather restraints seemed about to snap.

"Professor..."

"Yes?"

"If the subject is exhibiting intriguing new behaviors, wouldn't it make sense to observe him as a control before conducting any more experiments?"

"What do you think I've been doing? I've observed the subject for over twelve hours. He's done nothing out of the ordinary."

"But his face and abdomen show signs of having been beaten, and he's been tied to a gurney. Think of how an animal subject might react under the same circumstances."

Makepiece looked down at the leather strap in his hands. "Face and abdomen. You examined him, then?"

"I…"

"Of course you did. What else did you do?"

Lizzie glanced at the Bio-Mechanical, who was clearly comprehending every word that was said, and perhaps the ones that were not spoken, as well. She didn't understand how Makepiece hadn't noticed. But she knew better than to make the mistake of underestimating his intelligence. "I used my father's device," she admitted.

"I see," said Makepiece, pulling at his beard again. Yet this time, instead of concern, there was a speculative gleam in his eyes. "Very well, then. We mustn't confuse the experiment with too many variables. I will keep the subject here and observe him."

"Thank you," said Lizzie.

"Whatever for? I'm not doing you any favors, you know."

"Of course, sir. I know that."

The odd, stern note in Makepiece's voice made her uncomfortable, and she wondered what would have happened if she had admitted what she had overheard. As if reading her thoughts, the Bio-Mechanical caught her gaze and held it for a moment before giving the kind of formal nod a gentleman gives a lady. She wasn't sure what he was trying to communicate—gratitude, or acknowledgment, or some other, subtler message—but whatever his message was, one thing was certain: he was no mindless killing machine.

# 13

THE NEXT MORNING, THE FIRST YEARS WERE
scheduled to have a period of physical education. Because the
weather was so fine, they were going to have their class outside. Grimbald, who was in charge of athletics, was a great
believer in the benefits of fresh air.

The air turned out to be more brisk than fresh, and Lizzie
had to blow on her hands to keep them warm. Back home,
mid-September still seemed like summer, but here, even
though the sky was a cloudless blue, you could feel autumn
settling in. Some of the trees were even turning color. Pretty
to look at now, but if it got cold this early, it was going to be
a long winter.

*At least I don't have to stand out here with bare legs.* Except for
Byram, the boys were all shivering in striped shirts and black
short breeches that ended just above the knee. Byram, conspicuous in long trousers, had decided to make himself more
conspicuous by smoking a cigarette. As the smell of smoke
reached them, some of the other boys began muttering.

"Byram!" Grimbald's drill sergeant voice startled Lizzie, but Byram showed no visible reaction. "Put that out this instant!"

"Yes, sir." Byram took one last leisurely drag before crushing the cigarette butt under his heel.

"Why aren't you in gym uniform?" Grimbald was wearing the striped shirt and shorts himself, displaying a surprisingly trim and muscular form for a man in his late forties. A silver whistle dangled around his neck.

"Bad foot, sir."

"In the First Boer War, I had a corporal who had half his foot shot off. Didn't seem to stop him from wearing his uniform, or fighting with the best of them." Grimbald looked Byram up and down. "Your foot going to stand in the way of you becoming a doctor?"

"No, sir."

"Then next time you show up properly attired for exercise." Instead of leaving it at that, Grimbald leaned forward to say something only Byram could hear. A muscle twitched in the younger man's jaw, but he said, "Understood, sir."

Moving on to Will, Grimbald lifted up Will's baggy shirt and looked disapprovingly at the belt wrapped around his slender waist. In the oversize gym clothes, Will looked as skinny as a thirteen-year-old. "I take it your uniform doesn't fit properly?"

"No, sir."

"Was it your brother's?"

Will looked miserable. "No, they just didn't have my size, sir."

Grimbald's mustache twitched, as if he were suppressing a smile. "Make arrangements to have it altered." Turning to leave, he halted and looked over his shoulder at Lizzie. "You cannot participate in gym class without the proper attire."

She raised her eyebrows. "You want me to show my legs?"

Grimbald paused, and for a moment, she thought she'd scored that point. "I believe the Matron is in charge of the young ladies' physical education, *and* their attire. You are a young lady, are you not? In that case, you are Miss Shiercliffe's responsibility."

"But I'm not a nursing student, so my schedule isn't the same as theirs. I have Materia Medica on Wednesday afternoons, when they meet for their physical education class."

"Scheduling dilemmas are not my department. I suggest you take it up with Professor Moulsdale."

"But that's not…"

Before she could finish, Grimbald raised the silver whistle to his mouth and blew two sharp blasts. "The rest of you, fall in behind me! We'll take it easy and do three miles this first morning." With that, he set off at a punishing pace. After a moment, the rest of the class took off after him, their breath misting in the cool air.

"Come on, Lavenza." Byram tugged at her arm. "As the French say, 'if they're not going to feed you, leave the table.'" She followed him up the hill, watching as Will gave them a melancholy wave before running to catch up with the others.

Byram led Lizzie up the hill, around the back of Ingold's main building. There were the remains of an old tower there, but one side of the wall had crumbled away, exposing the winding stone stairs to the elements.

Pausing at the bottom, she watched Byram take the steps three at a time. She rested her hand on the curving stone wall—there was no banister—and paused with her foot on the first step. "Is it safe?"

"I've done it before without killing myself, if that's what you're asking."

It wasn't, but she followed him anyway, placing her feet with great care on the slickly sloping stairs. There were old names scratched into the stone beneath her hand—she could make out Crispin Weathersby, 1855, Roland March, 1804. Underneath were other names, too faded now to be legible. The clearest inscription was a quote: *It is dangerous to be right on matters in which the established authorities are wrong.*

That sounded true enough, but whoever had written it had declined to sign his name. "What is this place?"

Byram's voice came down to her like an echo. "It's just an old tower that was never refurbished. All the smokers know about it."

"Ah." Her legs were cramping from the tension of climbing, and she realized that this was Byram's way of showing her that he was both fit and resourceful. She caught up with him and sucked in a sharp breath; there was a gap where two stairs had crumbled away, which meant she would have to leap up and over to reach the landing. "How do you manage this last bit?"

"Watch me. Step there, at the edge, and jump." He demonstrated, only slipping a little on the landing, when his bad foot buckled. "Nothing to it," he said, as if nothing had happened.

"All right, then." She gathered her skirts in one hand and tried not to look down at the patch of distant grass and stone visible through the gap. She estimated that there were some sixty feet from the ground. *But if Byram did it with his bad foot, then so can I.* She bent her knees and leaped, and then Byram's hand was clasping her firmly around the arm, helping her up.

"Thanks," she said, not relishing the thought of climbing down again. Then she took in the view: miles and miles of countryside all around them, stretching as far as the eye could see. Over the crenelated battlements, she could also look down over the rest of Ingold's buildings. "It's incredible up here."

"Thought you'd appreciate it. You can make a bit more sense of the sprawl of buildings when you're looking down and not just another rat caught in the maze. Look over there, at that."

She squinted, not wanting to admit she couldn't really make out details. "There?" She pointed where he was pointing.

"That's an old smuggler's tunnel. You can sneak out of the school that way. Only problem is, the way is through Moulsdale's study."

She wondered how Byram knew all this but decided not to ask. After spending time with Will and Byram, she had learned that, outside a classroom, asking lots of questions made you seem unsophisticated and slightly foolish, and that it was better to just pick up bits of information as you went along.

Byram maneuvered himself into a seated position on the edge of the tower, which made her a little queasy. Still, she followed suit, noticing as she sat carefully on the ledge that there were old crushed cigarette butts crammed into the nooks and crannies. For a few minutes, the two just sat, looking out at the fields below. It was colder up here than down below, and she wondered whether Byram would try to put his arm around her, and what she would do if he did. Then she wondered if there was something wrong with her, because here she was, alone with an extremely good-looking young man, and she really had no desire to have his arms around her. Nervously playing with a loose strand of hair by her ear, she had an awful thought: perhaps the doctors who claimed that higher education shriveled a woman's reproductive organs were right. Would she know if her womb had already withered away inside her?

Byram was frowning at her. "Say, you're not about to go all hysterical on me, are you?"

"What? No!" She tucked the loose strand of hair back in place.

"Good. You looked a bit squirrelly there for a moment. Thought you were going to accuse me of luring you up here for nefarious purposes."

"Don't be absurd."

"Well, don't you get your dander up. Hey, look down there." He pointed at the path far below. "That's Will coming around the bend. Poor sap."

"I don't see him." Squinting, she could just make out the blurry dots that were the other students, tiny at this distance, running laps behind Grimbald.

"That's because you're looking in the wrong place. Look there." She followed the line of his pointing finger, and now she could see the blur that must be Will, lagging far behind.

"Poor Will."

"Indeed. So, have you recovered from your argle-bargle with old Grim?"

"Argle-what?"

"Row. Quarrel. Contretemps."

"Ah." She did feel a little better, sitting out in the cool air, watching the clouds scudding by. "Yes, I suppose so." Downhill, where the ground flattened out a bit, a farmer had built a massive haystack, well over six feet tall. Once upon a time, she would have attempted to climb it. Glancing sideways at Byram, who was rolling another cigarette, she noticed that the sole of his right shoe was thicker than that of the left.

With studied casualness, he tucked the bad foot back out

of sight before taking out a match and striking it against the sole of his shoe. She wished she could just go right ahead and ask what, exactly, was wrong, and if it had been the result of an accident, or was something he had been born with. He was so good-looking with those cheekbones, like an Italian Renaissance prince. If he hadn't had some flaw, she didn't think they would have been friends at all. For some reason, she found herself thinking of the Bio-Mechanical, and wondering what he looked like without the swollen eye and lip. She flashed on the memory of Grimbald from the night before, striking the bruised man's face again and again. She wouldn't have expected that of Grimbald. The former military man might be cruel, but in a calculated way. What she had seen last night had been raw emotion.

"You're awfully quiet all of a sudden," said Byram, offering a drag of his cigarette.

She considered it for a moment, then shook her head. No need to make herself even more shocking than she already was by adding the vice of smoking.

"Still upset about missing the dissection, or is Makepiece going to fix things for you so you can observe?"

"I don't think he can." With everything that had happened last night, she'd forgotten why she had gone to the lab in the first place until much later, when she was back in her room trying to settle down to sleep.

"Did you ask him?"

"Not exactly."

"Why ever not?"

"It was a strange evening." Taking a deep breath, she described finding the Bio-Mechanical.

"You can't tell anyone," she added. "I haven't even told Makepiece that he spoke to me."

Byram leaned back on his elbows, blew out a plume of smoke and contemplated the cloud formations. "Well, then, you're daft. You have one ally here on faculty. Don't go risking that for the sake of some little science project." He looked at her sharply. "Unless you've convinced yourself that this corpse walker's got feelings."

"You're making it sound ridiculous, but you weren't there. He wasn't like Igor. He seemed…aware. Intelligent."

"Like a dog? A good hunting spaniel's aware and intelligent, compared to Igor."

"It was more than that. He told me…"

"He actually spoke to you?"

"Yes. He said that his head was hurting… I mean, not as clearly as that, but I understood what he meant."

"So he grunted something and you interpreted it? Goodness, he does sound like a genius."

"There was more to it."

"I'm all agog. Did he inquire about the county cricket championships? Request a copy of *The Yorkshire Post*? Or, no, wait—did he inquire after the health of the queen?"

He was joking, but she felt prickly with unease. How much to reveal? "He told me to hide. Clearly. No slurring or grunting, and I did not imagine it."

"All right, then, for argument's sake let's just say he did. Any particular reason for this nugget of advice?"

"We heard Makepiece and Moulsdale and Grimbald talking as they came to the laboratory."

Byram stubbed out the butt of his cigarette on a rock. "I see. And so you hid?"

She nodded, uncomfortable. She hadn't intended to confide this much, but having gone this far, it seemed easier to just continue. "It was very strange. Grimbald seemed, I don't know, enraged at the creature. Upset. I got the impression that the Bio-Mechanicals aren't really working the way they want them to."

"Interesting."

"And then they said… They said something about the queen. They're bringing her in as a patient."

For the first time since she'd known him, Byram looked thoroughly shocked. "Are you certain?"

She nodded, and suddenly she wanted to tell him the rest of it. "There was something else, too."

"Do I want to know?"

The last secret seemed to jump off her tongue. "I think they might be intending to do something to the queen."

Byram stared at her for a frozen moment, then snorted and shook his head. "Well, I'll say one thing for you, Lizzie— you're never boring." He pushed himself to his feet. "Come on, we might as well head back down."

"So, what? You think I'm crazy?"

"I think you're…imaginative. In a way that's not particularly advisable for someone who wants a career in medicine."

"You're right, I suppose."

"Of course I'm right. I mean, even if the heads of school wanted to turn the queen into a scrapper, she's got guards and relatives and ladies-in-waiting all over the place. You don't think someone would notice if the queen went to Yorkshire for a treatment and came back with bolts coming out of her neck?"

"Maybe they're in on it? Or they could give her a ruff to wear, like Queen Elizabeth?"

"Fine. But even if they could get away with it, it's not like we're an absolute monarchy. We've got a prime minister, you know."

Now that Byram had spelled it out, she felt quite foolish. "I guess I wasn't thinking clearly."

"Look, lots of folks are uncomfortable with the idea of Bio-Mechanicals. My own father threatened to disown me if I came to Ingold. I'm all for taking the piss out of the institution, but we can't go spreading wild tales."

She waited a moment before following him across the gap. She had never been a part of anything before, and now she felt disloyal and stupid and more of an outsider than ever.

As they made their way past the section of the wall where previous generations of boys had scrawled their names, she couldn't help looking for the quote, its letters still fresh as if recently made: *It is dangerous to be right in matters in which the established authorities are wrong.* Perhaps Byram was right about the queen, but that didn't mean he was right about everything. She felt certain that the Bio-Mechanical in the laboratory was something unique. If she could encourage him to speak, then he might prove to be the breakthrough that Grimbald and the others were seeking, and she would receive part of the credit. Of course, she might win herself more enemies than allies: she could not forget what had happened with the etheric magnetometer, turned up to its highest level by some malicious hand. Yet what else could she do? If she didn't try something to change the status quo, she would wind up failing Gross Anatomy.

This time, when she shivered, it wasn't from the cold.

# 14

IT WAS LATE IN THE DAY WHEN SHE FINALLY HAD
a free period to check on the Bio-Mechanical.

"Professor? Hello?" She walked slowly around the cluttered
laboratory, but aside from the salamanders eyeing her from
their glass aquariums, the room appeared empty.

Then she turned, and there was the Bio-Mechanical, standing at his full and formidable height. *Lord, he's tall. Tall and
unhappy.* In fact, he looked downright menacing, scowling
at her with his lank black hair half-hiding his swollen eye.
She swallowed. The room was very quiet, and looking up at
the Bio-Mechanical's face, she tried not to imagine a newspaper headline reading: *Female Medical Student Falls Victim to
Homicidal Monster.*

No, that was ridiculous. Those were the sort of vaporish
feminine fears that she loathed. She would not give in to them.

"Hello?" No response, just that baleful, one-eyed glare.
She stiffened her spine. "Do you understand me?"

He gave a curt nod. For some reason, this made her feel less frightened.

"Good. I'm here to help you."

He narrowed his eyes.

"Honestly. You can trust me."

For a long moment, he didn't move. Then his right hand came out, palm open. She took a deep breath, then placed her hand in his. It felt warm, and muscular, and absolutely human. Then, unexpectedly, he placed his metal-gauntleted left hand over the top of her hand, trapping her. She thought about how, in this moment, she was utterly in his power. *But once I leave this room, he's at my mercy, too*, she realized. *He has no way of knowing if I'll tell what I know about him.* And wasn't that the definition of trust? *I put myself in your hands.*

She put her left hand over his, touching the darker skin where it melded with metal. "Does it hurt? The graft?"

He shook his head, looking bemused as she traced her fingers over the invisible seam that joined man to metal.

"Can you feel it, though? Where I'm touching you?"

He nodded, watching her fingers, so pale against his skin.

"It's amazing that there isn't more nerve damage." Suddenly, she realized what she was doing and withdrew her hands. "What is your name?"

He struggled visibly to form a word with his swollen mouth, but what came out was a strangled grunt that sounded like "Vunh."

"Oh, dear. I couldn't quite make that out. Did you say Van?"

He tried again, and this time managed to get out "Vunh-uh."

"Vanner? That's not really a name. Vance? No, it has to be two syllables." She tried to think of other names that began with the letter *v*. "Vernon?" He shook his head. "Vincent? Virgil? Valentine? No, that's three syllables. Vicary?" He blew

out an exasperated huff. "Vittorio? No that's also three." But
he was nodding at her. "Yes? Is that it? Vittorio… No, not
quite." He was shaking his head again. "Am I close, though?
Something like Vittorio?" For a moment, she wondered if
he really understood anything she was saying, but then he
made a gesture with his right hand she interpreted as meaning "go on."

"All right. Am I close? I'm close. Hmm, what's like Vittorio? Vito!" She clapped her hands with pleasure, but then
realized that the Bio-Mechanical was turning away, looking a bit deflated. "All right, not Vito, don't give up…let
me think… I was always so bad at charades." She tapped her
finger against her cheek, then looked up into that bruised,
distorted face. "Vittorio is Italian for victory… Is your name
Victor?" It seemed a cruelly ironic selection for a creature in
his straits, but he nodded vigorously.

"Well, then." She beamed at him, and he grimaced back at
her with his fat lip. "I am very pleased to make your acquain-
tance, Victor." She went over to the side table and picked up
her magnetometer. "You remember this, don't you?"

His left hand shot out, capturing her wrist and nearly making her drop the device. She knew he must be remembering
the way he blacked out the last time she used it on him. But
still, it did help, she thought. "I won't hurt you, Victor. I'm a
medical student, and I want to help you. Do you trust me?"

He nodded. And after a moment, his left hand unclenched.

"Good. Now, for what I have in mind, we need to stimulate your brain, not your arm." With her back to him, she
opened a wooden box that contained various configurations
of carbon-filament bulbs and glass wands and electrical leads.
"I'll need to change this around… Oh, of course, the perfect
thing." Walking over to the Galvanic Reanimator, she re-

moved the brass helmet and began unscrewing various pieces, and then reattaching elements from the wooden box so that now the wand was attached to a glowing glass semicircle. "That should work." As she raised the magnetometer to his head, he flinched, and his left hand shot up to seize her wrist.

"It's all right, Victor. It won't hurt you. I'm setting it very low." She smiled, and his hand released her.

She turned the dial, listening for the moment as the clicking noise gave way to a rising hum. Holding his gaze, she placed the glass on his head, disconcerted by the unexpected intimacy of touching him, unchaperoned by anyone other than Makepiece's cat, who observed them from a windowsill for a moment before closing her eyes.

That was the first of many sessions.

Miss Lavenza thought her device was painless, but she was wrong. Each time she passed the magnetometer over his neck, Victor offered up a small prayer, and remarkably, each time his left arm remained quiet by his side, the fingers sometimes trembling or tapping, but nothing more. *Good arm.* Perhaps it was a bit mad to think of the appendage as possessing a mind and will of its own, but there was no denying that, under duress, his Bio-Mechanical limb did seem to act of its own accord. In the Bible, Matthew admonished that "when thou doest alms, let not thy left hand know what thy right hand doeth," but in Victor's case, it was his left hand that seemed to make decisions independent of the rest of him. Yet for some reason, it allowed Miss Lavenza to do as she willed. Perhaps his sinister limb knew that she was only trying to help them. Or else he might not be the only one who admired the redoubtable medical student enough to endure a little torture, so long as she was the one meting out the punishment.

Yet, really, what were a few minutes of discomfort when he was compensated by what followed: an intelligent human being regarding him with compassion, touching him gently on hand and brow and speaking to him in a low, warm voice.

Besides, each time she used it, the magnetometer was becoming less painful. The first time she had used her device on him, back when he was recovering from the guard's beating, had been like getting zapped by lightning. The second time had felt more like putting his hand on a live wire. "So strange," Miss Lavenza had said. "It's not supposed to hurt, not at this setting." She had furrowed her brow and looked at him as if he were a puzzle she was trying to assemble. "Perhaps it's because of all the metal attached to your flesh." By the fifth and sixth session, however, the magnetometer no longer shocked him as badly, and afterward he felt bone-tired but relaxed.

He wondered if this meant that he was getting better, or if it meant he'd reached the limits of how much he was going to improve. Certainly, his speech was clearer—still slow and slightly slurred, but intelligible. That was also thanks to Miss Lavenza, or Lizzie, as she invited him to call her. The nickname didn't suit her—it was light and dizzy, a name for a barmaid or a hat girl. Elizabeth was a better choice—the name of a queen wiser and more spirited than most kings.

Despite Elizabeth's assurances, he couldn't bring himself to trust Makepiece, but the old scientist was so unobtrusive that half the time, Victor forgot he was even there.

Elizabeth seemed to forget, as well. After she put the magnetometer away, she would sit and talk with him. He still had trouble retrieving words—simple words, words even a five-year-old would know—which made him want to swear and break things, but Elizabeth was patient, and she had an easy way of speaking, as though they were friends. Over the course of their meetings, he learned random tidbits about her life. She had never had a pet, for example, although she had tried unsuccessfully to make friends with a neighbor's farm dog, a border collie who did not have time to waste on lonely children when she had work to do herding sheep.

She talked to him with the stunning frankness of an intimate, as if they had known each other for years. He did not know whether this was because she was American or because he was something less than human. In any event, he soon knew more about her than he knew about anyone, save Henry and his brother, Will. He knew, for example, that her mother died after catching measles from one of her husband's young patients. Mrs. Lavenza had quarantined herself so she wouldn't pass the disease on to her young daughter, but Lizzie came down with the rash all the same; by the time the spots had faded from her body, her mother was already gone. After that, Robert Lavenza decided to teach his daughter at home. At times, Elizabeth said, she felt as though she had made a bargain with the devil: no more torturous days in the schoolyard, but the price had been her mother's life.

She said she didn't miss the company of other children, but every once in a while, usually around birthdays or holidays, her father would say, "You need some friends your own age," and then drag her off to some neighbor's house, where she would be deposited with a bunch of unfamiliar children.

It usually took the children less than an hour to realize that she was as unfamiliar with the most basic rules of children's society as any adult. She didn't know that you never stop a game of tag to ask if you can play, or that bragging was reserved for pack leaders. She didn't comprehend that teasing was allowed, but that tattling to parents was not.

Adults liked her and commented on how mature she was, but until she was fourteen, she didn't have a single friend under the age of forty. That was the year she met Perry.

Perry had been one of the village's popular boys, moving in a circle so far removed from Lizzie's that he might as well have been the Prince of Wales. Then, at the age of sixteen, Perry was kicked by a horse. His family cared for him at home until gangrene set in. By the time they brought him to Dr. Lavenza, the infection had spread and the leg had to be amputated above the knee.

As Perry recovered, Elizabeth spent weeks sitting by his bedside, reading to him from *The Adventures of Tom Sawyer* and *Treasure Island*. For the better part of two weeks, Perry moved in and out of consciousness. Then, one morning, he interrupted her reading to say, "Always wanted to be a pirate. Now I suppose I can get a peg leg and hobble around like Long John Silver."

She put down the book, smiling. "Oh, I think my father's capable of fixing you up with something a little better than that."

"Depends what you mean by *better*." He sounded sour. "My uncle Ned lost his leg at Antietam. Got himself some highfalutin wooden contraption that buckled on with leather straps. Never wore the danged thing, though. Said it weighed a ton and chafed him worse than a scolding wife."

"We can do a *lot* better than that."

Working together, father and daughter came up with a design for a prosthesis that attached by means of a suction socket, and had a knee joint made of a lightweight alloy of brass and aluminum. They added a spring and rubber "tendons" so that Perry could control the movements of the articulated foot.

Once the artificial limb was constructed, Perry required weeks of work to strengthen his good leg and learn how to use "that infernal device," as he called it. Her father was insulted on her behalf, but she didn't mind. She didn't require compliments. She knew that deep down, Perry appreciated all she was doing for him. Besides, she enjoyed it.

Jealous, Victor listened as she rattled on and on about the other fellow.

As the autumn turned colder, Perry's condition improved, and by Thanksgiving he was able to move back home in time to celebrate with his family. She tried to be happy for him, or at least, to look as though she were happy for him instead of sorry for herself. In any case, she was sure he would come back. He would visit, perhaps introduce her to his other friends, take her along on picnics, maybe even fishing. It took her two months to realize that an older, healthier Perry was a Perry who no longer had time for her. Afterward, when she saw him in the village, he always smiled and asked how she was doing, but he never made any effort to see her again.

It was his illness, she explained to Victor, that had brought him down to her level. She was glad she hadn't known that at the time. She might have wished him sick again, just to have him back.

Hearing this, Victor longed to take her into his arms and declare his feelings. The first part was easy enough to imagine—even if she was likely to recoil from his embrace—but the second part was trickier. What was it exactly that he felt for her? That he understood her? That he admired her? That he wanted her as a man wants a woman, but also as a confidant, as a friend, as a partner? It was absurd, risible. At best, she would feel a kind of uncomfortable pity for him. At worst, she would feel repulsed.

That evening, however, when he was alone in his cot, he gave his imagination free rein.

Whenever she visited him, Elizabeth brought Victor some

new treat from the dining hall: a lady apple, a currant cake, even a cold Yorkshire pudding that tasted like ambrosia to Victor. He wasn't sure if his food had been drugged before, but after a few days of not eating the porridge, he seemed noticeably sharper, and his ability to recall words was greatly improved.

"You know, I should take you outside," she told him the last time she visited. "It can't be good for you, never seeing the sun."

Until she mentioned it, he hadn't realized how much he longed to go outside. He wanted to tell her how much she meant to him—her visits, the way she spoke to him like a human being and a friend, the fact that she was keeping his secret. He opened his mouth, but all the feelings seemed to form a bottleneck in his throat, and he got stuck on the word "I."

"Relax your throat," she reminded him. "Breathe."

Had he thought her merely pretty when they first met? She was beautiful to him now. But the harder he tried to get the words out, the worse it got, and then, in a burst of frustration and something else he couldn't name, he grabbed her hand and impulsively pressed a kiss to her palm.

*Oh, God, what have I done?* Why hadn't he at least kissed the back of her hand, like a gentleman? When he found the courage to look her in the eyes again, she was smiling at him gently, a kindly teacher to stammering schoolboy. Humiliating, yes, but at least she wasn't offended.

Or was she? She didn't come the day after, but he didn't lose hope until the third day. That was when he knew that he'd frightened her away. *Damn it.* He had to be more careful. He needed her as an ally, not a friend. He would be circumspect, when she returned, and not presume to take any liberties.

Assuming, of course, that she did return.

# 15

BY MID-OCTOBER, LIZZIE DISCOVERED WHY English people went on and on about the rain. The constant downpour stripped the trees of leaves, and there was a distinct chill in the air, but the tall, flower-embossed iron radiator in the corner of the room remained cool to the touch. "Radiators are purely for decoration in England," Byram had explained in his most sardonic tone. "We believe frigid temperatures build character."

She tried to take this in stride, the way Byram and Will did, but she wasn't used to being this cold; at home, her room had its own fireplace. *No longer my room, nor even my house, anymore. Someone else is living there now.*

The pace of work increased and, as midterm exams approached, Lizzie found she couldn't spare the time to go to the laboratory during her free periods. At home, her father had always told her she possessed an exceptional intellect, but now she was struggling to keep up with the torrent of new information coming her way. There were daily quizzes in human anatomy and organic chemistry, and the moment she learned something new, she forgot half the previous day's list. Moulsdale's comprehensive course on the history of botanical remedies, which had very little practical application, required that she spend hours every night translating medieval sources from the Latin in the dim light of her room. When she looked up from the page, her eyes stung and took ages to refocus. At this rate, she worried she was going to be the first blind female doctor. Will, Byram and other students formed study groups, which lightened their workload a bit, but she was not allowed near their dormitory after dinner, so she had to struggle along on her own. At first, when Lizzie started to feel the tickle in the back of her throat, she refused to believe that she had caught the upper respiratory inflammation that was making the rounds of the school. It was simply a matter of willpower; she could not afford to be sick.

By the third day, she realized she had no choice in the matter. It hurt to swallow, and the room began to spin when she tried to get out of bed. She had the grippe. Aggie, who usually acted as though Lizzie were invisible, paused on her way out of the room to ask if Lizzie needed anything. "No, no, I'll be fine, just need to rest," said Lizzie, assuming that her roommate would understand that of course she needed some tea with honey and lemon, and maybe a few lozenges, as well. The girl was studying to be a nurse, after all.

When hours passed and Aggie did not return, Lizzie found herself staring up at the ceiling, surrounded by crumpled, damp handkerchiefs, thinking about Victor. No one had ever kissed her hand before, and even though it seemed silly to think about it, she wondered if her patient was developing a sort of tenderness for her, the way some patients did for their nurses. Perhaps it was for the best that she had to stop seeing him for a while. She did worry about him, though. Had he managed to hold on to his gains in language? Was he able to practice on his own? She hated to think of him losing ground and having to start all over again.

She also worried about losing ground with Professor Makepiece. While she had kept Victor's progress a secret, she had told the professor about her idea of using the etheric magnetometer with a helmet attachment in order to stimulate the speech centers of the brain, and he had been extremely encouraging. Between studying for exams and getting sick, she had been away from the lab for nearly two weeks now. Might he be experimenting on Victor in her absence? Was he trying out the device on Igor or one of the other Bio-Mechanicals?

Unfortunately, at the moment, midterms were coming and she had other, more pressing concerns. Did the fat man in Wellington ward with the swollen foot have gout, arthritis or some sort of skin disease? Was the young girl in Alexandra ward suffering from cramps because she had ingested old mutton, as she claimed, or was there some other cause she was too embarrassed to admit? Just how much of Lizzie's histology grade depended on the final exam?

Lying in bed, feverish and stuffed up, she recited the names of the bones of the wrist to herself like a prayer: scaphoid, lunate, triquetrum, pisiform, trapezium, trapezoid, capitate, hamate. Will said his brother had taught him the mnemonic for them: Stop Letting Those People Touch the Cadaver's Hand. She thought of Victor's strange left arm, and the way he always kept it turned away from her.

Eventually she fell into a strange fever dream. She was looking at a ballroom filled with swirling, jewel-colored silk gowns, and then she was one of the dancers, whirling from partner to partner, moving from Perry to Will to Byram, who did not limp in the dream. She wanted to stay with Byram, but he spun her away, and then she turned and crashed into cold metal arms that closed around her waist and would not let her go. Startled, she found herself staring up at a helmeted medieval knight, but his visor was down and she could not tell if there was a man inside or not. It took all her strength to reach up to raise the visor, but as it came up, the movement of her own body jolted her awake.

The next morning, she felt a little better and when Aggie again asked if she needed anything, she replied with a curt, "No, thank you," and forced herself out of bed. When she made it to the dining room, however, she discovered that there was no hot food for breakfast. The constant rain had caused a delay in the coal delivery, and everyone had to make do with cold leftovers.

Her day did not improve. In Gross Anatomy class, some wag had scrawled Anatomy Killed Me on the blackboard and signed it Mortimer Graves III with an arrow pointing to the human skeleton. Grimbald erased the board without comment, then announced that their first cadaver dissection would take place the next day. Arrangements would be made for those who were not eligible to participate. Will gave Lizzie a sympathetic look as she sat beside him flushed with anger, but Byram calmly continued taking notes.

"This is completely unfair," she whispered. "I just got back, and now I'm going to miss another class."

Byram shook his head and wrote her a note in the margins of his notebook: *Forget about it*. Ever since his confrontation with Grimbald over wearing the correct uniform for running, he had been subdued. Whatever Grimbald has said to him, it seemed to have had the desired effect. If she wanted to fight back against Grimbald's rule, she was going to have to do it on her own.

★ ★ ★

By the end of the day, she still hadn't thought of a solution. Lizzie brushed her hair out with sharp, angry strokes, then hit a snarl that sent the brush flying across the room. She was picking it up when Aggie opened the door. Her roommate paused at the doorway, then walked over to the table they shared.

"Where's my brush gone?"

"I don't know." Lizzie picked up her brush from the floor and dusted it off on her skirt. A few of the boar's hair bristles were broken.

Aggie sat down and removed her nurse's cap. "Yes, you do. You're holding it."

"This is *my* brush."

Aggie, who had been looking in the small mirror, turned around to face Lizzie. "No, your brush is on your side of the table, where I put it every single day after you use it. You can tell it's your brush because it's filled with brown hair, which you never bother to comb out of the bristles."

Lizzie looked down at the brush in her hands. There were a few brown strands in it now, but it was very clean. And now that she looked at it more carefully, it was a slightly longer shape than her brush. She fought back the urge to apologize. Her roommate seemed to have made up her mind to be aggrieved with her on that first night, and nothing Lizzie said made any difference.

"I am sorry," Lizzie said with exaggerated politeness, handing Aggie the brush. "I must have taken this by mistake. I suppose I don't spend as much time thinking about my hair as you do."

Aggie muttered something under her breath and began

plucking Lizzie's brown hairs out of the bristles as though they were vermin.

"Let me do that. I know how tired you must be of cleaning things—after all, that's most of what you do in nursing school, isn't it? Scrub, scrub, scrub the surgical surfaces and the patients' beds and keep everything absolutely spic and span?"

"You have no idea…but since you're bringing up the subject of cleanliness…" Aggie looked up, her eyes meeting Lizzie's in the mirror. "Do you think you could manage to clean up all the soiled handkerchiefs lying around your bed? We nurses believe that such behavior is unhygienic and can spread disease."

Lizzie snatched up the offending articles and stuffed them into an empty pillowcase. All right, fine, she wasn't quite as neat as Aggie, but she had been sick for the better part of three days. Still, it wouldn't help matters to say that out loud. "Anything else bothering you?" She made her voice treacly sweet.

"Actually, yes." Aggie unpinned her hair. "While you were sick, you kept leaving your books out where I'd trip over them in the evening. I didn't say anything then, but since you're better now, do you think you'd mind putting them under your bed?"

"Not at all." Lizzie collected the textbooks, thinking that it wouldn't hurt Aggie to open a book every once in a while. "Please. Don't stop there. Let it all out."

"As a matter of fact, there is one more little detail." Aggie stood up and picked up a pair of Lizzie's drawers, which were hanging on the back of her bed next to her chemise. "Is there a reason why your knickers are always on parade?"

Lizzie snatched her drawers back and threw them on her bed. "Because I *wash* them. I don't know how many pairs of drawers you own, but I don't have enough to last me to laundry day." She had noticed that Aggie never hung out her underthings, but had assumed that English girls had different standards of hygiene.

"This is so typical. You really don't have a clue what's going on in front of your eyes, do you? We *all* wash our knickers, dearie. There's a clothesline in the nurse's bathroom."

"There is?" How was it possible she hadn't noticed it? This was just like being nine years old again, the odd, motherless girl, the only one whose hair wasn't braided or even brushed, the only one who didn't know better than to chew with her mouth open. "Why didn't anyone tell me?"

Aggie bent over to unlace her right shoe. "No one told me, either. I just paid attention to what other people were doing. In good weather you can pull the clothesline out into the little courtyard behind. That way, we don't stink up our rooms with the smell of mildew." She pulled the shoe off and wriggled her black-stockinged toes. "And we don't need to spray scent all over to disguise it."

*Oh, Lord.* Lizzie had noticed the faint odor of mildew in the room, but hadn't known what to do about it. The air here was always so damp. Then it occurred to Lizzie that she was in that bathroom every day and she had never seen a clothesline, or a bunch of nurse's underthings hanging out to dry. "Wait a moment. If there's a clothesline, why haven't I ever seen it?"

"It's around the back, behind the loo and the tub. Which you would know if you didn't act as though you was Lady Muck trapped amongst the peasants." Aggie arranged her shoes under her bed.

*So that's what they call me when I'm not around.* "I don't think of myself as Lady Muck. I'm American, remember? We got rid of all the lords and ladies."

"In that case, do you think you could make your bed in

the mornings?" She gestured at Lizzie's bed, which, as far as Lizzie could see, was made up: Blankets pulled up, at least.

"What are you talking about?" She'd pulled at the covers over the bed. "It's made."

"Are you serious? Look at the corners. And the sheet fold is completely lopsided. I can only imagine what Shiercliffe would say if one of us made up a patient's bed like this."

Lizzie stared at her roommate. The drawers, all right, that had been embarrassing. But this, *this* was petty. "Some of us," she said slowly, "have better things to do than perfect our hospital corners."

Aggie's mouth compressed into a hard line. "I'm not talking nursing-school standards, ducks. My eight-year-old sister could do better. No, I take that back—my six-year-old *brother* could do better."

Hands on her hips, Lizzie smiled at her roommate. "Then I am sure he will make an excellent nurse."

Aggie looked ferocious. "D'you think that's all that's required? Bed making?"

"You do seem to spend an awful lot of time on it. But of course, I know there's more to nursing."

"You 'ave no bloomin' idea, luv—" Lizzie had noticed that her roommate's accent thickened whenever the other girl was tired or upset. Right now, however, Lizzie didn't give a fig what Aggie was feeling.

"Emptying bedpans, giving sponge baths and making sure you don't mix up the food trays."

There was a moment of taut silence, and Lizzie braced, half expecting Aggie to slap her or pull her hair. It had been years since her last schoolyard fight, but her body remembered. But Aggie just shook her head.

"I thought, you being a woman and all, that you might

be a bit less thick than the other medical students. Truth is, you're worse."

"That's not true! I'm at least as good as any of the men."

"Which means you're not as good as any of the nurses. I've watched you doing rounds. Do you ever take the time to learn the patient's name? Do you stop a moment to hold someone's hand? When you ask them how they're feeling, do you listen to the answer?"

"I…" *No*, she realized. *I don't do any of that.*

"No, of course not, because that won't get you a good grade or impress your professors. And your professors are all men, and they think all that personal touch is just a load of malarkey. But stop and think a moment. Someone asks you, 'Where's the pain?' Maybe you're embarrassed to say where it is, so you say your belly instead of your breasts, and the doctor operates on the wrong bits. Or maybe you know where the pain is, it's in your leg, but the doctor never stops to hear the whole story about how a horse rolled over on you and broke your leg in two places. Because what does it matter how your leg got broke? Only the leg hurts so bad you don't savvy you've got a worse pain in your belly, where the horse rolled over on you and ruptured something vital, and that's what's going to kill you."

Lizzie stared at her roommate.

"Or maybe the doctor's so busy with his books and his charts that he orders the meds and doesn't bother to check the patient after, and now it's the nurse who sees the patient's turning blue, so she double-checks the order and realizes that someone put a period in the wrong place and so the poor thing's been given ten times the right dose."

"What happened to the patient?"

Aggie laughed. "Which time, darlin'?"

"It happens a lot?"

She shrugged. "Doctors are only human, and humans make mistakes. Sometimes it's trial and error, anyhow, but it's the nurses who are in the best position to observe the small changes, so we've got the best chance of catching something before it's too late." Aggie went over to her drawer and took out her little flask. "I came 'ere because doctors was always complaining about midwives not having proper training. And fair enough, I've learned a few things. But there are things I know that the doctors don't. Not that they'd ever admit it." She looked Lizzie over. "Ah, what's the point of even talking to you?" She raised the flask to her lips.

Lizzie sat down on the edge of her bed, her legs shaking. She wasn't used to arguing. She and her father had never argued. "I didn't know you worked as a midwife." Then she remembered that she had known, because Aggie had told her when they had first met.

Aggie didn't correct her. "Me mum was the midwife. I just assisted." She took another swig of the flask, then looked at Lizzie. "Want a nightcap?" Her voice had a mocking lilt. Without waiting for a reply, she replaced the cap. "Oh, no, of course not. A medical student is above such things."

"I'll try a little," said Lizzie, surprising herself. She was still sorting through all the accusations they had hurled at each other, but she was smart enough to recognize that all of Aggie's complaints had a common theme.

"Oh, will you stoop to drink my hooch? Big of you." Still, Aggie handed over the flask.

Lizzie took the flask and wiped the top off on her petticoat before bringing it to her nose. It smelled medicinal. "What is it?"

"Gin. Why, were you expecting after-dinner sherry? Here,

give it back if you don't like it." She reached out her hand, but Lizzie tilted her head back and took a sip. She coughed, hard, as the gin burned its way down her throat.

"Thanks." Her eyes were watering as she handed the flask back.

"Not your cup of poison, eh?" Aggie took another swallow.

"Not sure about the taste." Lizzie's voice was a bit hoarse, and Aggie laughed again. Actually, the aftertaste wasn't too bad—sort of like rubbing alcohol with a hint of pine needles. And the warmth spreading through Lizzie's chest wasn't awful, either. "I think I like the effect, though."

Aggie raised her eyebrows and handed Lizzie the flask again. This time, Lizzie took a more cautious sip. "So," she said, handing back the flask, "you think I need to spend more time with my patients?"

"Not just you, luv. All the med students." Aggie unbuttoned her dress and hung it in the wardrobe. "On my last rotation, I had this patient…sweet young girl, smart as a whip, can talk your ear off about how the prime minister's old as the queen and keeps falling asleep in Cabinet meetings, but her legs don't work."

"The queen?"

"No, luv, the girl." Aggie took another swig from her flask, then raised her eyebrows.

Lizzie held out her hand. She wanted her roommate's approval more than she wanted the gin, so she pretended to take a sip, then wiped the mouth of the flask before handing it back.

"Anyways, they get a Bio-Mechanical to move the girl in and out of this contraption they've got rigged up to help her breathe." She looked down at the flask. "Ah, better not." Capping it again, she set it aside, then flopped onto her belly, supporting her chin in her hands. "So of course she don't tell him that she's getting a bedsore on her hip."

"That could be dangerous, if it became infected." There was a pleasant sort of heat in her chest from the gin and the conversation. "Would you like me to take a look at the girl's wound?"

"Bless me, no! The trouble I'd be in then. You're still getting over the grippe and the girl's got weak lungs…they're ever so careful about letting folks in to see her."

"Must be lonely." She was struggling to keep her eyes open; Aggie's unexpected friendliness had left her relaxed and a little sleepy.

"Look at you, two sips of gin and you're half-rats."

"Mmm."

Aggie laughed. "G'night, Lizzie." She turned off the light, casting the room into a newly companionable darkness.

Lizzie turned on her side, resting her cheek on one hand, feeling a bit floaty. For some reason, her thoughts kept drifting back to Victor. She found herself thinking about all the times she'd talked and talked at him. She'd treated him the way she'd treated that old farm collie as a child. But he was a person, wasn't he, with his own thoughts and feelings. There was something wrong with this line of reasoning, but she was muzzy-headed and couldn't find the fault in her logic.

Unsettled, she turned over in bed. *I should really go check on him*, she thought. *He's probably wondering what happened to me.* She closed her eyes and felt an unaccustomed wave of guilt. Victor was her friend. He had kissed her hand, and then she had not gone back. She had treated him no better than Perry had treated her.

The next morning, she had a headache. She blamed it on the gin.

# 16

THE FIRST TIME THE CAT WOKE VICTOR, HE nearly killed it. He was still mostly asleep when Aldini jumped on his chest, and the first panicked thought was *Rats!* It wasn't his thought; he had never felt a rat's sharp nails scrabbling over his small body in the night. But the memory was there all the same, and his left hand was already in motion, ready to fling the nasty creature against the wall, when the cat began purring.

At that point, Victor came fully awake. The cat regarded him with a steady, golden gaze, as if she hadn't nearly lost another of her nine lives. "Can't say I think much of your intelligence," he said, surprising himself with the sound of his own voice. In response, Aldini kneaded her paws into the blankets covering his chest, and set up a low, rumbling purr. Over his heart, where the metal covered, he felt nothing, but then the cat stretched out her legs and began kneading over the surrounding skin, her claws extending and then retracting, her purr growing louder. *When was the last time anyone touched me with affection?*

Elizabeth did not count. She was a medical student, not his sweetheart, and he could not forget what he was and what he was not. It shamed him that the memory of her hands on him stirred feelings from another life. He had known a woman's caress once, but the woman's face and name were both lost in the mists that clouded his mind. When he tried to dredge up the other woman's image, all he could see was Miss Lavenza: thick, wavy brown hair pulled back in a loose bun, clever, probing eyes of some indeterminate shade of hazel, faint, childlike freckles scattered across her nose. She had a wide, full mouth—the sign of a sensual nature, they said. He couldn't remember who *they* were, but they might be right, considering the way she had pulled back the covers. An innocent, definitely, but a curious one. A man might be forgiven for thinking back to their first meeting and imagining what might have happened if he had shammed unconsciousness and let her uncover him completely.

*Except I'm not a man.* So easy to forget he was a monster now. Which begged the question of why he could think at all. According to no less an authority than the Archbishop of Canterbury, Bio-Mechanicals were like the beasts of the field, furnished with sensory capabilities, but no souls. They were not sensible, any more than cows were, and like cows, they could be disposed of for the greater good of mankind. Indeed, the archbishop had stated, it was easier to raise an objection to the slaughter of an innocent cow than to the slaughter of a Bio-Mechanical created from the body of a convicted thief or murderer. Bio-Mechanicals, he wrote, were only good or evil in as much as they were used for good or evil purposes by their creators. They were man's inventions, as were cows, which had been shaped by man through selective breeding to better suit his needs for milk and beef.

Yet for some reason, Victor was different—an aberration among aberrations. In one of the glowing green vats, there was a man's right arm. Was it the match to the devil's appendage that was attached to his left side? He longed to ask Makepiece the provenance of that limb, but every time he looked at the scientist, something stopped him.

There was something he could not remember, something hidden in the murky recesses of his mind that had to do with Makepiece and the other two middle-aged men who had gathered around him in the laboratory. Damn it, if only he could remember! His head began to pound, the way it had begun to lately whenever he thought of those three: Moulsdale, Makepiece and Grimbald.

The clue, he felt sure, was hidden in the conversation he had overheard that night in the laboratory. *We need them to be able to attack an enemy.* That had been Grimbald speaking. *We need to be able to control them.* That had been Moulsdale. But Makepiece had said nothing, until later, when he had been speaking to Miss Lavenza. What was it he had told her? *After all, what are we seeking to refine here, if not a modern version of what the alchemists called the elixir of life.*

*Please, God,* he prayed, *don't leave me here, suspended between knowing and not knowing.*

*Our royal visitor,* someone had said. The words evoked an image: a woman's small frame, covered by a thin blanket. His head throbbed with pain, and his eyes felt sore in their sockets, but he persisted, struggling to move the block in his mind. Who was the woman, and why did Victor feel that the answer would also tell him why he couldn't trust Makepiece? Until he could remember more, Victor averted his eyes whenever the scientist was around and pretended to be a mental defective.

The effort of concealing what he understood made his private moments with the cat all the more precious. He stroked his right hand over the Aldini's soft, black fur, and she responded by butting his hand with her head and rubbing her cheek against his knuckles. That was when he saw the electrodes and understood. *She's like me.*

And then, on the heels of that thought, came the realization of what this might mean. A purring, Bio-Mechanical cat, living proof that everything Moulsdale and the others believed about Bio-Mechanicals was wrong.

Victor and the cat developed an understanding. Now that the nights were colder, Aldini slept with him on his cot, ignoring Igor, possibly because the hunchback snored to wake the dead. Makepiece no longer kept Victor restrained at night, and he now worked alongside Igor, hauling coal buckets up for the little potbellied stove, moving boxes of equipment from the basement that smelled of fresh earth and formalin and, on one memorable occasion, even going outside to hammer the storm shutters into place. The leaves were almost all off the trees now, and soon it would be too cold to run away. Not that he was really ready to go anywhere at the moment, barefoot, dressed in thin rags and barely capable of coherent speech. In his current condition, he would be lucky to wind up in a workhouse.

Yet his speech was improving. Whenever Makepiece was not around, Victor practiced speaking to the cat or to Igor or just to himself. At times, he felt like a fool, but still he forced himself to keep going. The problem was, this sort of one-sided dialogue seemed to lend itself to confidences. Without intending to, he found himself telling Aldini he loved her, or, more embarrassing still, confiding his feelings of inadequacy to Igor. At times, Igor paused in his sweeping long enough to actually look at him and grunt, but Victor had no idea whether the sound was meant to communicate comfort or impatience or just a sign of indigestion. Comfort, he decided. He liked to imagine that Igor was becoming his friend as well as his companion.

To buoy himself up, he imagined the moment when Elizabeth would return—for surely she would return one of these days. Instead of greeting her in monosyllables, he would speak to her like a proper Englishman, and she would look at him with wide eyes and realize…what? He wasn't entirely certain just what he wanted her to realize. That he was an intelligent being, perhaps, capable of higher reasoning. That he was not just a science project. That he was, in some ways, still a man. Ah, but that was too much to hope for, even in his private fantasies. Better to just imagine impressing her with his abilities.

He stroked the cat's cheek. "Don' you hink…*think* so, Aldini?"

"Mrrowr," said Aldini, proving herself a far more satisfying conversationalist than Igor.

In any event, Victor wasn't the only one who talked to himself. Makepiece liked to think out loud while he worked in the laboratory, and Victor did his best to pay attention without appearing to comprehend. This was most challenging when Makepiece addressed him directly, saying, "Well, Victor, that didn't work," or, "What do you think? Is the theory at fault, or is it the experimental design that is lacking?" Victor kept careful track of the ingredients Makepiece used as he attempted to formulate a better version of ichor. The current formula appeared to have a half-life of about a fortnight. After that, Bio-Mechanicals needed a fresh infusion, or else they developed what the students used to call "corpse fever." It began with chills, fever and rash, and ended with convulsions and death.

If he did ever decide to make a break for freedom, he would have to find the correct ingredients, as well as the formula for producing the serum. Unless, of course, Makepiece succeeded in concocting a version that did not degrade so quickly.

Bit by bit, Makepiece began giving Victor more challenging tasks to do. He allowed him to mix the carbolic acid with water. He sent him on errands that took him to the main building and back. One morning, a pair of old leather boots appeared by the side of Victor's cot. Another day, he found a waistcoat and jacket, old and worn, but serviceable. *He's treating me more like a person.*

Then, one morning toward the end of the second week, Makepiece left the door open to his private rooms, exposing a small library that contained a wide, comfortable leather chair, a velvet love seat and a Dutch-tiled wood-burning fireplace. Leather-bound books lined the walls from floor to ceiling.

"Here. Use this." Makepiece handed him a feather duster and made a brushing gesture; he was to dust off the gilt-embossed titles, which were mostly scientific tomes, with some surprising exceptions: *Goethe's Faust, The Castle of Otranto, The Mysteries of Udolpho.* Makepiece, it seemed, had a taste for Gothic tales of devils and maidens.

As Victor dusted, he heard a loud clatter from the laboratory—Igor must have dropped something.

"Careful, Igor," said Makepiece, leaving Victor alone to see what his assistant had damaged. "Let me see—is it broken?" A moment later, the professor returned to the library, this time holding the box containing Elizabeth's magnetometer in his hands. Igor shuffled behind, carrying the brass helmet that usually sat atop the Galvanic Reanimator. Victor stiffened. Elizabeth had never used the device on him when the professor was around, but clearly, he must know of its use. Was he planning on resuming the experiments in her absence?

"All right, now, Victor. Enough dusting." Makepiece opened a door at the far end of the room, and reluctantly, Victor set the duster on a shelf and followed the professor, carefully blanking his expression so he showed no visible reaction to the six-foot-long metal cylinder standing on its side, or to the frail girl-child lying inside it like a magician's assistant, with only her head showing. There was a pressure gauge attached, and as a bellows moved air in and out of the chamber, he could watch how the pressure rose and fell inside. Victor had never seen the like in his life; it was like something out of a Jules Verne science-fiction novel.

"You are to watch this dial." Makepiece moved Victor, angling him so that he could see a pressure gauge. "If this line moves here, you must flip this switch. Do you understand?"

Victor inclined his head.

"Hello, Papa," said the girl, timing her words so that she spoke only on the exhale. "What are we doing today?"

Makepiece looked down at the girl, his expression softening. "A new sort of treatment, Justine, my child." He took the helmet from Igor and placed it over the girl's blond head while Igor rocked back and forth, making little chirruping sounds of distress. "Stop that, Igor."

"Don't worry so," said the girl softly, taking little sips of air between words. "I'll be fine."

When Makepiece turned on the magnetometer, Victor glanced up from the dial. The girl was watching him with huge pale eyes that seemed to absorb all available light, and then, abruptly, her eyes rolled back and she screamed. He did not remember yanking off the girl's helmet with his gauntleted left hand, but a moment later he was staring at the torn leather straps, dimly aware of Makepiece berating him.

After that, he was barred from the girl's room, although he

did hear the crackle of the etheric magnetometer being used from time to time. What would Elizabeth do, if she knew her mentor kept a girl prisoner as an experimental subject?

Outside the window, the darkening sky was streaked with rose and amber. What was Elizabeth doing now? Eating her dinner? Talking with her friends? Perhaps she had a beau. She might even have gotten engaged. Victor's left hand clenched involuntarily. *Stop it*, he told himself. *Just stop it. You have no right to think of her like that.* In his old life, he could have courted her, but in his old life, he probably wouldn't have bothered. He had been too preoccupied with his studies, with sports, with thoughts of the future and what he hoped to achieve to spend his days mooning over some bluestocking. Would he have even seen Elizabeth in a romantic light? Probably not. It was only now, trapped in this shadow existence, that feelings had become more important to him than facts and stratagems.

Above his head, there was a flittering of wings—bats, stirring from their sleeping place in the rafters. How he envied them. If only he had a special sense that allowed him to navigate through all the dark places, inside and out.

Aldini usually left in the mornings when Makepiece arrived, then returned late in the evening to spend the night curled up next to Victor on his cot. Then, one day, Aldini didn't come back in the evening. Days passed without any sign of the cat, and Victor was ashamed by how much he missed her. He hadn't realized how much he had come to rely on her presence until she was absent. Without her, the hours dragged by, and he felt surges of despair. *This tedious room*, he thought, *will be my whole world till I die.*

Aldini returned as abruptly as she had disappeared, yowling and purring, winding herself against Makepiece's legs for a moment, then going over to Victor and rubbing her cheek against his ankle. Victor was so happy to see her he nearly smiled and gave himself away.

"She seems to like you," said Makepiece. "Curious, as she never pays any attention to Igor."

Victor attempted to ignore the cat without actually tripping over her as he stacked crates in a corner. Makepiece scratched his beard, looking away as though solving some problem that had nothing to do with Bio-Mechanicals or cats. Then, very casually, he said, "Stop."

Victor stopped, still holding a crate of glass vials in his hands.

"Put that down." Victor obeyed. "Now, pick up the cat." Victor stared straight ahead, then bent and scooped up the cat. Too late, he realized his mistake; he had picked up Aldini with two hands, one under her hind legs. Surely a mindless automaton would have simply hoisted the creature by its scruff.

"Now, put it on the table." Makepiece moved, giving Victor room to move past him. Victor placed the cat on the cast iron operating table, trying to keep the tension from showing on his face.

"Now, take this." Makepiece handed him the scalpel, and now an icy shock washed away all his frantic speculation. "Take it. Like this." Makepiece demonstrated. Victor had to shift his grip on the cat to take the scalpel, and he hoped Aldini would take advantage of his one-handed grasp to break free.

Instead, the stupid animal butted his hand with her nose and began purring.

"Good. Now, cut its throat."

Victor stared at Makepiece, certain he had misunderstood.

CADAVER & QUEEN  **145**

Makepiece loved this cat. He fed it and pet it and cleaned up after it. Surely he didn't mean for Victor to slit its throat.

"Here, I'll help." Makepiece grabbed Aldini by the scruff of her neck and pinned her to the table, baring her throat. For a moment, the cat acquiesced, then she tried to roll over. "Go on. Cut."

Victor tried to think. The only reason he could think of for Makepiece to sacrifice his cat this way was that the scientist suspected that Victor was more intelligent than he was letting on. That meant that Victor had two choices: kill the cat and keep his secret, or spare the animal and reveal it. Or perhaps Makepiece intended to spare Aldini at the last moment, crying out "Hold!" like the angel of God who told Abraham that he did not, after all, need to sacrifice his son.

*If you reveal yourself, old man, it will be you on that table under the knife.* The voice in his head sounded like the Henry of his memories. It sounded like a trusted friend.

So, what to do? Victor's right hand, holding the scalpel, began to tremble. His left hand reached out to steady it. *No.* He would not let his left hand take over this time.

The cat squirmed to get free of Makepiece's grip, then relaxed. She had a lovely, trusting disposition; another cat would have hissed and struggled.

"What is it, Victor? Do you like the cat? Do you care for her?" Makepiece's gaze was sharp and all too knowing.

*Victor. He used my name.* With a sudden, sharp move, Victor's left hand shot out, seizing the scalpel. Unable to stop his rogue limb, Victor threw himself sideways, slamming his hip bone into the side of the table and causing the knife strike to miss the cat, brushing by the tips of the cat's sensitive whiskers instead of severing her jugular. The cat howled and turned sharply in her skin, startling Makepiece into releasing her.

The terrified feline seemed to explode off the table, skittering across the wood floor with claws still extended before disappearing from view. Makepiece cursed under his breath and examined the scratch on his hand.

"Well, that didn't exactly go as I intended." He gave Victor a wary look as he put antiseptic on the cut and bandaged it. "But did it go as you intended, that is the question." Victor kept his face carefully blank. "I suppose not. Ah, well. Nothing to do but keep trying."

*Safe.* That was all that mattered, thought Victor. He did not know what Makepiece would do with him if he knew that he was not a mindless automaton, but until he knew, he intended to keep that information to himself.

But that night, when Makepiece left, the cat shot out the door as if chased by unseen dangers. She did not return the following morning, or the one after that.

Preoccupied by the loss of his one companion, Victor didn't recognize the second test until it was too late.

# 17

THE DOOR TO THE ANATOMY CLASSROOM WAS bolted shut. Lizzie stood outside in the hall, her heart pounding. Today the first year students were being given actual cadavers to dissect, and even though Grimbald had said that female students would be excluded, Lizzie had figured that she would, at least, be permitted to observe. But when she tried the doorknob one more time, just to make sure, she knew there was no mistake—she had been locked out.

*Damn it.* She felt as though she had been punched in the stomach. She took a deep breath, her ribs pressing against the boning of her corset. If she gave up and walked away, she would be behind all her classmates. If she pounded on the door and made a scene, she would make a fool of herself. *Women,* they would say. *So emotional. No control.* Of course they can't be permitted around sharp knives, except in the kitchen.

*Damn, damn, damn.*

Pressing her hands onto her stomach and forcing herself to breathe slowly and think, Lizzie considered her other options.

Appeal to Moulsdale? No, he would just pat her on the head and tell her to run along.

Appeal to Makepiece? "You're my right hand," he told her when they worked together on the Reanimator. "Indispensable."

Surely he would intervene on her behalf for something as important as this.

With a course of action decided, Lizzie straightened her blouse and set off down the hall to the laboratory.

It had finally stopped raining, and the sky was actually blue. Lizzie had never been to the laboratory in midmorning, and she was surprised by how attractive the building looked in the bright October sunshine. There was ivy growing up one of the walls, and on one corner she spotted an endearingly ugly little stone gargoyle, sticking out its curled waterspout tongue at her. Somewhere close by, a robin warbled, paused, then warbled again. There was a whole world of lovely hidden things going on all around her, while she, oblivious, obsessed about cadavers.

They were probably cutting into them right now back in anatomy class. *Oh, Lord*, she thought, hand on the doorknob, *I do not call on you often, so just this once, do me a favor and let Makepiece be in the laboratory and the door unlocked.*

The door was unlocked and as she opened it, she heard someone moving around in the back of the laboratory. Her prayers were answered.

"Professor Makepiece," she began, "I am so glad to find you in. I need to speak to you about..." She stopped midsentence, because the figure that turned around was not Professor Makepiece.

For a moment, all she saw was a big man standing in the

shadows, and she thought he must be one of the local labor-ers who came to haul rocks. There was endless construction going on at Ingold, with roughly dressed men pushing wheel-barrows or shouting orders at each other, and watching her with a steady, unblinking, predatory stare if she walked past them on one of their breaks.

Nervous, she lifted her chin and tried for a tone of com-mand. "Excuse me, but are you supposed to be in this build-ing?" The man stepped forward out of the shadows, and she saw it was Victor.

In the three weeks since she had last seen him, he had bulked up, especially around the shoulders and chest. The bruises on his face had faded, and the swelling around his eye and mouth had gone down, revealing a surprisingly patrician appearance—high cheekbones, a sharp blade of a nose, a strong jaw.

"'Lo," he said, "Miss Lavenza." The words were thickened and distorted, but recognizable nevertheless. Then he smiled, and suddenly he was *handsome*. Distractingly so.

"Oh! Hello," she said, annoyed to hear how breathless she sounded. Her heart gave a little kick as he turned toward her. He was holding a vial in his good hand, while the Bio-Mechanical arm hung loosely at his side. "You startled me." Why had she said that? It was so unprofessional.

"Sorry."

"It's not your fault. Midterms are around the corner and I'm on my last nerve, as you Brits say." He frowned, looking confused. "What were you doing?"

"Working." He gave her a slightly crooked smile. "Like Igor." As she gaped at his response—he had never uttered more than a one syllable word before, let alone strung three words together—he nodded to a corner of the room where she spotted the distinctive, twisted shape of the man's back as he dusted a vat of green liquid. The comparison was patently absurd. Both might be Bio-Mechanicals, but that was where the similarities ended.

"Your speech has improved a great deal. Have you been working with Professor Makepiece?"

"No."

"All this progress on your own?"

He nodded, then added, "Yes. On my own."

"Oh, my goodness, you sound so…so…*articulate*," she said, although the first word that had come to mind was "human." Was he upset that she had deserted him? "I'm sorry I couldn't come before now. I just got swamped by schoolwork." He didn't reply, but continued looking at her with an intensity that left her flustered. "But in the end, you didn't need me, did you?" Absurdly enough, that made her feel a bit bothered. Wanting something to do with her hands, she began sorting through the vial rack on the table in front of her, moving the glass tubes around so they were graduated from small to large, instead of the other way around.

"Yes," he said. "Thanks to you." He replaced the vial he was holding into the wooden rack she was sorting. He had superb fine motor coordination with his right hand, she noticed, but his left hand remained limp by his side.

"I didn't do much." She replaced the vial rack in the cabinet where it belonged.

He smiled and shook his head.

She didn't know what to say. Before, he had seemed like a patient. Now, suddenly, he seemed like…like any other man. A good-looking man. Not as perfectly handsome as Byram, perhaps, but somehow more…more *something*. Something that made her breath catch with nervousness, which was ridiculous. "Makepiece must be thrilled with your progress," she decided to say. Yet he hadn't bothered to send her a message. She felt a bit stung by that.

"I do not speak to Makepiece."

"Really? After all this time?"

Victor hesitated. "I do not trust him."

"But why? If he knows that you are the breakthrough that he's been looking for, that can only be better for you, can't it?"

"He's a scientist. Scientists like to experiment."

She gave a startled laugh. "You make him sound like some sort of mad vivisectionist! He may be a little obsessive, but he's not evil."

He looked away, and she felt there was something he wasn't telling her.

"Perhaps not. But you haven't told him what you overheard that night, have you?"

It startled her to hear him mention it. He had seemed like such a different creature then. "No, but the more I think about it, the more absurd it seems not to. I mean, so what if the queen is a patient?" Unless Makepiece planned to do more than cure the ailing monarch…but, as Byram had pointed out, what would the school gain by it? Victoria didn't rule the country on her own. "It's not *that* dark a secret."

"Keep it anyway. Better not to say anything about the queen…or about my being able to speak." He smiled, and she could feel him trying to lighten the mood. "After all, you wouldn't want me telling your secrets—even though they're not dark."

"My secrets?" For a moment, she had no idea what he meant, and then the room felt too warm as she recalled all the things she had said to him. Dear Lord, had she really nattered on about Perry as if confiding to a sympathetic dog?

Fidgeting with the button on her cuff, she said, "Speaking of Makepiece, where is he now? I was hoping to speak to him."

"He went to York. For supplies. Ch-chemicals."

*Oh, terrific*, she thought. *Just my luck.* The trip to York took an hour, at least, and another hour back. No chance of her observing the dissection now.

"Is something wrong?"

She was caught off guard by how quickly he picked up on what wasn't said. "Oh, no." She smiled reflexively. "It's quite all right."

"Liar."

Lizzie gave a startled choke of a laugh. "All right, fine. I'm supposed to be in Grimbald's anatomy class, where the rest of the first years are getting their hands on cadavers."

Victor frowned. "Grimbald? You are not—" he paused, clearly searching for a word "—not permitted to be there? But why?"

Lizzie sighed and sat down on the stool by one of the long tables.

"Because my presence could negatively impact on the learning experience of the other students," she said, parroting Grimbald's explanation. "According to my professor, it is unseemly to discuss such vulgar things as *legs* in the presence of a lady." She looked up at him and laughed. "Oh, the expression on your face! I suppose you're scandalized, as well." Another thought occurred. "Or was I speaking too quickly?"

"No." He suddenly seemed preoccupied.

"I just don't know how I'm supposed to learn anything if I'm not allowed to participate," she said, more to herself than to Victor. "It's one thing to read about anatomy in a book, or to see an illustration, but I've seen enough of medicine to know that the reality is always messier and more difficult."

He didn't say anything, but seemed to be listening intently again, so she went on. It helped to talk this out, whether or not her companion comprehended her.

"I've studied the pectoral girdle, but I need to actually see where the tendons attach the clavicle to the scapula. I understand that the temporomandibular joint is there so the mandible can move, but all I've ever touched are skeletons, so I've never seen the articular disk or the ligaments that connect to it." *I'm babbling*, she thought, but she couldn't seem to stop herself. Something about the way Victor seemed to be listening to her, attentively, with a glint of good-natured humor in his eyes, made her want to divulge everything—all the little insecurities and doubts she kept hidden from everyone else, even Byram and Will. *Especially* Byram and Will. "I know some people think the charts in the books are actually better than the physical specimens, but I've studied the diagrams six ways from Sunday, and I'm still a little confused about the precise location of some of the abdominal organs. I mean, I've got a general sense, but that's not good enough once you're digging around with a scalpel." Which was what all her classmates were doing, right now at this very moment. "Damn it."

She felt the flush creeping up her cheeks. Had she really cursed in front of a man? Well, not a man in the most literal sense of the word, she supposed. Yet enough like a man that she couldn't stop blushing.

"I understand."

"That's very kind," she mumbled, looking at the scuffed toes of her boots.

His hoarse laugh startled her, but not as much as what he did next. Bending down so that his head was on a level with hers, Victor took her hand in his. "I mean I understand." Distracted by the sensation of her bare hand resting in his, she forced herself to pay attention to what he was saying. "I understand how the median and ulnar nerves run through the hand," he said, turning her palm up and tracing their path with one finger. "I know where the abductor and adductor muscles are." He pressed his thumb into the pad of muscle below her thumb. "I know anatomy." He stroked his thumb across the center of her palm, causing the nerves to tingle in a way they never had before. Then, giving a low whoop, he clasped her just above the waist, lifted her off her feet and swung her around in a wide circle. "I know anatomy!"

# 18

VICTOR'S HEART WAS RACING AS HE LOWERED Elizabeth so her feet touched the floor again. She gave a gurgle of laughter as a lock of hair came loose from its pins and suddenly her face was inches from his, her body pressed against him for one breathless moment. Then she broke away, still laughing as she attempted to pin her hair back.

"Well!" She was blushing scarlet, and no wonder. He tried to slow his breathing and not look as though he was about to grab her again.

*You should have kissed her, old man.* That would have been Henry's advice. He was always giving romantic advice, although as far as Victor knew, he had never even held a girl's hand.

"Here," said Victor, seeing that Elizabeth was struggling. He twisted her thick hair and then pinned it back, a little haphazardly, but at least it was staying put.

"Thank you. My hair has a mind of its own."

*It should meet my left hand.* A sudden image of his hand tangling in her unbound hair, pulling her head back for his kiss, made him feel light-headed, and as it was, his pulse was still pounding. He wondered if his heart, brought back from the grave, could handle the strain. Not that it mattered; there were so many other things that could go wrong right now that cardiac arrest felt like the least of his problems.

"Sorry," he said, feeling awkward.

"No need to apologize. I'm sure I would have done the same, if I were in your position. But how do you know anatomy?"

He hesitated, then decided to risk confiding in her. "I think I was a student. Like you."

Her eyes widened. "A medical student? But Victor, this is incredible! What else do you remember?"

She was so innocent, gazing at him with admiration and wonder. Had he ever been that fresh and unspoiled? "I remember this place."

She frowned. "You mean you were a student here, at Ingold? I suppose that makes sense. It's just that Professor Grimbald taught us that Bio-Mechanicals are usually created from the unclaimed corpses of workhouse paupers, convicts and lunatics. The most successful specimens were claimed straight from the prison gallows. Well, never mind." She waved her hand, as if batting away an annoying insect. "Your case must have been an exception. Perhaps that's what makes you so unique. Do you remember anything else?"

"Not certain." He concentrated, and suddenly he recalled being struck by what felt like a bolt of lightning, and the searing pain that had exploded in every cell of his body. The force of the electricity firing through his brain must have destroyed certain memories, but others had just been buried somewhere in his mind. And now, finally, those memories were coming back.

Elizabeth was speaking to him again. "So, if you were a medical student here, it stands to reason you must have friends who are still classmates here."

*Yes. That made sense.* Yet it didn't feel quite right. If only he could remember more about his life before the transformation.

A rush of images assailed him: hands tied behind his back, trying not to stumble on the rough wood stairs leading up to a platform, the sun shining in his eyes. He could hear the low roar of the crowd below, punctuated by jeers and catcalls: *Give us a jig! Let's see you twist!* The big man in the black hood was waiting for him, noose in hand.

The memory faded, leaving Victor feeling dizzy and disoriented. A trickle of cold sweat ran down the back of his neck. His initial sense of exhilaration faded, leaving a sour taste in his mouth as he realized the truth: somehow his left arm, grafted from another's man body, was possessed of that man's memories. He was not just Victor, a former medical student. He might feel like him, might share his name and resemble him superficially, but in reality he was something new and strange—an amalgam of metal and flesh, of student and criminal, of good and evil.

Elizabeth, oblivious to his convoluted thoughts, was beaming at him. "This is so incredible, Victor!" Her fingers squeezed his, and suddenly, that shock of awareness was back again, replacing the icy fear with something warmer. "You are a breakthrough, you know. A medical marvel." Well, that was putting him in his place. Still, being seen as a medical marvel might not be as good as being perceived as a man, but at least it was better than being lumped in the same category with Igor, who was still sweeping the same corner of the floor, oblivious to everything going on around him.

"Victor, surely we need to tell someone now. We need to tell Makepiece."

He shook his head. "Not yet." Hearing how abrupt that sounded, he turned it into a request. "Please."

Her brow furrowed. "But why not? Victor, this is too big to keep between us."

"There's something else. Something I need to remember." He concentrated, trying to dredge up the memory. "I don't know."

"Well, why not enlist Makepiece's help? I can see why you might not trust Moulsdale and Grimbald, especially since Grimbald seems to have it in for you, but I've gotten to know Professor Makepiece, and I think we should trust him."

Victor was still trying to parse the rapid-fire burst of words, but his left hand was miles of ahead of him. Reaching out, it seized her right wrist. "No!"

She stared at him, openmouthed with shock. Obviously, she assumed that he was shouting at her, instead of his own rogue limbs.

He swallowed, fighting to unclench his gauntleted fingers. "I mean to say...don't tell him. Yet. *Please.*" It would have sounded better if his huge monster hand wasn't still clamped around her wrist like a vise. Her bones were so slender, so fragile. *Don't hurt her. It would be so easy to hurt her by mistake.* His hand relaxed, but did not let go. So it could be reasoned with, if not controlled.

She glanced down at his hand, then back at his face. "I wasn't going to tell Makepiece without your permission." She spoke slowly, as if reasoning with a small child, or an idiot.

"Besides, the professor is in York today, remember? You told me so yourself."

"I did… Of course." And still his hand held her. *Let her go*, he thought. *You're going to frighten her.* But this time, the hand didn't listen to him.

"I'll wait until you're ready, if that's what you want."

Her face was tipped up to his, as if in anticipation of a kiss. He was still holding her gaze when he felt his hand release her, gauntleted fingers sliding down the outside of her arm and making her shiver, even through the cotton of her blouse.

"Forgive me," he said.

She licked her lips, a nervous gesture that nonetheless made his blood rush south. "There is nothing to forgive." She paused for a moment. "But do you really imagine that Professor Makepiece would treat you like…like some sort of giant salamander?" She said it as if it were the most absurd idea imaginable.

*Or like his own child.* Should he tell her about Justine? No, he couldn't do it. If Elizabeth were to learn about the pain Makepiece was inflicting on his own daughter with the etheric magnetometer, she would feel obliged to step in, to speak out, to do something. "I know you are fond of Makepiece," he said carefully, "but when it comes to getting what he desires, he is more ruthless than you might imagine."

"Let's say he is as callous as you suspect. How much longer can you keep your intelligence a secret from him? A week? A month?"

"Long enough to remember what it is that I know."

She walked over to the window, and stood for a moment, lost in thought. "So you want me to lie to Professor Make-piece."

"You've already lied to him once."

She looked over her shoulder at him. "And if I say no?" If she had been another, less earnest woman, he might have thought she was flirting with him.

"How about I offer you a deal?" The words were out, unplanned, before he could consider them.

She raised her eyebrows, as if skeptical that he had anything to bargain with. "What kind of deal?"

He smiled, because something had clicked in the back of his mind. "You keep my secret for a little while longer, and I'll teach you gross anatomy."

# 19

LIZZIE HAD HOPED THAT SHE WOULD BE ABLE to have her first anatomy lesson the same day as the rest of her class, but Victor was more pragmatic, explaining that he needed to plan a little in advance. In the end, it took two weeks of clandestine meetings before they found the right opportunity. Grimbald announced that the cadavers were being brought out of the cold room again, as the class had not made many inroads during their first session. The plan was for Victor to take her to the dissection room right as the rest of the class departed, but before the Bio-Mechanicals came to clear up the room.

"We'll have about twenty minutes, maybe thirty," said Victor, "so we had better make the most of it."

She nodded, aware that over the past fortnight, the student had become the teacher. Victor had been coaching her with anatomy diagrams and growing more and more confident as the material sparked old memories. There was one thing she didn't understand, though. "So how, precisely, will we get in and out without being seen?"

Victor grinned like a pirate and opened a door in the back of the laboratory. "We travel like Bio-Mechanicals."

Heart pounding, Lizzie followed Victor out of the laboratory and through a side door in the main building that led to a long, low passageway. She knew that Ingold contained a hidden network of servants' tunnels, originally built by the abbey's monks in case of attack and now used by the Bio-Mechanicals to move about the four main buildings, unobtrusively entering common rooms in order to clean them or take away rubbish.

Some of the more daring students had attempted to navigate between the buildings this way, but no one made a habit of it—the tunnels had been scaled to accommodate diminutive medieval monks, and if you ran into a Bio-Mechanical, one of you would have to back up until there was some sort of switchback. In more than one section, the ceiling was so low that Victor had to bow his head to keep from scraping it on the ceiling, but the tunnel widened and sloped upward right before he stopped rather abruptly beside a door. To Lizzie, it looked exactly like all the other doors they had passed.

"This is it," he said. "But we have to wait. They're still inside. Look." He gestured to a decorative metal grille that was set at her eye level in the wooden door. The grille had a vaguely Ottoman design of swirls and curlicues, and allowed a person to stand unobserved while spying on the occupants of the other room. Pressing her face closer to the latticed grille, Lizzie could see that all twenty of her fellow first year students were present, divided into groups of four around five cadavers. Byram and Will had been placed with Outhwaite and Mothersole, and it was impossible to tell which pair was more unhappy with the arrangement. They had all removed their jackets and rolled up their sleeves, and were wearing long white aprons flecked and stained with bits of brownish blood and gore. Despite the scalpels they held, they looked more like butchers than doctors.

"By now, you should have located the inferior vena cava and the descending aorta." Grimbald's voice held an edge of exasperation.

"I don't think this fellow has one," complained Will. He was making an uneven sawing motion, like an inexperienced cook carving a joint of mutton. Beside her, Victor made a strange, muffled sound of surprise. She looked at him, but he didn't spare her a glance, all his focus on the classroom.

"I found a kidney," said Outhwaite, holding up the dark pink organ in the palm of one hand.

"I could murder a steak and kidney pie right now." That was Mothersole, a sheen of sweat on his plump face as he pulled a handful of greasy yellow fat out of the cadaver.

"How can you talk about food," said Byram. "The smell of this place is making me gag." His movements were more precise and controlled than the others, but he looked appalled by his corpse, as though it were doing something vaguely offensive just by lying there.

"Well, I'm hungry," whined Mothersole.

"And my hand is cramping from trying to saw through this tough old bugger," said Will. He continued sawing with vigor.

"That's good, Shanley," Grimbald was saying to someone out of view. "No, no, Jenkins, that's the esophagus." As he came into view behind Byram, Lizzie saw that Grimbald looked drawn and tired, with dark shadows underneath his eyes. "Now, what's this?" He twirled the edges of his mustache as he bent over Byram and Will's cadaver. "Artery and vein, and neither one damaged. Not bad, Frankenstein, not bad at all."

"Ac-ac-actually, Byram's the one who did all the work," said Will, but Grimbald had already moved on to the cadaver's lower half, where Outhwaite and Mothersole were working.

"Good Lord, boys! What a pig's ear you've made of this fellow's innards." Grimbald took a probe and moved a flap of flesh to one side. "I don't understand. He's almost completely empty. Where's his liver? Where's the large intestine?"

"I think we might have mistaken some of it for fat. I removed a lot of adipose tissue," said Mothersole.

Grimbald just stared at Mothersole, the right side of his mustache twitching.

"Here's his kidney," offered Outhwaite, trying to make a joke of it.

Grimbald wasn't amused. "You're supposed to be training to be a doctor, not preparing a body for Egyptian burial." He shook his head. "Study your charts, boys. Go to the kitchens if you must, and ask the cook to point out the bits of offal to you."

"Oh, I should have thought of that," said Lizzie, turning her head and nearly bumping noses with Victor. She hadn't realized how close he was standing, watching through the grille alongside her. With a jolt, she saw that their mouths were just inches apart, and she forgot what she was saying.

It was only after staring at his mouth for a moment that she took in the fact that his jaw was clenched, causing a muscle to jump in his lean cheek. "What's wrong?"

"That young man." He closed his eyes for a moment, took a deep breath. "William Frankenstein."

"Will? He's my friend. What about him?"

Victor closed his eyes for a moment, then said, "He's my brother."

She stared at him for a moment. "Are you certain?"

He scowled at her. "Yes, I'm certain. What did you think? That I was grown in a vat like yeast?"

"No, of course not." Suddenly it all seemed painfully obvious, and she wondered why she hadn't made the connection herself. Will's exceptional older brother, the school's star student—no wonder he was defying what everyone thought they knew about Bio-Mechanicals. "Oh, God," she said. "He'll be... He talks about you all the time," she whispered. "He thinks he can't live up to your example."

Victor wasn't even looking at her. "Enough."

"He's going to faint dead away when he finds out."

That got her his attention. "No," he said, his words so soft she could barely hear them.

"No, he's not going to faint, or...?"

"We're not going to tell him."

"But why? Don't you know how much it would mean to him?"

He held up one hand, and the grandfather clock in the corner chimed the noon hour a moment before the bell tower followed suit. That caused a flurry of activity as medical students hurried to hang up their aprons and put away their instruments. A few threw rumpled sheets over their cadavers, but Mothersole and a few others left the bodies where they lay in their rush to be first in line for lunch.

Grimbald gave a "tsk" of disapproval and scribbled notes in his book.

Lizzie turned back from the grate and gave a squeal of surprise; there were three Bio-Mechanicals standing behind Victor. "Sorry," she whispered.

Victor's expression told her to be more careful. She tried not to stare at the Bio-Mechanicals, who wore flat caps and dark, shapeless jackets, but it was hard not to keep stealing glances at their scarred, seamed faces, corpse-pallid where they weren't smudged with dirt. At first, they looked like miners, but then she began to notice their blank stares and slack mouths, and something else—something indefinable that felt wrong and raised the small hairs on the back of her neck. She had gotten used to Igor, she supposed, but there was still something a little unsavory about these Bio-Mechanicals. She wondered if, in life, they had committed crimes more serious than Igor's.

There was a rattling of the door from the other side, and Victor stepped aside to let the other Bio-Mechanicals through. All three shambled past her without any discernible change in expression. Victor surreptitiously took a strip of surgical gauze out of his pocket and slipped it between the door and the frame, allowing it to close without locking. Then Lizzie peered through the grate again.

"You and you, take the cadavers back to the morgue," Grimbald barked at one of the Bio-Mechanicals. "You, put the dirty instruments in the bucket."

The Bio-Mechanicals swayed in place.

"Ah, damn it, where's the guard? It's like talking to monkeys. You, take the feet. You, take the head. No, not the head, the arms. Good. Now take him to the morgue. The cold room, yes? Then come back for the next one."

Grimbald left the autopsy room, muttering to himself.

Lizzie waited for Victor's nod before she followed him into the Gross Anatomy classroom. "Why don't they have a guard, like usual?"

"Part of the training. So the Bio-Mechanicals can function on their own in battle."

"And can they?" The two Bio-Mechanicals carrying the cadaver were having trouble navigating the doorway, repeatedly slamming their corpse's head into the door frame.

"Jury's still out." Victor gestured for the Bio-Mechanical holding the cadaver's hands to wait, then moved the head so it was no longer lolling sideways. Without a glance or a nod, the two Bio-Mechanicals carried their burden out the back door and disappeared back into a tunnel. "All right," he said, standing beside the cadaver Will and Byram had been dissecting. "Ready? We won't have long."

"I'm ready, but if you don't feel up to doing this now, I understand." She kept trying to see Will in Victor's features, and thought she might detect a resemblance around the shape of the eyebrows and eyes. All in all, though, Victor's was a darker, far more masculine face, and she couldn't imagine him as a child, the way she could with Will.

"I am up to this. Are you?" It was a challenge.

"I'm not getting an attack of the vapors. I just thought, given what you just told me about Will…"

"Do you want to dissect or gossip?"

"Dissect."

"All right," he said to Lizzie. "Find an apron."

The used aprons were hanging from hooks along the wall. She selected one that appeared relatively free of splatter, and was still tying the strings around her waist when she realized that Victor was already starting on a cadaver. "Now, pay attention." With one neat, economical movement, he widened the opening, exposing the thoracic cavity. "Can you identify the respiratory organs?"

"Trachea, bronchi and lungs." Lizzie pointed to each one in turn. "Are we going to talk about Will, or just pretend it never happened?"

"Digestive system."

All right, then. She had her answer. "Liver, stomach, small intestine, large intestine." She could play this British game of cool containment as well as he could.

"Esophagus."

"There."

"Gall bladder."

That one threw her. She looked down at the cadaver, and suddenly all the organs looked like a collection of gray rubber toys jumbled together. "It looks so different in the chart."

"Think about your location. Consider the landmarks."

Lizzie summoned a mental image of the diagram that divided the human body into territories. "Caudal, so it's the appendix."

"Good. So you're still trying to locate the gall bladder."

She paused, looking up at his face as he looked down at the cadaver. He seemed so sure of himself here, more like an assistant professor than a student, and nothing like a Bio-Mechanical. She had no idea how to act around him from one moment to the next. He was like some sort of shape-shifter, always surprising her by revealing some new side of his personality. Right now, he seemed very aloof and British upper class. "I'm being rude and American, aren't I? Asking you personal questions."

"I don't know the answers."

"You know that Will is your brother. He can help you figure this out."

Victor gave a small twist of a smile that had absolutely no humor in it. "You mean, I can put him in harm's way. Just like I did to you."

"What do you mean?"

There was a sound behind them, and Victor's head whipped

around. It was only the two Bio-Mechanicals, back for another cadaver, but when Lizzie looked back at Victor, she saw he was holding the scalpel in his left hand now, as though it were a weapon.

"That's it," he said, untying her apron strings. "Come with me."

"But we've just begun."

"I must have been mad." His eyes were fierce. "We have to leave. A guard might come any moment."

"I have to hang up the apron!"

"Hurry." He put his hand at the small of her back and propelled her out the back door. The Bio-Mechanicals ignored them, and Lizzie could not see the cause of all this panic.

"What is it? Victor, what's wrong?"

He pulled her down the corridors after him, not pausing until they were back at the lab. Igor was gone, and they were alone, but Victor's pale, set face did not invite thoughts of intimacy. "I don't understand. Are you angry at me? What have I done?"

"Wash your hands."

She went over to the cast-iron sink and ran the water. After a moment, he joined her, scrubbing at his nails so harshly she winced. She must have done something to set him off, but what? When he ran his hands under the tap, she felt his fingers brush hers and moved to get out of his way. He grabbed her wrist, then interlaced his fingers with hers, pressing her palm to his. The look on his face was anger, she realized, but not at her. At himself.

"What was I thinking? If someone had seen us…"

Her heart was pounding, and she couldn't stop looking at her hand, so small and pale inside his. "So I might have gotten in a little trouble? I don't mind. I knew I was taking a risk."

"Not just a little trouble. Elizabeth, I think they killed me because I knew something. If they think I've talked to you… if they think you know what I know…"

"But I don't know anything!"

He gave a harsh laugh. "Doesn't matter." His eyes were a little wild, and this was yet another Victor, one haunted and distressed. She tried to think of something she could say to soothe him.

"I don't mind," she said, giving his arm a squeeze. His bicep was so hard her fingers barely made a dent. "I know if it came down to that, you'd do whatever you could to protect me."

A shiver ran through him, and suddenly she was in his arms, held so tightly she could hardly catch her breath. The metal on his left arm dug into her back, but she didn't care.

"I am so sorry," he said, whether for endangering her or embracing her she could not tell.

"I'm not." A dozen different thoughts and sensations raced through her. He was pressed against her. It was most inappropriate, she supposed. She wasn't used to being touched at all, and this should feel odd and wrong, but instead, it felt incredibly, stirringly right. She felt as if she had discovered that she was ravenously hungry, but hungry for some food she hadn't realized existed. "I'll protect you, too, Victor."

"Elizabeth." He pressed his face into her hair as though he wanted to breathe her in and trembled, and then suddenly he pushed her back, making her stumble. "Sorry, sorry," he said, voice hoarse and chest heaving as if he'd just finished a race. And then he pushed her out the door and bolted it after her, as though she were the one who had lost control of the situation.

She stood outside the laboratory, blinking in the sunshine as her eyes tried to adjust to the sudden change.

# 28

"WILL, TELL ME MORE ABOUT YOUR BROTHER," Lizzie said as she sat across from him in the dining hall, too keyed up to eat the baked beans on toast that constituted the evening's supper.

Will, who had been drinking a cup of tea while checking his notes on cranial nerves, began spluttering and choking.

Byram glared at her as he pounded his friend between the shoulder blades. "What are you trying to do, kill him?"

She refused to be intimidated. "Oh, stop it. He had a brother who died. He knows it, you know it, everyone knows it. So why are we supposed to act as though it's some unspeakable secret?"

Byram smiled mirthlessly. "Oh, of course, you're going to give us a lesson in American etiquette. Care to tell me all about your dead mother and father, then?"

Lizzie stuck her chin out. "Certainly. And then you can tell me what's wrong with your—"

Will coughed into his napkin, interrupting her. "Now stop

it, Byram. I don't mind discussing Victor. I just swallowed the wrong way. What do you want to know, Lizzie?"

She hesitated. There were so many questions tumbling through her mind. She wanted to ask: What was he like? Did he say anything about discovering something important shortly before he died? Had he kept a journal or a lesson planner? Yet behind these legitimate questions, there were others, slyly insinuating their way to the front of the line. Questions such as: What sort of girls did he like, and did he have one special girl, and if he did, where was she now?

"What was he like?" There. That covered both valid curiosity about the chain of events that had led to Victor's transformation into a Bio-Mechanical, and the less honorable desire to know whether or not he just embraced girls as a matter of course.

"I've already told you. Top of the class. Perfect test scores. Captain of the rugby team. He was three years older than me, but before he went off to school I tagged along with him everywhere. He was patient with me, for the most part." Will crumbled a bit of toast between his fingers, then looked down at what he was doing. "Sorry. What else do you want to know?"

"You make him sound perfect."

"I don't!"

"You do, you know." Byram was uncharacteristically serious. "You talk about him as though he were some sort of godlike youth, beloved by all, while you're the weakling runt that crawled around after him."

"Do I? Well, let's see, then. Victor's shortcomings. He was a passable rider, but he didn't like horses much. And he had a bit of tunnel vision."

Lizzie leaned forward, resting her chin on her hands. Talking about Victor was nearly as good as being near him. "What do you mean?"

"Things came easily to him, so he never understood how difficult it could be for other people. When I got to Eton, I found out that some of the chaps at school resented him a bit, but they never said so to his face and Victor never twigged to it."

"What about here? Did he have any enemies here?"

Will looked puzzled. "Enemies? I wouldn't say that Victor had *enemies* anywhere."

Byram shook his head. "Of course he had enemies, Will. He was top of his class. People in power always have enemies." He poured himself some more tea, then frowned as he picked up his cup. "Cold. Of course."

"I suppose he might have had enemies," said Will. "But I never knew about it. In his letters, he always sounded very happy, and if he complained, it was in a joking sort of way." He looked pensive. "I think that's what made the news of his death easier to take—we knew he'd been happy, right up to the end."

Laying her hand on his Will's arm, she asked the question she realized she should have asked all along. "How did Victor die? You never said."

"Septicemia. He had a putrid inflammation of the vermiform appendix, which ruptured."

"But didn't they operate? I have heard there was a successful operation in London a few years back."

"They might have tried. I didn't inquire. We were all too distraught at the time." Will looked pale, and Lizzie knew she should leave him alone.

"You could ask now, though," she said softly. "Is there anyone who might be able to tell you more, besides the professors? A friend, or roommate?"

"I suppose," said Will. "Henry Clerval was his best friend and roommate. I could speak with him."

"Henry Clerval? The supercilious toad-face who helps grade our papers in Materia Medica?" Lizzie couldn't imagine him being Victor's friend.

"I know, he's an odd sort of chap—arrogant to the first years, unctuous to the professors. But he and Victor were friends ever since they were small, like Byram and me."

"Bite your tongue," Byram said, but Will was lost in thought.

"I could talk to him, I suppose." Will raked his hands through his hair, and for a moment, Lizzie could see the resemblance to Victor. "Yes, why *not* learn more about what happened?"

"Because some things are better off left alone," said Byram. He cleared his plates and stalked off, apparently more upset than Will by the conversation.

"What's wrong with him?" Byram was usually broody, but Lizzie had never seen him like this.

"He has these black moods. Strangest things set him off. Don't worry about it, Lizzie." Will's smile didn't quite reach his eyes. "You haven't done anything wrong."

They knew each other so well, better than she had ever known anyone. Sometimes it surprised her that she had even been admitted into the tight circle of their friendship. Though perhaps that was enough to explain why they included her: they were all black sheep, clinging together because they were separate from the rest of the herd.

"So," she said, "when do you want to approach Henry

Clerval? I don't see him in the dining hall at the moment, but why don't we look for him tomorrow after class?"

Will swallowed, then nodded. "Certainly," he said. "If you think we should, then…certainly."

As he walked away, she wondered if she was a bad friend for pressing him to speak with Henry about his brother when clearly the memories were still fresh and painful. Then another thought intruded, darker than the first: perhaps she shouldn't be poking around, openly asking questions about Victor's death.

*Elizabeth, I think they killed me because I knew something. If they think I've talked to you…if they think you know what I know…*

Would Victor approve of her talking to Henry Clerval? Probably not. But then, it wasn't as though she were talking to the faculty. Whatever the big secret was, it wasn't as though Clerval could be a part of it, or he would have been changed into a Bio-Mechanical, as well.

Besides, ignorance was its own kind of hazard. In medicine as in life, what you didn't know could most certainly hurt you. Any man of science, any person of science, would know it was always better to bring things out of the shadows and into the light.

The next day, Will sat next to Lizzie in Materia Medica while Byram sat closer to the front row, near Temple and some other boys. She wondered if Will and Byram had argued about something, but she couldn't exactly ask during class.

After the lecture, she was about to say something, but before she could get the words out, Will stood up and said, "You ready?"

Lizzie nodded and followed her friend to the front of the lecture hall as the other students, including Byram, filed out.

"Clerval," said Will. "Do you have a moment?"

Henry looked up from the papers he was grading. "A moment, yes, but that amount of time has already passed." He smiled smugly at his own joke.

*What an utter toad.* Lizzie had no idea how Victor could have been friends with the man, unless he was less of an ass around people of the same gender. Or perhaps the loss of his friend and roommate had changed Henry.

She decided to try again. "Mr. Clerval," she said, clutching her books to her chest, "I know you are busy, but if you could just spare me a few minutes, I would be very grateful."

"You would, eh? Just how grateful?" Putting down the test papers he had been grading, Henry leered at her. She exchanged a quick look with Will, who seemed as uncomfortable with the situation as she was. Too bad Byram had already filed out of the classroom with the other students.

She cleared her throat and tried again. "What I mean to say is, I have a few questions."

"Oh, I see." Henry went back to grading papers, revealing a bald patch at the top of his ginger hair. "Sorry, old girl, but I'm a bit snowed under at the moment."

Will started to head toward the door, but she stopped him with a look.

"I understand, but I think you may feel differently when I tell you it's about Victor Frankenstein."

"Victor's dead." There was no hint of smugness or humor in Henry's manner now.

Lizzie forced herself to plow through her embarrassment. "This is Will, Victor's younger brother."

Henry's eyes flickered over to Will, then back. "I am well aware of that fact."

"Then you should also understand why we…why *he* might have a few questions to ask you."

Henry looked coldly furious. "So who has the questions? You, or Miss Lavenza?"

Will took a deep breath. "I do."

"I see. And do you always let a woman do your talking for you?"

"No, sir. I do not." Will squared his shoulders. "But talking about Victor is difficult for me, as I'm sure it is for you. Miss Lavenza never knew my brother. She is here as a friend, to encourage me."

Henry's lips thinned. "All right, then. Seeing as how you've been encouraged…what is it I can help you with, Frankenstein?"

"I wanted to know more about my brother's final days. What he was doing, how he was feeling…" Will glanced at Lizzie, and she motioned for him to go on. "If there were any signs that might have been caught earlier…"

Henry pushed his chair back hard, as though readying himself for a fight. "Are you suggesting that the school is in some way to blame for your brother's death?"

"I… I…no, not at all. I just…"

Lizzie took a step forward. "Just out of curiosity, why did no one suggest operating to drain the vermiform appendix? Ingold is meant to be at the cutting edge of medical care, after all."

Henry's eyes darted from Will to Lizzie and back again. Standing this close to him, she caught a whiff of acrid sweat.

"What is this?" Henry slammed down his pencil. "Some sort of interrogation? You think I didn't care for Victor? You think perhaps I ignored signs that he was unwell?"

"Not at all," Will said quickly.

"I don't know," said Lizzie. "I wasn't there. Do you think that, Mr. Clerval? Do you believe that you could, or should, have done more?"

Will stared at her as though she had lost her mind, and it occurred to Lizzie that he might not be wrong. Henry Clerval might not have as much power as a professor, but he was still an upperclassman and a teaching assistant. He could certainly influence Moulsdale against her, not that the head of medicine required much of a push, as he was already inclined to disapprove of her.

"I do think that, at times," said Henry, surprising her. "I look back and wonder what I might have done differently."

"Did he complain of abdominal pain?" Will spoke without hesitation this time.

"Abdominal pain?" For a moment, Henry seemed utterly confused, as if he had forgotten that they were talking about Victor's appendicitis. "No. No, he never complained. He seemed fine at the time. No one had any idea he was so unwell until it was too late to save him."

"Of course not," said Will. "He wasn't the sort to make a fuss."

"But isn't an inflamed appendix meant to be terribly painful?" Both men turned to look at Lizzie. "Not to cast aspersions on Victor's manly ability to withstand discomfort," she said with a touch of sarcasm, "but if the appendix was inflamed, he would at least have winced or lost his appetite or groaned a little when he sat down or stood up."

Will took a moment to think that over; clearly, the heroic image he had of his brother did not include groaning, even when in acute physical distress. "That's true, I suppose." He sounded unconvinced.

"Oh, for goodness' sake! Mr. Clerval, tell him! Nobody

with an appendix about to rupture just walks around as though everything's fine!" Henry Clerval had the strangest look on his face: fear, but with a touch of something else that seemed almost like longing. *It's as though part of him wants to be blamed,* she thought. "Has it occurred to you that Victor Frankenstein might not have had a ruptured appendix at all?"

"I don't understand," said Will. "You think he was misdiagnosed?"

Taking a deep breath, Lizzie forced herself to look at Will, because it made her too nervous to address Henry. "Misdiagnosis is one possibility."

"Are you suggesting that someone *deliberately* harmed Victor?" Henry's voice rose in indignation, as though she had insulted him personally.

"I'm saying," she said with deliberate calm, "that we should investigate the circumstances surrounding his death."

"But why?" Will's voice was as plaintive as a child's. "Why on God's green earth do you think anyone would want to hurt my brother?"

"Yes, Miss Lavenza," said Henry, steepling his fingers in a gesture copied from Moulsdale. "Why do you think someone would want to murder Ingold's most promising medical student?"

"I don't know," she admitted, feeling the burn of indigestion low in her chest. Even to her own ears, her suspicions sounded unfounded and more than a little preposterous. Unfortunately, she couldn't just come out and say that it was Victor himself who had planted the seeds of doubt in her mind. "It's just a hunch, really."

"Woman's intuition?" Henry laced both words with equal amounts of contempt. "I think, Miss Lavenza," he said slowly, "that this disordered thinking may be attributable to anemia.

You young women are frequently anemic, are you not?" He raised an eyebrow.

It took her a moment, and then, when she saw how Will looked as though he wanted the floor to swallow him up, she understood. *He means I'm irrational because I'm menstruating.* She could feel the shaming rush of blood to her face. No gentleman ever mentioned a woman's monthly courses in mixed company. It was more than crude—it was demeaning.

"I won't take up any more of your time." She strode out with as much dignity as she could muster, but she could not help overhearing Henry giving an audible sniff, as if he were smelling something unpleasant, and saying to Will, "Definitely on the rag."

# 21

IT CAME TO LIZZIE IN THE MIDDLE OF THE night: Victor had been a medical student, which meant that there had to be a file somewhere containing his medical records. The logical place for current files would be in Moulsdale's study. If she could get in there for fifteen minutes or more, she could read what had happened to Victor in the days leading up to his death. Of course, records could be falsified, but at the very least she could see whether the official report matched the story about Victor's appendicitis. She might find some answers or at least something that might spark his memory. At worst, she would miss one lousy dining hall meal. Considering the effect all those starchy suppers were having on the fit of her corset, that might not be such a bad thing.

She waited until she was sure that everyone else was at supper before making her way to Moulsdale's office. She didn't think she knew how to navigate the back corridors, so she took the main staircase, then turned left. She had only been to Moulsdale's office once, at the beginning of term, to have her schedule of courses approved and signed. Now, as then, she was struck by how the upper floor seemed more like a mansion than a monastery. The heavy oak banister, the age-darkened oil portraits of bewigged dignitaries and the Italian marble underfoot were all improvements that had been added long after the monks had been removed from their home.

Moulsdale's study, predictably, was the most ornately decorated room of all. Just as she had hoped, the heavily carved door was unlocked. Lizzie slipped in and then paused to catch her breath. There were no cleaners here yet, and the air was still thick with the odor of Moulsdale's cigars. On the far side of the room, a faint, reddish glow from the setting sun illuminated the high, arched Palladian windows, and on the other side, a fire was burning low in the tiled fireplace. She didn't have long to find what she was looking for, as the room was settling into evening shadow.

She didn't want to turn on any lamps, but in the fading light it was hard to make out details, and for a moment she mistook the crouched shape in the corner for another heavy, dark oak and leather chair. Then the figure moved and her heart skipped a beat before she realized it was a Bio-Mechanical. Now she could make out the rough jacket and workman's cap, as well as the feather duster and broom propped against the filing cabinet. He was so intent on his work that he hadn't noticed her presence.

*Just my luck the brute would be cleaning right where I need to be.* Her heels made no sound on the thick Persian carpet, and it was not until she was standing a few feet away that the cleaner grunted in surprise.

"Don't worry," she said in the voice she used for small children and large dogs. "I'm not going to hurt you."

"Elizabeth?" He stood up, pulling back the cap's brim so she could see his face.

"Victor!" Her broad smile wavered, confronted by his frown.

"What are you doing here?" He glanced behind her, at the slightly open door, then back. There was a shadow of stubble on his jaw, giving his handsomeness a harder edge.

"Trying to find out what really caused your death. What are *you* doing here?"

"Trying to find out what it was that got me killed."

His disapproving tone made her want to back down, so she made herself do the opposite. "Did you remember something else?"

"Just bits and pieces. Nothing that would explain why someone would have wanted to murder me."

"You're certain it was murder, though?"

He gave a humorless laugh. "I'm not certain of anything. Perhaps my appendix did rupture. Perhaps there's a perfectly innocent explanation for all of this." He met her gaze. "But what if there isn't?"

"Then we need to find out the truth." She lifted her chin. "Would you do any differently, if you were in my shoes?"

"No, of course not. I would do exactly what you're doing." There was something new in his expression now—a gentling of his eyes and mouth. "But I am not now, nor ever have been, a young woman. Do you have any idea how dangerous this is?"

He had leaned in, looming over her, and although she tried to ignore this, she felt the tingle of awareness waking every nerve ending in her body.

"If it's dangerous for me, then it's dangerous for you. The fact that I'm a woman has nothing to do with it."

His scowl turned into a look of pain. "I'm a lost cause, Elizabeth."

"That's not true. You deserve to know what happened to you and why."

He gave a humorless huff of laughter. "When you're a little older, you'll realize that what one deserves and what one gets are seldom the same thing." He looked down at her, and his gaze felt like a caress. "You need to get out of here, Elizabeth."

She put her hand on his right arm, aware of the strength of his bicep even through the rough material of his shirt. "I want to help you."

"I don't need your help."

"Then why are you holding on to me?"

His blue eyes registered surprise, and then a bleak hint of humor. His left hand had come around her waist, drawing her in to him. She became aware of the scent of him, a hint of masculine perspiration. He'd probably been doing hard physical labor all day and hadn't had a chance to wash. This should have repulsed her, she supposed, but instead, she had the urge to inhale the saltiness on his skin, or possibly even...taste it.

"You know why I'm still touching you. I'm part of the danger you're in."

She could see the shadow of a beard on his chin, and wondered what it would feel like against her cheek. "You wouldn't do anything to hurt me," she said, her voice a little breathless.

He met her gaze. "Wouldn't I?"

His tone made her think of frightening, thrilling things: brides and grooms and wedding nights. Except that he wasn't offering marriage—in fact, he couldn't, even if he wanted to, since Bio-Mechanicals were not considered human. "Now you're just trying to scare me off." She planted her hand on his chest and gave him a push, and he let go of her. "It's not working." She tried not to focus on how much she wanted his hands back on her.

"I can see that." He shook his head, but he was smiling now. "Don't you have any sense of self-preservation?"

"Yes, I do, which is why I think we ought to spend our time looking in that file cabinet. One of us should stand watch while the other locates your file."

He took a deep breath, raked his right hand through his hair and then nodded. "All right. Two minutes, no more. I'll stand watch." He took the broom and moved in front of the fireplace, but it was hard to believe that anyone would be fooled into thinking he was a mindless drudge. He stood like a soldier—broad shoulders back, spine straight and powerful arms holding the long broom more like a weapon than a cleaning implement. For some reason, that thought made her want to touch him again, to feel the contained violence in him combust into passion instead of pain.

Looking back over his shoulder, he said, "What are you waiting for?"

"Nothing." Lizzie knelt where Victor had been and forced her mind to the task at hand. As she rifled through the files, she realized they weren't all in proper alphabetical order. *Someone needs a secretary*, she thought, squinting in the dim light as she checked again: Fink, Ferguson, Frank, Franken, Franks, Frobisher. She fought the urge to alphabetize them.

"Do you see it?" Victor's voice was low and tense.

"No. I'm sorry. Do you think they would have thrown it out?"

"Possibly. But where's my... Where's William Frankenstein's file? Surely they wouldn't have discarded that one."

Lizzie rocked back on her heels, thinking. "Could they

have misfiled both under a different letter? I can go through all the *f*'s again from the beginning."

"No. Wait." Victor strode over to Moulsdale's desk. "What are those papers there?"

"What papers— Oh." She now saw that there were a number of papers on the desk. Picking them up, she read out the name. "They're your files!"

"And Will's. Damnation. What have you got yourself into, Will?"

As he stood behind her, looking over his brother's file, she picked up the report marked Victor Frankenstein. Underneath the typed name, address, height, weight and general physical condition—excellent—someone had written out a character assessment in flowing cursive. *Personality: V.F. is an exceptional surgical student, motivated and confident to a fault. "Driven," "talented," and "a bit of a cold fish," according to his peers.*

Not exactly the noble older brother Will had described. Nothing like the man she had come to know. Her Victor was cautious rather than cold, inquisitive but not ambitious and carried himself more with determination than arrogance. Her Victor cared passionately about his brother. Could the author of this report have gotten his character completely wrong, or had the transformation from human being to Bio-Mechanical changed his heart as well as his mind?

"Damn and blast."

Startled, she looked up at Victor, who shook his brother's file. "This says that Will approached Henry, asking questions about the circumstances of my death."

Her stomach contracted as though she'd been punched. "Oh, um…" She tried to swallow. "Does it say anything else?"

"Such as the fact that a certain Elizabeth Lavenza accompanied him on his fool's errand? It doesn't need to. I could figure that one out for myself." She had seen him angry before, but only at himself. Never at her.

"I'm sorry, Victor, but it made sense to go to your old roommate to learn a bit more about—"

"*You* went to Henry?" His voice rose, turning the last word into an epithet.

"Quiet, Victor, they might hear—"

"You daft, reckless… Tell me, what gave you that brilliant idea?"

"I… Will said you were roommates…"

"I am fairly certain that *Henry's* the one who murdered me."

She took an instinctive step back. "I thought… Didn't you both… Weren't you *friends*?"

Victor's lip curled in an expression she had never seen before—one of contempt. "Funny thing about betrayal—only intimates can do it to you."

Now it was her turn to be angry. "If you're trying to say that I betrayed your trust, take a look in a mirror! You never told me anything about Henry that would lead me to believe he betrayed you!" She slammed her palm against his chest. "No wonder your file called you arrogant!"

"Arrogance is what thick people call the truth when they don't like it."

"Are you calling me stupid?" Too angry to come up with a coherent response, she slammed her palm against his chest again, and this time his hand shot out and caught hers, the metal gauntlet biting into her fingers. "Let go of me," she said, trying to wrench her hand free. "You're hurting me!"

"Elizabeth." There was a note of strain in his voice. He no longer sounded angry; he sounded raw. "It's not your fault. I should have told you about Henry."

"Let go of me! I hate you! I don't know why I ever bothered to try to help you." But something had shifted in her, gone from fury to something quieter, and she stopped struggling. What was the point? She was only going to scrape her skin against his unyielding metal. He used his good arm to draw her into his embrace. "I hate you," she said again, her forehead moving forward to rest on his chest.

"Of course you do." His right hand was making soothing circles on her back.

She moved her head so her nose was in the hollow of his throat, and she could inhale the unique scent of his skin. "Now you're furious at me," she said.

His chest rose under her palm as he laughed. "Try again."

She tilted her head back. "You're angry at me?"

"I was." He tucked a loose strand of hair back behind her ear. "For a smart girl, you've been remarkably stupid."

She opened her mouth to argue, but he silenced her by saying, "But not as stupid as I've been. You're like some damnable female mirror of me. I should know what to expect from you—the same thing I'd expect from myself."

It wasn't precisely a declaration of love, but Lizzie's whole body warmed to his words as though it were. Was it normal to feel a hot rush of desire for a man who'd just been yelling at her?

"Victor," she said, not at all sure what she meant to say next.

"Oh, no," he said, stepping back and holding up his hands as if warding off an attack. "You do not say my name like that. Not with that look in your eyes. God almighty, woman, do you have no sense of self-preservation at all?"

"I think we've already established that I do not."

One side of his mouth quirked up in a reluctant smile, but his eyes remained serious. "Elizabeth, we need to leave before someone catches us. And you have to promise me not to speak to Henry again. Neither you nor Will. Are you listening? This is important. You have to convince him that you're not a threat."

"I'm listening."

"Promise me you won't do any more snooping."

"But the file… Victor, we haven't read the rest of your file yet!"

"You have one minute. I'll go back to guarding the door, and then we need to leave here."

"A minute is all I need." She had just gotten to the part of the file titled *Cause of Death* when she heard the door open.

"Someone's coming," said Victor in a low, urgent voice. "Hide!"

With no time to think, she did what she would have done at the age of six: she darted under Moulsdale's large oak desk and held her breath.

"Good Lord," she heard the intruder say. "You're like Marley's ghost, aren't you? Come to remind me of all my sins?"

It was Henry Clerval, Victor's former friend, and his possible murderer.

# 22

VICTOR SCHOOLED HIS EXPRESSION INTO BLANK-
ness, and then began to push the broom in jerky, uncoordinated
mechanical motions.

"I don't suppose you've been doing a bit of reading?"

Henry removed his hat and his jacket and hung them on a
coatrack. His clothes carried a slight smell of damp earth and
charred twigs. Whatever he had been doing, it had involved
digging things up and then burning them.

"I suppose not, old chum."

Henry picked up the files from the desk and stared at them
for a moment. Could he tell that they had been handled? Victor forced himself to keep at his task, as mindless as Igor, as
oblivious as Aldini the cat to the currents of ambition and
intrigue that surrounded her.

"Arrogant and a cold fish," Henry mused as he perused
the file. Looking directly at Victor, he said, "They gave me
brandy, you know. Right in this very room, as a matter of fact.
A very fine Calvados, Moulsdale called it, with some sort of

smoky cheese. Can't recall the name. There were these tiny little slices of dark bread, and pickles…just enough to keep me from getting completely obfuscated. Still, I had a glorious shine on, if you take my meaning."

*I taught him that bit of slang*, thought Victor. Like most middle-class boys, Henry had grown up trying to speak properly, only to learn that the upper classes garnished their speech with liberal dashes of workman's slang.

Victor realized he had swept himself into a corner. He turned around and began work his way back across the room.

Henry wasn't paying attention, however. He was looking at the leather chairs beside the fireplace as if seeing his own ghost sitting there.

"You have to give the old man credit," Henry continued. "Had me talking for hours. At first it was all about me—how I was doing at school, my hopes and aspirations. Then he moved on to you. Did I like having you as a roommate, did you have any peculiarities, that sort of thing." He shook his head as he moved around the desk. "Funny what they chose to pick out from all that jabber."

*Hilarious.* Victor tried to keep Henry in his peripheral vision without appearing to do so. If his old roommate moved three feet to the left, his feet would come in contact with Elizabeth, curled up under the desk.

It was like some monstrous version of hide-and-seek.

"Take that line about us not being friends. I said that in a burst of maudlin appreciation of you. I went on and on, as I recall, about how I considered you my friend, but could never really tell if you held me in the same esteem." Henry tapped the sheets to line them up. "My own file, by the way, is fairly thin. I don't think they were prepping me for anything particularly important, the way they were you." Henry slid the files into the drawer. "I took my fate into my own hands, though. You have to agree about that."

It was so close to an admission of guilt that a chill ran down Victor's neck. So, Moulsdale had approached Henry, but only to assess Victor's character. Henry must have been simmering with jealousy before that interview, but that tantalizing brush with preferment had tipped the balance.

A jumble of emotions roiled in Victor's stomach, but he was able to keep a poker face as he continued sweeping the floor. He couldn't prevent his left hand from tightening on the broom handle until the wood creaked, but Henry didn't seem to notice. Out of the corner of his eye, Victor saw his former friend take a thick cigar from a brass standing ashtray.

"I keep thinking there's something left of you in there," Henry mused out loud as he lifted a box of matches out of a brass holder affixed to the wall. Victor heard rather than saw Henry strike the match. "You look so much the same. I expected you to look like a mindless, shuffling automaton after. But you look…like you." A faint, sulfurous smell filled the air in the closed room, followed by the spicy-sweet, burned-oak and leather fragrance of expensive cigar smoke.

Victor looked down at the floor and found the broom scraping up against the Persian rug. He had run out of room again. He turned and found that Henry had moved up behind him, effectively trapping him.

"Is there anything of you left, Victor?" He puffed on the cigar, exhaling the heavy smoke in a cloud that stung Victor's eyes.

*Don't look up. If you meet his eyes, he'll know what you are.*

But Henry's hand was under his chin, forcing his head up. Victor kept his gaze trained downward. "I didn't think they would do this to you. I want you to know that. I thought they would simply kill you. I didn't want your death, but I made my peace with it. But this…" Henry shuddered, the vibration of it traveling down his arm to the hand that still held Victor's jaw. "I am so sorry, my old friend." Henry took in a ragged intake of breath, and Victor couldn't help it—he looked up.

Henry was crying. His pudgy face was reddened, the protuberant blue eyes bloodshot and moist. "Is there anything of you left? Are you… Do you suffer, being as you are?" He took a quick puff of the cigar, and at first Victor thought it was to comfort himself, but then Henry held the glowing cigar tip so close to Victor's face that the heat of it burned his cheekbone.

"Do you feel fear anymore? Hatred? Do you feel anything, Victor?"

A test. One more test to pass. He'd always been good at tests. There were students who weren't, students who spent all their waking hours in the library, studying and preparing, but balked when the appointed hour came and the exams were passed out. There were others who didn't study until the last moment but met the challenge with raw nerves and adrenaline. Victor had been the third kind of student, the kind who was always working, so that tests required no additional preparation, the kind who turned the paper over and faced the ticking clock with neither fear nor bravado. He had been, in effect, a student Bio-Mechanical, emotionless and determined.

He faced the test of the burning cigar with a stone face. What did a burn matter to him, now? It was nothing. It would heal.

He hoped that Elizabeth couldn't see anything from underneath the desk.

"God damn it, Victor, don't you even have a shred of self-preservation left?" Ironic, that echo of his own words to

Elizabeth. "What if I take out your eye? Will that make an impression?"

From underneath the desk, Elizabeth gave an audible gasp, and Henry turned toward the sound, his voice shrill with surprise. "Who's that? Who's hiding in here?"

"It's me," she said as she came out from her hiding place under the desk. She confronted him, shoulders back and chin up.

Henry's face was mottled with angry red. "You stupid *bitch*. What are you doing here?" He spat the words at her.

"I could ask you the same thing."

Henry shoved her back against the desk, cornering her. "You brainless whore—" he began, but that was as far as he got. A low growl issued from Victor's mouth as his left hand hauled back and smashed into Henry's chin. There was a look of almost comical surprise on Henry's face as he fell back, his head striking the wood floor with a sharp crack.

As Victor stood, stunned, Elizabeth crouched beside Henry. His old friend was sprawled with his arms over his head, face wiped clean of all expression. *He used to sleep like that.* For a moment, Victor was transported back to Eton, lying in the bed across from Henry's, listening to his breathing deepen into snores. They had been as close as brothers then. How had it come to this?

Elizabeth placed two fingers over Henry's carotid, then looked up him. "I feel a pulse, but it's weak."

He knelt beside her, then leaned over to check for breath sounds. Nothing. "Here," he said, pulling off his jacket and rolling it under Henry's neck, to open the airway. His hands came away stained with red.

"Should I try to staunch the bleeding?"

"First, we have to get him breathing." Sitting behind Henry's head, Victor began to mechanically go through the motions of the Silvester method of resuscitation, crossing Henry's palms over his chest, then lifting them high over his head.

"It's not working," said Elizabeth. "What about trying Fothergill's method of mouth to mouth?"

He moved aside to give her room. "Show me."

Elizabeth tilted Henry's head back and pinched his nose shut before covering his mouth with hers. She blew into his mouth, paused to take a breath, and then repeated the process three more times. "Is it working? Is he breathing?"

Victor put his ear to Henry's mouth. "Wait...yes!"

She sat back on her heels as Henry opened his eyes and blinked. His gaze was vague and unfocused for a moment, and then his throat worked. Just in time, Victor turned him so that he could vomit onto the floor.

Henry wiped his mouth with the back of his hand, then looked back and forth from Elizabeth to Victor. "What... what happened?"

"You don't remember?" Elizabeth asked. Victor met her gaze for a moment, and then, as if by unspoken agreement, he stood and shuffled off to a corner.

Henry frowned and looked around the room. "Are we in Moulsdale's office?"

"Yes."

He must have amnesia from the head injury, thought Victor.

Elizabeth must have understood at once, because she added, "You asked me to meet you here."

*Oh, clever girl*, thought Victor. Henry would be suggestible now.

"I did?" Henry winced, as if thinking were physically painful.

"Yes, and then you...you tried to kiss me, and when I pushed you away, you fell back and hit your head."

It was plausible enough, but would Henry believe it?

Elizabeth played her part well, looking down as if embarrassed. "I am so sorry. I didn't mean to hurt you."

"No…no, I don't seem to recall…" Henry put his hand down in the pool of his own vomit, flinched, and then looked up at her in embarrassment. "I seem to have been ill."

"Yes. A side effect of the head injury. Do you want me to help tidy or…?"

"No, no, just leave me, I'll take care of it."

She stood up, a little unsteadily, and walked toward the door. Victor found himself holding his breath, and then, just when he thought she was safe, Henry called out.

"Miss Lavenza."

To her credit, she didn't flinch as she looked back over her shoulder at Henry. "Yes?"

"Do you mind not speaking of this?"

She nodded, as composed as any English lady at tea. "Of course not. It was all a misunderstanding."

"Yes. Thank you."

Then she was gone, leaving Henry and Victor alone. Henry got up slowly, holding on to the edge of the table for support, and then swayed for a moment. He gave a visible start as he noticed Victor in the corner. "Victor!" He hesitated and then repeated his name, this time as a question. "Victor?"

Victor shuffled over with the broom, and began clearing away the vomit. The broom wasn't the right tool for the job, and he was really only making things worse by spreading the sour-smelling liquid around until it mixed with the blood from Henry's laceration, but that only added to the impression that he was a dull-witted moron.

After a moment, Henry straightened his coat and left

Moulsdale's office, giving Victor one last inscrutable look before he closed the door.

Once he was alone, Victor found some paper in Moulsdale's private lavatory and used it to clean up properly. He thought, on balance, that he was relieved that he hadn't actually killed his murderer. Perhaps he did have a trace of conscience left after all.

# 23

HENRY CLERVAL SPENT A WEEK RECUPERATING from his injury, but no one seemed to miss him or ask after his welfare. When he returned to class, he was more subdued and polite with Lizzie than he had been previously. She hadn't seen Victor either of the two times she had gone to the laboratory, but once she had seen the back door slam just as she arrived, and she knew that he was avoiding her, either because he thought he would hurt her...or because he thought something else might happen if they were alone together.

She wanted to tell him she wasn't afraid, but what could she do? Demand that he spend time with her again?

Most unsettling of all, these thoughts were wrapped up in fantasies of Victor holding her in his arms again. Kissing, it seemed, was as intoxicating as gin, at least for her. Other girls didn't seem quite so obsessed with it, although boys were meant to have nothing else on their minds. Late at night, when she lay in bed, she imagined Victor's body, both the parts she had seen and the parts she had yet to see, and then worried that this was yet another strange and mannish thing about her.

She had to fight back the urge to confide at least some of this to Aggie. Her roommate might seem sophisticated in the ways of men and women, but Lizzie didn't think that Aggie's broadmindedness extended to Bio-Mechanicals. Yet the temptation to talk to Aggie kept growing stronger, particularly now that she worked alongside her in the infirmary two days a week. All the other medical students had been paired with older nurses— to prevent any hanky panky—but an exception was made for Lizzie.

Not that there was much time to talk about personal matters on infirmary days. By eight in the morning, there was usually a small line of people already waiting outside Ingold's gates to be admitted. The second years and the more experienced nursing students were given the job of sorting the urgent complaints, usually broken and dislocated bones, burns, miscarriages and acute appendix cases, from the chronic complaints, which usually consisted of older people with various kinds of bronchial difficulties. Most of the patients were seen and then discharged within the same day, unlike the soldiers who remained in their ward for months, receiving surgeries and prosthetics and learning how to use them.

The infirmary was one of the brightest areas at Ingold, set in a long hall lined with large windows. Proper circulation of air was considered of paramount importance in treating the sick, but drafts were dangerous for patients, so there was a small potbellied coal stove in the center of the room. There were twenty-eight beds in the ward, but only five of them were occupied at the moment, Lizzie noticed as she entered. On one, an elderly gentleman with a bandage on his forehead was reading the *York Herald* and tutting to himself. Across from him, a middle-aged man with a long, narrow face was drinking a cup of tea and tucking into a plate of eggs, while his neighbor, a heavyset man with a thick mustache that met his sideburns, looked on with obvious jealousy. He had a bowl of what smelled like beef broth and nothing more.

"But why, Mama?" This complaint came from a young boy with his arm in a plaster cast. His mother, a thin woman in a dark dress, looked absolutely exhausted. "I can't stay more than another five minutes, luv. Your sister can't watch the babies for more than a few hours. She's only nine."

Aggie and another student nurse were stripping one of the narrow beds, while the patient observed them from a cane-backed wheelchair that creaked under his muscular frame. One of his feet was bandaged and visibly shorter than the other.

"Hello, Lizzie," said Aggie, looking up as she shoved the soiled sheets into a laundry cart. There was a fine sheen of perspiration on her forehead. "Come to watch us nurses and see what real work looks like?"

"You're acting as though this is my first time here."

"First time in ages," muttered Aggie. "Suppose doctors don't really need to spend any time with actual patients."

Lizzie knew better than to take this bait. When it came to a battle of insults, Aggie was sure to win. "And how is the patient feeling today?"

"Better now I've got another pretty girl to look after me!" This patient's round baby face seemed a bit incongruous atop his solid blacksmith's physique. He was probably no more than sixteen or seventeen, and possibly younger even than that. His short, fair hair was the buttery blond that usually darkened with age.

"None of that, now," said Sabina in her lilting Jamaican accent. "You're going to make me jealous."

"Say the word and I'll post the banns."

Sabina laughed as she and Aggie shook out a fresh sheet. "And what would your mother say?" Sabina sometimes did homework with Aggie, and Lizzie had learned that she had been inspired by Mother Seacole, a Jamaican woman who had tended wounded soldiers in the Crimean War, like Florence Nightingale. Sabina never complained about other students or professors treating her differently, but she didn't seem to have many friends other than Aggie and Lizzie. Still, it was probably better for her here than it would have been back in the States.

"My mother would be shocked that any book-smart girl would have me."

Sabina's eyes sparkled with humor as she shook a pillow into its case. "Well, now, we don't want to shock the poor woman."

The young man glanced over at Lizzie. "What about you, miss? You look kindhearted."

Aggie tucked the corner of the sheet neatly underneath the thin mattress. "Afraid she's out of your league, Billy. Lavenza's going to be a doctor."

The young man whistled in surprise. "A lady doctor! Will wonders never cease. Don't suppose you can discharge me? I'm right as rain now, just need a bit of cotton stuffed into the toe of my boot."

The truth was, she felt useless on the ward. Unlike Aggie and Sabina, she wasn't supposed to change bandages or make beds, and she couldn't really diagnose an illness yet, or modify a real doctor's orders. "Let me see what I can find out."

She walked across to the room to speak to Sister Tuttle,

more commonly known as the Turtle. The older nurse was standing by a large oak desk and writing in a ledger. She was a solid woman, built square rather than round, with a large bosom that seemed to have been formed out of granite rather than flesh. Even her iron-gray hair had a slightly helmet-like appearance under her nurse's cap and veil.

After standing for two minutes while Sister Tuttle continued writing notes, Lizzie cleared her throat. "I beg your pardon, Sister."

"Yes?" Sister Tuttle reluctantly dragged her eyes away from her figures. "May I help you?"

"I have a question about Billy Collins. He was asking when he could be discharged."

A ripple of annoyance crossed Tuttle's impassive features, and she turned back to her papers. "Can't you see I'm busy? The patient will be seen in his turn."

"Sister Tuttle?"

Lizzie and the Turtle both whirled at the sound of Shiercliffe's severe voice. The head of the Nursing School looked unusually haggard and, for once, her lace veil was not lying perfectly straight down her back. "I'm here to do an inspection." She walked down the center aisle between the beds, pulling off a glove to use one finger to check for dust along the bed frames. She moved past the little boy and the man with the heavy mustache before pausing at Billy Collins's chair. "Your eyes seem a bit glassy. May I ask you to extend your tongue?"

"Seems a bit rude."

"Nevertheless."

Billy shrugged and opened his mouth. "Should I say 'aah'?"

"That will do." Shiercliffe's heels clicked sharply on the floor as she made her way back to the Turtle's desk. "Were you aware that you have a case of scarlatina on this ward, Sister?"

Tuttle looked confused for a moment, then said, "No, Matron."

Shiercliffe sniffed, unimpressed. "We'll need to isolate this floor, as a precaution." Turning to Aggie, she added, "DeLacey, Lavenza, Hillier, you'll need to leave immediately. Wash your hands and arms thoroughly with a carbolic solution."

"Don't worry, Billy. The sisters will take good care of you," Aggie called over her shoulder. She kept the smile on her face until the ward door closed behind them.

"Now that was just plain strange."

Sabina looked worried. "I know. Do you think we missed something?"

"I suppose. Poor Billy. He was dying to get back to work."

The next day Lizzie learned that the blacksmith's apprentice was gone, his bed already stripped. Billy Collins, she was informed, had died in the night.

# 24

LIZZIE HAD JUST SAT DOWN TO LUNCH WHEN she saw a resident run up to the dais where the faculty sat and whisper something in Moulsdale's ear. The head of medicine looked down at his plate of cold ham for a moment, then dabbed the corners of his mouth with his napkin before pushing his chair back from the table. Grimbald and Shiercliffe were already up and moving toward the door. There were a few other professors at the table, mostly men in their mid to late thirties, and they waited for Moulsdale to move before following suit. Makepiece, of course, lived by his own schedule, and was not sitting with the rest of the senior faculty.

"Something's going on," said Byram, pushing away his half-eaten biscuit.

"What do you think it is?" Lizzie watched Moulsdale, who was now walking purposefully down the hall.

Will sat back with his tea, as if taking in a show. "Whatever it is, it's got the faculty in a flap."

"Come on," said Byram, getting to his feet. "Let's go find out."

Will looked worried. "Won't we get in trouble?"

"For following our professors?" Lizzie didn't pause to see if Will was following. Instead, she lengthened her strides and quickly caught up with Byram. They were in the school's main hall, standing beneath the massive iron candelabrum, just in front of the winding staircase that led up to the faculty rooms. "Where did they go? Did you see?"

"Front gates." Byram, who usually walked slowly to disguise his limp in public, was lurching toward the heavy oak and steel doors. He pulled them open with surprising ease; Lizzie hadn't realized how strong he was.

"Wait up," said Will, but Lizzie was already following Byram out the doors and through the black iron front gates. The sky was gray and overcast with darker clouds rolling in, and a strong wind was blowing leaves off trees and forcing Moulsdale to keep one hand on the brim of his tall black hat. Grimsbald, hatless, seemed wary of the small crowd of villagers, his hand going to his hip as if expecting to find a sidearm holstered there.

Lizzie was now close enough to hear that one of the crowd, a woman, was shrieking abuse in a high, hoarse voice. "Give 'im back! Murderers! Thieves! Give me back my child! I seen 'im just yesterday and 'e were fine! Give 'im back, I say!"

"My good woman, please, calm yourself." Moulsdale's calm, authoritative voice seemed to subdue the woman for a moment. "I am terribly sorry, but your son cannot go home."

The woman collapsed, sobbing so loudly that two men had to help support her.

Moulsdale cleared his throat. "Mrs. Collins, our doctors labored with all their might to save your son, but despite their best efforts, I am afraid we could not save him."

Mrs. Collins breathed out sharply, as if she'd been punched.

"No," she said. "There 'as to be some mistake." In her tired face and dishwater blond hair was the faintest resemblance to the cheerful blond boy from the infirmary.

"I am terribly sorry," said Moulsdale. "I wish it were a mistake."

"All 'e 'ad was a cough, and it was gettin' better," said Mrs. Collins flatly. "And now you tell me 'e's dead." Her eyes went vague and unfocused for a moment. "I should never 'ave brung 'im 'ere. Everyone told me. They steal the body parts of the poor, they told me." Suddenly focused and fierce, she looked past Moulsdale at Grimbald and Shiercliffe. "And that's what you've done wif my Bill. Where's the body to bury?" Her eyes searched Lizzie's face, as if she might hold the answer, and Lizzie felt suddenly guilty, as if she were somehow responsible for this woman's awful distress.

Moulsdale held out a gloved hand. "My dear woman… this is grief speaking, not sense. Surely you do not believe that our hospital trades in such gruesome practices. Your son died of an infectious disease, and had to be disposed of with particular care."

"The 'ell you say!" This was from a burly blond man. "Bill's my nephew. You say 'e's snuffed it?" The man jerked his chin up, revealing the battered, flattened nose of a fighting man. "I say, gif us back the body."

Moulsdale exchanged a look with Grimbald.

"I'm afraid that's impossible," said Grimbald. "As Professor Moulsdale already explained, the boy died of an outbreak of contagious fever. He had to be buried immediately, and all his clothes and linens had to be burned. If you like, we can show you the spot so you may place flowers." His tone, cold and dismissive, made flowers seem an absurd ritual, like sacrificing a pig.

Now there were angry murmurs from the rest of the crowd. Lizzie had never seen a mob before, but she had read about race riots in the *New York Times*. There were about twenty villagers gathered now, and each of them was looking at her as if she belonged to some alien race. *They're afraid of us*, she realized. *And that makes them want to hurt us.*

"Lies!" Mrs. Collins was shrieking now, spittle flying from her lips. "Gif us our Billy back!"

"'For, behold, the Lord will come with fire,'" said an old man, his voice hoarse with tears, "'and with His chariots like a whirlwind, to render His anger with fury, and His rebuke with flames of fire.'"

"Aye, ye ha' the right of it," said the quiet man with the pugilist's nose. "Burn the lot of them."

The crowd picked up the word *burn* and passed it back and forth.

"Billy will have his revenge," said the old man.

"I don't think they like Grimbald any more than you do," Byram said in a low voice.

"Nice to agree on something," she whispered back, as if her knees weren't shaking. Forcing herself to lock them, she realized that whatever had happened to Billy was only the spark. The locals here did not view Ingold as a hospital, or a medical school. They saw it as something sinister.

"Miss Lavenza." Shiercliffe looked younger with her hair coming loose from the wind. She leaned in, so that only Lizzie could hear what she was saying. "Go and fetch your roommate. Bring her here at once. Do you understand? At *once*. But do not run. Walk."

She held Lizzie's gaze for a moment, and then Lizzie was off, walking as swiftly as she could back up to the school.

It felt like ages to find Aggie, who had left breakfast and was busy rolling bandages with a few of the other newer nursing students. The ward sister seemed annoyed at the interruption, but when Lizzie explained that there were a group of angry townspeople gathered by the gate, she nodded brusquely to Aggie, who threw aside her bandages and moved so quickly that Lizzie had to struggle to follow her.

"Did you get any names?"

"Mrs. Collins, the blacksmith's wife." Lizzie fought to speak around the stitch in her side; she hadn't had much exercise in the past month. "There was an old man, too... He said something about burning Ingold down."

Aggie's eyes widened, then narrowed. "Right," she said, pulling down her sleeves as she walked.

They pulled open the heavy doors together and then raced down the hill. "Nancy," Aggie called out. "Miles, Mr. Connelly." What she said next came out in a thick, North country accent that Lizzie could barely understand, filled with "tha" and "thee" and words that didn't even sound like English.

"What's she saying?"

Byram shook his head. "They're talking in dialect."

"She's telling them that we aren't killing off their loved ones," said Will. "She's reassuring them."

Byram raised an eyebrow. "You speak Yorkshire?"

"I don't have to. Just look."

Following his gaze, Lizzie saw that Mrs. Collins was listening to Aggie, and so were the men.

"If you say these city folk aren't butcherin' our kin, lass, I believes ye," said Mrs. Collins, looking defeated.

"I don't," growled the flat-nosed man.

"Pack it in! Her ma came fer yer wife's lying in, and yer ma's layin' out. Aggie 'ere came with 'er, as I recall. Sewed up the shroud."

"As is right and proper. We wants our loved ones to bury," said the man in a low growl.

"I understand," said Shiercliffe, "but there is a risk of contagion. Please try to understand." She looked at Aggie, as if appealing to a peer, but the man broke in.

"I understand all too well. Ye cut the limbs off our folk and sew 'em onto yers. Spare parts, that's what we are to ye." He spat on the ground. "Out of respeck fer yer ma, Aggie, I'll leave. But learn what ye mun, and then leave this place." He stared at Grimbald and Moulsdale, then turned on his heel and began to march back down toward the village. After a moment, the rest of the crowd began to peel away and follow him.

"Miss DeLacey, thank you." Shiercliffe leaned forward and said something in a low voice near Aggie's ear. Lizzie wasn't sure, but she thought it sounded like the same dialect the villagers had been using. Aggie's eyes widened. "'Tweren't nothing," she said.

Shiercliffe straightened and her face assumed its usual forbidding expression. "It was nothing, you mean. Proper English, Miss DeLacey." She turned and began walking up the hill, while Moulsdale and Grimbald stood a moment longer, looking down at the dwindling forms of the departing villagers.

"That was unfortunate, Ambrose," said Grimsbald.

"Indeed. But what can one expect from the superstitious lower classes?" He began to lumber up the hill, and Byram and Will fell into place beside him, while Grimbald walked just behind them.

Lizzie glanced at Aggie, who was looking back down at the village. There was a worried crease between her eyebrows. "Is he right? They won't actually try to burn the school down, will they? They don't really think we're all a bunch of ghouls, do they?"

"What do you mean, *we*?" Aggie looked at Lizzie. "We live up here at Ingold, sure, but just how much do they tell us about what's going on?"

"We're only first years, though. After we pass the end of year exam…"

Aggie snorted derisively. "They won't ever tell the likes of me what's really going on." The sky, which had been cloud-free moments before, was suddenly overcast. "I should've known what they were about. I shouldn't have left Billy."

Lizzie reached for the other girl's hand, which was icy cold. "It's not your fault, Aggie. He had scarlatina."

The wind whipped Aggie's red hair into her face, making her look like some romantic painting of Ophelia, distraught and a little wild with grief. "That's the odd thing," said Aggie. "Even if he did have the fever, it wouldn't have killed him overnight. And they wouldn't have had to dispose of the body, neither." She met Lizzie's eyes. "What if they did steal the body, Lizzie. Or worse…"

She didn't say the words out loud, but her meaning was unmistakable.

What if the faculty had killed him?

## 25

VICTOR SETTLED DOWN BEHIND THE ROW OF triple-stacked specimen cages, using an unopened crate of fish food as a chair. Then, setting a bowl of soup on his lap and balancing a mug of tea on the corner of a salamander's cage, he tucked into his dinner. Experience had taught him that whenever he or Igor sat down to eat, Makepiece was likely to barge in and assign them some new task. He and Igor had gotten quite creative about finding secluded corners so they could consume their meals in relative peace, but this time, Igor was off on an errand, and Victor wasn't really hiding from the professor.

Over the past week, he had managed to avoid Elizabeth, hoping that the time apart would clear his head and give him a chance to figure out what to do next. She was so damn stubborn about putting herself in harm's way in order to help him. He wasn't even sure what posed the greater danger—the cabal of professors who ran the school, or his own craving to touch her. It would have been easier to resist if he weren't aware that she craved his touch, as well. Didn't she realize the consequences if she were found in his arms? She would be expelled from the school, outcast from polite society, reviled, ruined.

He had to stay away. If only he could find a way to unlock the secrets concealed inside his head before he saw her again.

He swallowed a spoonful of soup and wondered what the school cook had against the use of salt and herbs. Probably thought they were wasted on Bio-Mechanicals. Pushing the bowl aside, he watched the salamanders as they scrabbled at the glass walls of their cages. *Know how you feel*, he thought. *I can't figure a way out, either.*

The laboratory door opened with a squeal of unoiled hinges, and Victor froze for a moment, listening. "Are we alone?" Moulsdale's voice was instantly recognizable.

"As good as," replied Makepiece.

"What about…?" Moulsdale's voice trailed off.

"All taken care of."

"Do we have everything we need for tonight? Ichor? Organs? What about the electrical equipment? We don't want the circuits to overload, like last time." There was a clink of glass, and Victor suspected that Moulsdale was inspecting things.

"If you don't mind," said Makepiece, "these are in a particular order." There was more clinking as Makepiece presumably restored the vials to their rightful places. "And yes, we are prepared for tonight, but you keep demanding instantaneous results. For the kind of outcome you desire, we will need to space out the treatments."

"We don't have time for that, I'm afraid." Moulsdale sighed. "Still, you know what I always tell the students—'*Le mieux est l'ennemi du bien.*' That is to say, 'Do not let the perfect be the enemy of the good.'"

"I know Voltaire as well as you do, Moulsdale. I also suspect that while neither of us is perfect, we might both be considered enemies of the good."

The two continued talking as they left the room, their voices fading into silence as the door closed after them.

Now there was something new to worry about. It sounded as though they intended to perform a Bio-Mechanical procedure tonight, but that didn't explain why Moulsdale was so interested in the outcome, or why Makepiece sounded defensive. Victor turned his mug so the unchipped side faced him and took a sip of his tea, yearning for something stronger. He imagined a glass of beer, the distinctive yeasty taste of it on his tongue, and was startled to find the room whirling around him. Christ, how strong was his imagination?

Suddenly, it hit him. Moulsdale had asked if they were alone. What had Makepiece said? "As good as." *He knew I was here. He knew, and he didn't care, because he'd taken care of me.*

Victor was sure of it; he'd been drugged. He stood up and managed to take one staggering step before losing his balance. He dropped his tea mug, but before it hit the floor he was off and gone, soaring through the air, looking down at the Thames River and the crenelated towers of Windsor Castle.

Victor was inside the castle, moving briskly down a long hallway. On one side of him, curtained windows stretched from the ornate rococo gilded ceiling to the bloodred carpet underfoot. On the other side of the hall, there were oil paintings darkened by age, and white marble busts.

It was as much mausoleum as palace, with all the monuments to the past.

"You understand that at no point are you to speak to Her Majesty," said Grimbald, appearing beside him.

"Unless she directs a comment to you," amended Moulsdale, huffing with the effort of walking at the pace Grimbald had set. His heavily jowled face was red with exertion. "If she asks you a question, answer as briefly as possible and then look to us to elaborate if necessary."

There were dreams that you recognized as stews created from the stock of memory. This, he could tell, was one of those dreams.

"I don't understand," Victor said in the dream. "Why does she want to have me there at all?"

"Because she's smarter than many credit," said Grimbald, sounding none too pleased about this. "Because she's read Machiavelli."

"You know that Her Majesty is considering appointing us to be her personal physicians," said Moulsdale, pausing to dab at his brow. "Well, by meeting one of our most promising students, she is taking our measure."

Surprised and pleased by this unexpected praise, he was startled when Moulsdale gripped him hard by the shoulder.

"You're an arrogant young whippersnapper, and the queen knows that. She will play on your pride, boy, and your ambition."

"What do you want me to do?"

Moulsdale's grin was unexpectedly boyish. "Why, be your own cocksure self, of course. Tell her the truth. Earn her trust." He leaned forward, and Victor forced himself not to flinch from the sour-sweet odor of Moulsdale's breath. "But do not forget that in the end, you must make Her Majesty trust us to serve her as loyal and capable servants of the throne."

Victor nodded. *How could I have forgotten all this?* The corridor seemed draftier and darker than it had a moment before, and the candle flames flickered in their wall sconces as he passed. At the far end of the hallway, a pair of gilt-embossed doors flew open, revealing a bearded Indian man in a turban. He pointed at Victor and said, "He is to enter alone. You two must wait outside."

Before Victor could assimilate what was happening, he was ushered into the queen's sitting room, and the heavy doors were shut, sealing Moulsdale and Grimbald out in the corridor.

It was even darker inside than it had been in the hallway, with a candle-bearing chandelier the only source of light in the shadow-filled chamber. The old queen, it seemed, did not approve of gaslight, let alone electricity.

As his eyes adjusted to the gloom, Victor saw that he was in a room cluttered with side tables and knickknacks and painted screens, every surface covered by a lace doily and every lace doily covered by cluster of small, framed miniatures. Victor noted that the royal children all seemed to have inherited the unfortunate combination of their mother's protuberant eyes and their father's weak chin. There was a faint doggy odor in the room, combined with the subtle hint of old-person smell. Despite all its riches, Victor felt as though he were in the drawing room of a fusty maiden aunt rather than the reigning monarch of an empire that spanned the globe.

The bearded Indian man said, "Is that all?"

It was only then that Victor noticed the old woman in the wicker wheelchair. "Thank you, Munshi." Queen Victoria's voice was breathy, but still held the ring of command.

The munshi took hold of the curved, cane-shaped handles on the back of the wheelchair and moved her to the center of the room before bowing and stepping back against the wall. For a long moment, the monarch said nothing, staring at Victor as though taking his measure. He stood very still, keeping his eyes slightly downcast. The woman who had ruled much of the world for longer than Victor had been alive was much older and shorter and fatter than he had expected. She also did not look healthy. Her white hair was thin under her lace cap, her heavily jowled face sallow, her body unhealthily stout beneath the heavy black cloth of her dress. The Widow of Windsor, still in mourning for a husband dead forty years. It was difficult to imagine this forbidding old woman carrying such a passionate torch for any man.

"So you are the young doctor whom I have heard spoken of with such effusive praise." Queen Victoria's pale, slightly protuberant eyes were clouded with cataracts, but something in the way she regarded him let him know that he was in the presence of a sharp intelligence.

"Your Majesty, I am only a student."

She beckoned him closer with her swollen and arthritic hand, and he saw that her fingers were so bloated that if she wanted to remove any of her diamond, sapphire and ruby rings, the gold would have to be carefully cut.

"Come closer," she said impatiently. "I won't bite." Obediently, he took a step forward, and was greeted by a low growl from the vicinity of the monarch's lap. With a start, Victor realized that she held a small white dog, its lip curled back in a snarl. "Turi, please," said the queen, giving the Pomeranian an indulgent smile. "We did promise him not to bite. Let us see what this young man has to say before we drive him off." Her voice had a phlegmy rattle in it. "Now, young man. Speak to me. How long do we have to live?"

Startled, Victor tried to think of what to say. "Your Majesty, surely it would be wiser to consult with my professors."

"So you presume to teach us wisdom." The shrewd old queen gave a short laugh. The munshi stepped forward, ready to assist, but the queen waved him away. "Your professors think highly of you, young man, and you think highly of yourself as well."

"Your M–Majesty, I..."

"Do not interrupt. We have already spoken with Doctors Moulsdale and Grimbald. They have given us their wise diagnosis, but now we want yours. Wisdom is for politicians, you see, and you are young and clever and arrogant enough to tell us the truth."

"Majesty, I will do my best." He bowed his head, feeling anything but clever in front of this intimidating woman.

"None of that false modesty. By all reports, you are not a modest person, Mr. Frankenstein. Not that you are vain— you act like a man who does not know how good-looking he is. Your flat stomach tells us that unlike our eldest son, you do not indulge yourself with food and drink, and your stiff manner tells us that you do not rely on charm to get your way. He is a great disappointment to us, you know, with his cavorting and carousing and loose women."

*Dear Lord, that's the crown prince she is disparaging.* Victor schooled his face into impassivity, knowing that to agree with the queen was to insult the heir to the throne. He had the uncomfortable feeling that she knew what he was thinking; nevertheless, there was something more than a little witchy about the Widow of Windsor, with her black clothes and all-seeing, cataract-opaque eyes and her little dog sitting like a familiar in her lap.

"We came to the throne at a dangerous time. All over Europe, the old order is giving way to anarchy. But Prince Albert and I steered England away from those treacherous shoals. We are the world's great power now, a shining beacon to other nations."

She beckoned him closer, and underneath the cloying tea rose perfume she wore, he caught the sour odor of her skin.

"Prince Albert and I wanted to create a new Camelot here at Windsor, but our son is like Mordred." Mordred, Victor recalled, had murdered his father, King Arthur. It was common knowledge that Prince Albert had gone off to Cambridge to speak to his eldest son about a romantic indiscretion, and had become ill after walking with Bertie and getting caught in a cold rain. Albert had died three weeks later, plunging Victoria into mourning.

"When we die, Bertie will become king. But the people have no patience with monarchs who indulge their senses and squander their wealth. They will not respect a king who sins with other men's wives and pays for his lust with jewels from the country's coffers. And our enemies will see us growing weak and make their move." Queen Victoria leaned forward and the wicker wheelchair creaked under her shifting weight. "Do you understand what we are saying, young man? We cannot leave the throne at this time, do you understand? All of England's fate lies in the balance. Now tell us, and tell us true—how long do we have to live?"

Victor had not been prepared for this. "Your Majesty, without an examination of your person, I cannot make a diagnosis."

"You may take our pulse." She held out one plump, trembling, beringed hand, the fingers twisted by rheumatism.

"Your Majesty, I will need to do more than that."

She stared at him out of those milky eyes and then nodded. "You have our permission to touch our person."

Over her head, Victor found himself meeting the steady brown gaze of the munshi. *Whatever I'm about to find out,* thought Victor, *he already knows.* He had no stethoscope, so he hesitated a moment before requesting that the queen loosen the front of her gown. He was sure he would be executed for pressing his ear to the plump royal bosom, but she made no comment as he listened to her heart, then moved around to her back, tapping her to check the lung sounds. Finally, moving back to her front and kneeling, he carefully lifted the hem of the queen's heavy black skirt and examined her swollen feet and ankles. She made a small sound when he prodded the underside of her left foot, and the little Pomeranian growled, but the queen shushed him.

"Well? Have you poked at us enough?"

He straightened and began to awkwardly attempt to refasten the queen's bodice. "Yes, thank you, Your Majesty."

"Leave that alone and tell us how long we have to live!"

It came to him in a flash; Mousdale and Grimbald must have told her something about the state of her health, and for some reason, she was using him to give her a second opinion. *Am I wrong? Did I miss something?* "Your Majesty, I am afraid that in a few months, your vision will begin to fail. Additionally, I am sorry to report the detection of preternatural pulsation in the epigastric area."

"It does us no good to hear our health reported in some foreign language, you know. Tell us what you must." She paused, then added, "We can see by your face that it is not good."

"Your heart is under some strain, ma'am, and its rhythm is erratic."

"How long do we have?"

"There are medications, like digitalis, extracted from the foxglove. If it proved efficacious, and if you were to receive some gentle exercise, in a bathing pool, you could perhaps expect to rule for years to come."

"If, if, and perhaps. What might we expect if the medication were not efficacious?" Those filmy, bulging eyes held his, unblinking.

"I cannot say. If your condition were to worsen, though…"

"And does this condition tend to worsen?"

How did one tell the monarch of most of the Western world that her heart was likely to become her executioner? He remembered Moulsdale's words as they walked here: *Do not forget that in the end, you must make Her Majesty trust us to serve her as loyal and capable servants of the throne.*

"Your Majesty, if left untreated, you will die before the year is out."

There was a short, sharp intake of breath—hers, he thought—and suddenly he was flying again, out of the queen's dark sitting room, down the long hallway with its gold ceiling and bloodred carpet, around a corner and into a small room where a trapdoor flew open. He was plunging down an ancient stone staircase now, the smell of earth and damp rock in his nostrils, darkness rising up to swallow him.

He woke up in his cot in the back of the laboratory, soaked in sweat and breathing hard. When his heart rate slowed, he turned his head and saw a corpse lying on the gurney beside him, covered by a white sheet. He sat up, gripping the edge of his cot for support. He didn't really need to pull back the cover to know who it was, because his dreaming mind had already pieced together the clues. He did it anyway, slowly uncovering the queen's plump and waxen face, her gray hair frizzing at the temples and the telltale bolts at the side of her neck.

She blinked one eye like a parrot. "Cockcrow victual?"

Here it was—the secret that had died with him. The secret that had been reborn as their creature.

There was a sound and before Victor could compose his features to blankness, Makepiece walked in, carrying the helmet of the Galvanic Reanimator.

"Ah," he said, "good. You're awake at last."

# 26

THE COMMON ROOM WAS CROWDED, AND THE noise level seemed to rise and fall in waves. Besides the background conversation and bursts of laughter, there was a group of medical students gathered around the upright piano in the corner, singing to impress Aggie and Sabina and a couple of other probationary nurses.

"'Casey would waltz with a strawberry blonde,'" they sang, "'and the band played on! He'd glide cross the floor with the girl he adored, and the band played aaaahhhhnnn!'" They finished with an attempt at harmony.

To a casual observer, Aggie looked completely at her ease as she laughed and flirted with the young men, but Lizzie, who knew her better, could see the hint of steel in her gaze and the shadows under her eyes.

In another corner of the room, a boisterous study group was testing its members on the muscles of the larynx, loudly cheering and jeering right and wrong answers.

"I should be over there, studying," said Will.

"Relax, old man. Too much revision dulls the brain. Look what it's done to Outhwaite—he's chatting up a girl who doesn't appear to be in possession of a chin."

"Oh, I don't know, that might not be a bad thing," said Lizzie. "Between the two of them, they might have a chance at a child with a normal jawline." She glanced over at their nemesis again, and noticed that Mothersole was sitting lumpishly on the couch beside Outhwaite, methodically eating his way through a tin of shortbread biscuits. He wasn't the only one feeling unlucky in love. She had gone to the laboratory after classes to try to speak to Victor, but Makepiece had opened the door a crack and explained that he was asleep.

"Isn't it awfully early for that?" she'd asked.

"Afraid we've all been exposed to scarlatina. Best to stay away for a day or two, just to be safe." He had shut the door in her face before she could ask another question.

At that point, she'd decided enough was enough. Makepiece hadn't sounded *ill.* He had sounded ready to jump out of his skin with anxiety. Something strange was going on, and it no longer just involved Victor. She had gone back to her room and, looking for advice, told Aggie a slightly censored version of the truth, starting with the night over two months ago when she had first discovered Victor.

Aggie's initial reaction had not been encouraging.

"Are you serious? You heard them talk about the queen and needing cadavers and you just thought you'd keep it to yourself?"

"Not exactly. Byram explained why the idea didn't make any sense."

Aggie planted her hands on her hips. "And why ever not?"

"Because somebody would notice, and because the queen

doesn't actually have all that much power. It's the prime minister who really rules the country."

"So maybe he's in on it. Or maybe he's next. Look, Lizzie, I don't know what it's like where you come from, but in my experience, people do perfectly horrible things if they think it'll get them something they want."

At first, Aggie had wanted to investigate on their own, but Lizzie had convinced her to include Byram and Will. If something did go wrong, it would be safer to have a little insurance, and Byram's father was in the House of Lords.

"As long as he doesn't start talking like Sherlock Holmes," had been Aggie's grudging concession.

Byram, of course, had instantly started talking like the master detective, sending Aggie over to sing at the piano—"so you don't look preoccupied"—and insisting that Will play him in chess.

"White or black?"

"White," said Will, looking miserable. He moved a pawn as if he already knew the game was lost.

Aggie said something to the medical students at the piano and walked across the room to where Lizzie sat. "All right," she said. "I've done my little performance for Shiercliffe." She nodded at the tall, thin matron who was sitting in the corner, knitting something long and gray. "You ready?"

"Of course," said Lizzie, getting to her feet. "I think we can go together, since everyone will assume we're just heading back to our room. Will, Byram, you'll probably want to wait a few moments before following us to the laboratory."

Will stared at her. "I'm sorry, but this insane. What do you expect to find? A jar with Billy's head in it? You can't really think that the faculty would murder people for spare parts."

"Not murder, no," said Aggie. "But they might decide not

to return a body to the family if they thought they could put it to better use."

Byron took one of Will's pawns. "What's really the matter? You afraid your head might wind up in a jar, too?"

Will picked up his rook and then hesitated, as if unsure of his next move. "I'm thinking of more garden variety dangers, such as disciplinary action or expulsion. Not to mention the fact that if I don't spend tonight working on the bones and muscles of the face and cranium, I'm likely to fail tomorrow's test. Some of us actually need to do the work to survive here, you know."

"Sorry, but that dog won't hunt," said Lizzie. "You've already studied for at least two days straight."

"We can't just stand here for much longer," Aggie cut in, "so tell me now if you're going to join us."

"We'll join you," said Byram, taking Will's white rook with his black knight.

She looked at Will, who shrugged. "Oh, *fine*. Why do I let myself be talked into these things?"

Byram grinned at him from across the table. "Because you revere me, old chap. And because you know how dull life would be if you went your own way."

Will smiled and shook his head, but of course, Lizzie knew, Byram was right. Will went along with Byram because he loved his friend, and in the end, love was the reason why *all* sensible people did reckless things.

Old buildings are never quiet at night. They sigh and creak and rustle back down like restless sleepers. Lizzie was convinced that the four of them would never make it down the corridor and into the main foyer without being detected, and the sense of impending capture reminded her of some high-stakes game of tag. In the end, though, no one stopped them before they opened the heavy portal and stepped out onto the path that led to the laboratory.

There was only a crescent moon tonight, and none of them had thought to bring a lamp, making it almost impossible to see.

Byram struggled to catch up to Aggie. "Need an arm?"

"Not necessary, thanks."

"You're very brave, you know. To be doing this."

"You joking? I'm terrified. To think they might've used Billy to make one of those...creatures."

"I know what you mean," said Will. "They're bad enough when you don't know what they were like before."

"But what if a Bio-Mechanical still retained all its old memories and intelligence," said Lizzie, the knot in her stomach drawing tighter. It was only occurring to her now that bringing Will into the laboratory meant that he would finally meet Victor. No, that was a lie. She hadn't *let* herself think about it because, deep down, she really wanted the two to meet. Will deserved to know that his brother was alive. *If I were really brave*, she thought, *I would just tell Will about Victor instead of engineering this chance encounter.*

"But they don't retain their memories," said Will as they reached the laboratory. "They're corpse walkers."

She didn't try to argue. He would feel differently when he saw Victor and had a chance to talk to him.

"All right," Byram was saying. "Let me take a look in the window first to scout out the situation." He craned his neck. "Can't see anyone...in—" He ducked down, grim-faced. "Blast it. Makepiece is there...and so are Moulsdale and Grimbald. You may be right about something going on."

"That settles it," said Will. "Let's go back before someone finds us missing from our rooms."

Aggie folded her arms. "You can go back. Billy and his mum are my people. I'm staying."

"So what's your plan?" Will sounded uncharacteristically snide. "Stand around and wait till they come out?"

Aggie took a step toward him; she was taller, and broader about the shoulders, as well. "Do you have a better one?"

"The tunnels," said Lizzie.

Will shook his head. "Right. You get lost walking to the dining hall in broad daylight. Do you even know where the nearest entrance is?"

"Actually, I do." At least, she thought she did. Victor had shown her where one of the tunnels exited, some distance from the building. "Do you see a pile of leaves, right around where the roof slopes down? It's there."

"This is *absurd*," said Will.

Byram made a dismissive gesture. "Don't be so wet."

Aggie was already brushing away leaves. "Over here, Lizzie. There's a trapdoor."

"I've got it." Byram moved closer, then lifted the door by a metal handle. The creak of the hinges seemed unnaturally loud.

"I'll go first," said Lizzie. "No talking once we're down there. Voices echo." She stepped gingerly onto the old stairs, feeling her way down. It was so dark that being shortsighted made no difference; they were all as blind as moles. Then she saw the gleam of greenish light from above: the laboratory.

There was a slight scuffle as Byram bumped into her. "Sorry!"

"Shh," the other three said in unison, and Lizzie fought back a nervous giggle. She inched up the stairs until she was standing by the trapdoor that opened into the laboratory floor. Holding her breath, she opened it a crack, peered up at the room…and lost all desire to laugh.

# 27

PEERING THROUGH THE PARTIALLY OPENED trapdoor, Lizzie could just make out Moulsdale and Grimbald as they contemplated something in the corner of the laboratory.

"I still don't understand," Moulsdale was saying, and for once, his booming voice was muted. "I thought you said the critical factor was the freshness of the subject. The parts we got her couldn't have been fresher, so why didn't it work?"

"In a sense, it did," said Grimbald. "I mean, she's speaking. She just isn't making much sense." They all looked at the figure hunched in the shadows, which made it growl and rattle its chains.

"Yes, what a great advance. She's a mindless lunatic instead of a mindless moron."

"And we're out of time." There was a tapping sound, then the sound of a match striking, followed by the overpowering scent of bay rum pipe tobacco. "I've just received information from our source at Windsor that the kaiser has produced a battle-ready prototype. Wilhelm is calling it the Dreadnaught."

"Damnation!" Moulsdale's voice reverberated through the room, making the unseen figure moan and shake. "Makepiece, what if you use the modified magnetometer on her again?"

"We could make her worse."

"Try it anyway."

Lizzie bit her lip as Makepiece came into view. He had a livid bruise darkening one eye, a gash on his cheek and a swollen lip. What had happened to him? And where was Victor? Neither he nor Igor appeared to be in the room.

"Come on, Makepiece. Hurry up."

"Be patient. Do you want this to work or not?" Makepiece did something out of her line of vision, and then turned so she could see that he was holding her etheric magnetometer—and the Galvanic Reanimator's helmet.

Moulsdale pushed a wheelchair forward, and now Lizzie could see the chair's occupant more clearly: a small, plump, elderly woman with slightly protuberant eyes…and electrodes visible at her neck. She glanced back at Byram, recalling all his wonderfully rational arguments about why the heads of school would never turn the queen into a Bio-Mechanical.

The heads of school, it seemed, had seen things differently.

Makepiece put the helmet on the queen's head in what looked like a grotesque parody of a coronation. As he stepped back, the queen blinked once.

"And how does your garden grow?"

Moulsdale flicked another switch, and the queen lurched forward in her chair, then listed to one side.

"Silver shells and cockle bells."

"Pathetic," said Moulsdale. "We must find a way before

we have a go at Salisbury. Folks may excuse a dotty monarch, but the prime minister's got to speak some sense."

The others were growing restless behind her. "What's happening?"

She glared over her shoulder at Byram and brought her finger to her lips.

In the laboratory, Grimbald was pacing. "It's no use. We need to figure out what makes the other one's brain different."

"We need to find him first." Makepiece touched his swollen jaw.

"I still can't believe you were so careless."

"How was I to know he would attack me?"

"After you drugged him? Anyone who knew Victor would expect it." Grimbald walked out of her line of sight, but she could hear his heavy footfalls coming closer. "Has Igor checked the tunnels?"

Startled, Lizzie released the trapdoor. The sound seemed to echo in the tunnel.

"Scatter!" Byram said.

Lizzie scrambled after the others, but within moments she could hear them farther down the tunnel. She still couldn't see a thing—her eyes were taking forever to readjust to the dark. She reached in front of her, hoping to feel the stairs, and instead felt a cool breeze. The passageway branched off in two directions…she must have stumbled the wrong way.

She tried to feel her way with her right hand—she remembered reading somewhere that you were supposed to always bear right in a maze. But where were the others? Should she risk calling their names? Suddenly she slammed into something so hard it made her cry out. A rough hand yanked her back, another hand covering her mouth so she couldn't scream. She bit down, and the man holding her muttered a curse and shifted his grip. She inhaled the clean scent of skin washed with harsh carbolic soap and, underneath that, something subtle, masculine and familiar. *Victor?* She stopped struggling and let Victor pull her back into a dark cell that smelled of dust and stone. She could feel his chest moving with long, even breaths, behind her. Footsteps thundered past them, and someone shouted, but then the sounds grew more distant, then disappeared. She strained to hear if someone was coming back, but no one did.

There was a moment of ringing silence.

Only then did the hands holding her finally release their hard grip. Turning in his arms, Lizzie was close enough to make out the rough outline of Victor's familiar features. He didn't say anything, and neither did she, because she was suddenly aware that she was in his arms, his mouth inches from hers. Perhaps he did not realize, because he did not remove his hands. Or perhaps he was very much aware of what he was doing. A shiver of excitement raced down her spine.

"Victor," she said. "Thank God you found me." She reached up to touch his jaw, surprised at her own temerity.

"Victor's not 'ere, darlin'." He turned her back to the wall and placed his arms on either side of her shoulders, hemming her in. "But I'm ready and willin' to take 'is place."

# 28

THE GIRL DIDN'T SLAP HIM, WHICH WAS EN-couraging. But she didn't flutter her eyelashes or put her hand out for cash, so that was a bit of a puzzlement. In his admittedly limited experience with the fairer sex, one either got smacked down or got down to business.

This girl, though, seemed to follow her own rules. Frowning up at him, she said, "Very funny. I take it this is your way of apologizing for last time?" Before he could reply, she put her finger over his mouth. "Wait! I think I hear something." In the corridor outside there were voices, and footsteps pounding past. They listened together, and when the footsteps faded, she looked up at him and smiled. "I think we're safe, for the moment."

Safe? He had her trapped between his arms in the dark, with no one around to stop him from doing whatever he liked, and she was smiling up at him. Whoever Victor was, she was more than fond of the bugger.

"I should be yelling at you, you know. Shoving me away like that. Are you even going to say anything about it?"

"Must've been out of me loaf," he said. Why would any man put this tasty crumpet aside? Suddenly, the right side of his temple throbbed as though he'd been coshed by a two-by-four. He felt a wave of light-headedness, and a voice in his head said, *Don't you touch her.*

"Loaf?"

"Loaf of bread, 'ead." He tried to smile at her, but his head was still throbbing. It occurred to him that he didn't really know where he was, or what he was doing here. This wasn't the first time he'd woken up after shore leave in a bit of a fog, but he'd never come to in a place as strange as this before. First there had been that strange old man with the bushy eyebrows, and the dead-eyed fellow with the twisty back, and then he'd heard that same voice in his head telling him to *run!* How much had he drunk last night? He'd never woken up hearing voices before. "Ye don't know where we are, do ye, lass? I'm a bit lost."

"No, it's my first time down here." She frowned. "You sound different."

"So do you." He thought he knew the lass, which was strange; she was too fresh-faced and wholesome to be one of the dollymops that worked the docks, but she wasn't a girl from back in his village, either. Not with that accent. So how did he know her? He didn't see many women in his line of work, other than the ones he paid to pretend they liked his touch. A battleship was a world of men.

"*I* sound different?"

"Yeah. American." Her accent conjured up a memory of sailing into New York harbor and gazing up at the copper-colored statue of Lady Liberty rising up out of the waves like the goddess of a new age. The folds of her robe were already oxidizing green. He remembered thinking that in a few more years, the Statue of Liberty would be green all over, and in a hundred, no one would remember that she was ever anything different.

"Very funny. You're a regular vaudevillian tonight."

The American girl's voice brought him back to the present moment. She lifted her chin and looked at him expectantly. *Does she want me to kiss her?* The pain in his head faded, and now he felt like he'd just taken a swig of rum, sweet heat and thickened thoughts. The dollymops objected to kissing unless you paid extra, and he never had the dosh to spare. He was no virgin, but he'd never been kissed on the mouth.

"Victor," she said. "I thought you were angry at me." In the dark, her pupils were enormous.

"Not at you." Memories pushed at him from that last time, touching her, his consciousness rising up out of the shadows, the other one, Victor, shoving her away. *My turn now.* He pressed his body into her and kissed her hard, his stomach muscles tensing—she wouldn't be the first girl to try to slip a knife under his ribs whilst he was distracted—but to his amazement, her lips opened under his, and he felt the tip of her tongue. *Sweet Jesus.* He felt the shock of that contact zip down his spine and pulled his head away, trying to get himself back under control. *This* was kissing? *This* was what his mate Lou called "a sop to the ladies"? This was bloody amazing, was what this was. He'd gone his whole life without knowing what he was missing.

"What are you laughing at?" Her eyes smiled up at him.

*Sheer joy*, he thought. "No idea," he said. He traced her plump lower lip with his thumb.

"Hmm." She raised herself up on tiptoe, her little hand cupping his jaw, and by all that was holy, this time she was kissing *him*. She had her head tilted at an angle now, and somehow that made things even better, for now their tongues were tangling and sending sparks down his spine. No bleedin' wonder the working girls charged extra for this! He was shaking from head to toe, and she hadn't even touched him anywhere but his face.

"Lizzie. Kiss me again." The words came out in a growl, but she didn't seem to mind. She lifted her chin and kissed him, her hands tangling in his hair. It was the best feeling in the world. Better than a bite of a sweet, ripe mango after a month of weak tea and hard tack. Better than climbing to the top of the rigging and finally, *finally* seeing land. Better than diving into an ocean the color of sky and air, and feeling as good as baptized. It wasn't just the feel of her; he *knew* this girl, down to his bones. Somehow, she could see right through all the bad he'd done.

*Don't think about it. Touch the girl. Drown in her.* He pulled her in to him, hard. She gasped.

"Wait, stop, what are you...?" Her voice was whisper soft. She did not want them to be discovered. *She trusts me.*

It stopped him cold, and he pulled away, looking down at her bewildered expression. He stroked her cheek in wordless apology, and she kissed him again. Tightening his arms around her, he kissed her back with wild tenderness, his hand cradling the back of her head, the side of her jaw. She inhaled sharply, and oh, blimey, there was no mistaking the sound for fear. "Oh, Victor."

*Victor.* A tremor went through him. He was in the laboratory with Henry, arguing. *Moulsdale is the one pulling the strings. That fat lushington?* The room spinning him into darkness. *Damn it,* those were not his memories. He rested his forehead against hers. *Lie to her again*, he thought. But he couldn't. The throbbing pain in his head was back, worse than before. "I ain't Victor. Don't know who I am," he admitted as she smoothed back her hair where it had come loose. "But I know I was hanged for murder."

He waited for her to scream, to cringe, to run as far and as fast as she could. Instead, all she did was suck in a sharp breath, then frown as if she were working through a problem in her head. On second thought, of course she wasn't screaming. After all, this was the same redoubtable lass who had followed him through dark tunnels without a qualm and cut into her first cadaver without flinching. *No. Not followed him. Followed Victor.* "Ah, Jesus," he said, bringing his fist up to his head as if he could pound out the pain and the voice and the thoughts that weren't his. "I don't know who I am, but I think I'm supposed to be dead."

Her cool fingers closed over his wrist, stopping him from hurting himself further. "That's all right," she said. "I can help."

# 29

LIZZIE TUCKED HER BLOUSE BACK INTO HER skirt's waistband with trembling fingers. She was wearing gloves, but the cold had penetrated the thin material, and she felt clumsy. Of course, some of that could be attributed to nerves.

*I know I was hanged for murder.*

It had to be some sort of delusion or nightmare. No wonder he kissed so differently this time, with an edge of ragged desperation. *Never mind that*, she thought. *Focus on coming up with a plan to restore him to himself.*

"I think if we wait a little longer," she said, "it should be safe to go back to the laboratory. I have my magnetometer there, and perhaps, with another treatment…"

"No." His hands gripped her wrists, and there was something fierce and urgent in his tone. "I don't want you to send me away."

"I won't send you away."

"No," he said in a low, gruff voice. "Don't know who I am,

but I know there's two of us in 'ere, me an' the other one. I know I was on a ship."

She frowned. "A ship?"

"We brought the ammo to Ladysmith."

"Lady Smith? Who is…?"

"Ladysmith, Mafeking… Ah, Jesus, the camp. They made me a guard. Why'd they do that? I'm a sailor, not a bloody soldier."

"Mafeking? Wait, that's in the South African Republic, isn't it?"

"Fighting for queen and country, they said." He gave a derisive snort, releasing her wrists and turning away from her. "I was supposed to stand guard over a bunch of women and children. Said they would treat 'em with full 'umanitarian care, seein' as 'ow they was white."

"I don't understand. What are you talking about?"

That made him turn around. "The camps, woman. Don't tell me you 'aven't 'eard?"

Lizzie shook her head. She had not even been aware that Great Britain was fighting a war until she had heard about it on her trip across the Atlantic. In the *Oceanic's* second-class dining room, seated at a table set with white linen and good china, Lizzie had discovered that there was a war going on in the South African Republic between English soldiers and Dutch farmers, or Boers. For some reason, this was causing tension between England and Germany, and the only thing keeping the situation from blowing up was the fact that Kaiser Wilhelm was Queen Victoria's grandson.

Still, what could all this have to do with Victor? He had been a medical student at Ingold, not a sailor. "I'm sorry, but I don't understand what you're talking about. What women and children?"

"Why, the wives of the Boer fighters, o' course. And the kiddies, as well. Skeletons in skin and rags, six to a tent. Filthy rags, at that. No soap, and precious little food. I 'ad to cart off the bodies. The officers said it was the typhoid and dysentery, but we was the ones 'olding them prisoner, all clumped together so they caught it off one another." His voice shook. "I killed the guard. I'm not sorry, neither, but I'm going to 'ell all the same, for what I done." His eyes were unfocused, or rather focused on something far off. "I'm damned, all the same. Knew it when they put the noose around my neck. Only thing I don't understand is why I'm not in 'ell yet, 'cause far as I can recall, they strung me up and killed me. So why am I not dead?"

Lizzie stared at him, his face so close she could see the bleak flatness in his gaze, and behind it, something hungry and hard. She felt a moment of real fear, and had to work not to give in to panic. This was a man on the brink. She had let him kiss her before, and more. Some would say she deserved whatever he did to her now.

In her head, she could hear Aggie telling her, *Don't be daft*.

Then, to her astonishment, he sank slowly to his knees on the frozen ground. "The boys too young to shave. Little girls, too… Ah, God, I remember it all." He lifted his face, and even in the shadows, she could see the anguish there. "Do whatever you like wi' me, lass. Bring back your Victor. Sorry I touched you wi' my filth."

The rough accent, the stories he was telling about the Boer War—he sounded as though he really had been there. Yet Victor had never said anything about serving in the navy. Perhaps he had read something in a newspaper, and confused imagination with reality.

She looked down at Victor, who was kneeling beside her,

holding his brass-encased left hand in his right. "Victor? Have you sustained an injury lately? A blow to the head?" No response. Hesitating only a moment, she ran her fingers through his hair, searching for some bump or cut that would indicate trauma to the skull.

He sighed at her touch, placing his hand over hers, either to stop her from examining him, or to keep her hand in contact with his head. Her hand appeared almost childlike, covered by the metal gauntlet of his sinistral limb, but as he removed her hand, tracing his thumb over her palm, she did not feel anything like a child.

In a low, gravelly voice, he said, "Ye must stop, lass. For I like yer touch. More than like. And if ye keep touching me so…" He looked up and met her gaze, his blue eyes black in the darkness, and what was in them was stark and primitive and required no words. She could feel desire rising up off him like heat, and an answering heat pooled low in her belly, which was wrong. *Because this is not Victor.* She felt it in her body, in nerves and pathways that bypassed the higher brain and spoke directly to ancient centers of reflex and survival. This was a stranger. A stranger she had kissed. Suddenly, she realized something she had noticed before about the arm; the difference in skin tone. *It was not Victor's arm.* Was it possible that another man's memories, even his essence, remained embedded in its cells?

Another, less scientific thought occurred: What if the borrowed flesh carried traces of its original soul?

She shivered and began to back away from the kneeling man. She didn't understand how or why, but this was Victor's body, but not Victor. But then the man's wide shoulders began to shake, and she realized that he was crying. *You're not a frightened girl*, she told herself. *You're a doctor, and a scientist.*

Taking a deep breath, she made herself take a step forward. "What's your name, sailor?"

He shook his head, as if to clear it. "I don't know. I think... it might've been Jack."

Whatever lingering doubts Lizzie had felt, the name made it official somehow. Made it real. This wasn't Victor with amnesia. This was a different person. A murderer. But not an evil man—she'd stake her life on that. She put her hand under his chin, forcing him to look up at her. "I don't think you're going to hell, Jack. Not if you tried to help those people. But more people are going to get hurt if we don't bring back Victor. Are you prepared to do that?"

He took a breath that inflated his chest, then slowly got to his feet. "Yes."

"All right," she began, and then they both stiffened as they heard the sound of footsteps.

Shoving Lizzie behind him, the sailor sank into a fighter's crouch. Someone called, "Byram?" and before Lizzie could call out, there was the sound of flesh hitting flesh, a moan of pain, and the loud whump of a body hitting the ground.

The man on the ground groaned and rolled over, then gave an incredulous gasp. "Oh, my God." It was Will, whose night vision was clearly much better than hers. "Victor?"

# 38

AFTER THE FIRST SHOCK OF DISCOVERY, WILL lurched to his feet and threw himself into his brother's arms as though they were both still children. "They said you were dead!" He clung for a moment, while Jack stood stiffly, looking over Will's back at Lizzie as if to say, *Any advice?* After a moment, Will pulled back, frowning a little as he took in his brother's lack of response. "Victor?"

Jack shook his head. "Sorry, mate, I'm…"

"He has amnesia," Lizzie interjected before he could say more. Discovering a resurrected brother was shock enough. No need to burden Will with the knowledge that a new personality had taken over Victor's body. "He still doesn't remember very much about the past."

"Oh, my God. But you know me?"

"'Course I do," said Jack.

"Can you tell me anything? What have you been doing this past year? Mother and Father will be overjoyed!"

"Of course," said Lizzie, "and you must tell them as soon

as possible, but right now, we should probably head back before we freeze."

Will turned to his brother, wordlessly waiting for him to
show the way. Clearly, a lifetime of training had left him
ready to follow his sibling's lead, even if he'd just returned
from the land of the dead.

"Don't look at me, mate." Jack gave a little shrug. "She
seems to 'ave all the answers."

Will frowned at that, but only for a moment. "All, right, then,
Lizzie," he said. "Seems you're in charge. What's the plan?"

"Can you lead us back through the tunnels to our rooms?"

Jack shook his head. "Sorry. I only know the way to the
laboratory."

"We can't go back there," said Will. "What if Moulsdale
and Grimbald are still there?"

"Don't worry. All we need to do is get back outside the
way we came in."

"This is a disaster. They've probably caught Byram and
your friend."

With no other plan at hand, they moved silently through
the tunnels for what felt like a very long time.

"These are the stairs," Jack said eventually. "Wait here a
moment."

Lizzie could just about make out Will's face. He looked as
though he might be in shock, and she reached out to find his
hand and squeeze it. "We'll be all right."

Jack came back down a moment later. "We can't go out
that way now. I just heard heard Grimbald tell Moulsdale to
stand guard at the exit."

"What do we do now, Victor?" Will sounded scared and
young.

"I've got an idea. Follow me."

★ ★ ★

They stepped out of the clammy darkness of the tunnels into what felt like a different world: a library with a Dutch-tiled fireplace and comfortable upholstered chairs and leather-bound books. It took her a moment to understand that they must be in Makepiece's private quarters.

"What if he comes back?"

"They're too busy chasing their tails out there. Give it a half hour, then we'll try the exit again." Jack ambled over to a liquor cabinet and lifted the top off a crystal container so he could sniff the amber liquid inside. "Perfect." Pouring three shots, he handed the first to Will. "Liquid courage?"

"Thanks." Will tipped the glass back, emptying it, and then coughed.

Lizzie took her shot glass and sipped more cautiously as she looked around. On the wall, there was a framed photograph of a wan-faced woman in an old-fashioned bustle dress, and a small oil painting of a cherubic blond child, aged three or four and holding a pug dog. That must be Makepiece's daughter. Strange that he never mentioned her.

"Bottoms up." Jack knocked back the drink in one swallow, closed his eyes, then smacked his lips in apparent satisfaction. "Fancy another?" This said to Will, who was walking slowly around the room, as if taking inventory.

"I probably shouldn't."

"Go on with you." Jack held out the drink.

"Well...I suppose one more won't hurt."

"How about you?" he said to Lizzie. "Wet your whistle?"

"Still working on this one, thanks." The taste was sweeter and richer than Aggie's gin, and nicer, but it burned the same warm feeling down her throat.

"Victor. Where does this lead to?"

Lizzie turned and saw that Will had discovered a door behind one of the bookcases.

Jack frowned and pressed the glass to his temples. "I'm not sure. I've been in there, I think, but I can't quite recall..."

Lizzie approached the door swiftly. "So let's find out." She turned the doorknob, hoping for a way out while expecting to see Makepiece's bedroom, but instead, she was confronted by a huge metal contraption that resembled a small submarine, attached to a mechanical arm that pressed a bellows in and out. In this room, the library's smell of leather and woodsmoke and brandy was replaced by carbolic acid and ozone.

Will came up beside her. "What is that?"

"Papa?" It was a girl's voice, light, thin, breathless. "Is that you?"

It was only as they moved farther into the room that they could see that the girl was lying inside the metal tube, her head emerging from an opening at the far end.

# 31

"WH-WHO ARE YOU?" THE GIRL'S EYES WERE enormous in her thin face. She could not turn her head to see them better—the enormous metal cylinder that concealed her body from the neck down prevented any movement—but a mirror positioned above her face gave her a little peripheral vision.

"Easy, now," said Will. "We're not going to hurt you."

"Oh." The girl appeared young, perhaps thirteen or so, but with only her face showing it was impossible to know for certain. Someone had braided her dark blond hair into a neat Dutch crown, but there were mauve shadows under her eyes, her skin had a consumptive's pallor and her cheekbones were as painfully sharp as an old woman's.

"She's already hurt," said Jack, his voice rough. "Looks like someone's starving her."

"I'm afraid I'm just not very robust." The girl was staring at him. "Don't I know you?"

Jack looked uncomfortable, then smiled, instantly affable. "Of course. Just refresh my memory, that was when…?"

"You attacked my father."

That threw him. "But how did you…?"

"I was right there. When my father began the…the new treatments. It's all right—I know you were trying to protect me."

Jack tapped his temple with one finger and then pointed it at her, grinning as if she'd tricked him with a riddle. "Oh! Right. That time. Yes."

The girl dragged in a deep breath, timed with the contraction of bellows. "But forgive me, I don't recognize either of you." The metal box had a pressure gauge, and suddenly Lizzie understood what it was being used for: the thing was like a metal lung, helping the girl breathe.

"I'm so sorry. I'm Elizabeth Lavenza, and this is my friend Will. I work with—"

"Oh, I know who you are! Father's told me all about you. I'm Justine. I was so hoping we would meet, but he's always worried I'm going to catch something."

Lizzie leaned away. "Oh, I didn't even think. Of course, your lungs must be quite delicate." So this was Makepiece's daughter. Because he never spoke of the girl, Lizzie had assumed she must be intellectually impaired, but there was clearly nothing wrong with this girl's mind.

"Oh, please, don't be frightened! I'm not *that* fragile. In fact, I don't really need to be in here all day anymore." She paused for breath. "I don't suppose… Could you help me out?"

"I'm sorry," said Will, speaking directly to Lizzie. "But we need to get out of here before Makepiece gets back."

Far from looking upset at these revelations, Justine appeared fascinated, as if she had just been given a front seat at the theater. "Why are you avoiding my father?"

"It's complicated," said Will, turning back to her. "We may have broken a few rules."

Jack snorted. "Not as many as her father."

"It's about the queen, isn't it?" Justine laughed, a quick, breathy sound. "Yes, my father confides in me. After all, whom could I tell his secrets to?"

Will was shaking his head. "This is not good, Lizzie. We need to get out of here."

Justine sucked in a breath. "Take me with you."

Lizzie bit her lip. "Oh, Justine, I don't know if that's such a good idea…"

"Of course," said Jack, ignoring her. "How do we get you out of this contraption?"

"Turn the…the handles."

On the end of the metal tube nearest her feet, there was a lever. Jack pressed down on it, and a hatch opened. "Got it." He extracted her carefully, pulling off the cloth hood that covered her head before putting her arms around his neck so he could lift her. Her wasted legs were concealed by a lace-embroidered white lawn nightgown that seemed fit for a princess. "All right there?"

She beamed up at him. "Perfectly."

"You must be out of your mind," said Will. "She's not a puppy that's fallen down a well. What are we going to do, carry her down through the tunnels?"

"A very good question, that." Makepiece's voice seemed to steal all the air in the room as he calmly stepped through the door. The bruises on his face were livid, his hair was tangled with leaves and twigs and his jacket was torn at the shoulder, but he appeared not to notice any of this. "Justine, have you taken leave of your senses?"

"Papa, what happened? Your eye…"

"Never mind me! I'm not the one suffocating myself just to prove a point! Now, put her back inside before she passes out." Makepiece watched with a critical eye as Jack placed his daughter inside. "Not like that…support her head… Yes, fine." He watched as Justine reluctantly released her grip on Jack's hand, then resealed the hatch.

Makepiece waited until the bellows started up again before speaking again. "A classic case of infantile paralysis, or Heine-Medin disease." He moved around to adjust the support under Justine's head. "Comfortable, my dear?"

"F-fine, Papa."

"So," said Lizzie, "the device…it's essentially a negative pressure ventilator? To aid respiration?"

"I like the term spiro…phore better," Justine said, her eyes meeting Lizzie's. As the bellows did the work her lungs could not, Justine's pale cheeks grew rosier. The girl might look like an angelic invalid straight out of a Dickens novel, but within that frail body there was a spirited young woman, capable of humor and desire.

"This is the reason why you're so interested in regeneration," Lizzie said to Makepiece as the realization hit her.

"Yes, indeed. Given time, I believe we will find a way for patients like Justine to regrow a healthy pair of lungs, or even a pair of limbs." Makepiece smiled at his daughter. "But like so much research, mine is taking too much time," he added, no longer smiling. "And in the meanwhile, my child lives out her youth in this windowless dungeon."

"If I am a prisoner, Papa, it's because you keep me that way."

"I know you're lonely, child. But not for much longer. Miss

Lavenza here showed me that there could be a quicker remedy for your condition."

"I did?"

"I've watched you stimulate Victor's brain. If we could just strengthen her mind before the procedure, then Justine could live out a full life as a healthy young girl."

"The procedure? You mean to turn her into a...a Bio-Mechanical?" Will's voice broke on the last word.

"You say that with such disgust," said Makepiece. "But I see you've become reunited with your brother. Surely seeing Victor again has convinced you that not all Bio-Mechanicals are shambling hulks?"

"You *knew*," said Lizzie, shocked. "How long have you known about Victor?"

"That our patient was Victor Frankenstein? Oh, no, you want to know how long I knew that he was special. Long before you did. I was following his progress for weeks before you encountered him in the laboratory. But he trusted you, and I wanted to encourage that. In truth, he made much greater progress with your gentle ministrations than he would have done with my more direct methods."

Makepiece didn't have to specify what those direct methods would have been: Lizzie understood all too well that he would have used experimental drugs and surgeries to achieve his goals.

"You're both wrong," said Will, a muscle jumping in his jaw. He looked older and harder all of a sudden, as though he had aged years in a matter of moments. "That thing may look like my brother, but it's *not* Victor."

# 32

JACK'S EXPRESSION WAS AFFABLE, AS THOUGH Will had said something mildly intriguing. He was standing in front of a small wooden washstand, and he trailed his hand casually over the blue Willow china jug and bowl, as if admiring the familiar pattern. "Who am I, then?"

"I don't know who you are or what you are," he told Jack. "I only know that you're riding around in my dead brother's body like a filthy parasite."

Jack shook his head, smile still in place. His hand had closed over the handle of the jug. "Easy there, old son. No use throwing around the big words. They just go right over my head."

"God damn you, what have you done to Victor?"

Without any warning, Will reached inside his jacket pocket and pulled out a pistol. In response, Jack raised his left arm and smashed the jug against a sharp table corner, instantly transforming the piece of pottery into a jagged weapon.

"Will," Lizzie said, wanting to put a hand on his arm but

suddenly wary of her friend. "Why do you have a gun with you?"

Will kept his eyes trained on Jack, who held the shattered jug as though it were a weapon he had used before. "Why do you think? You and Byram and Aggie were all acting as though this were some kind of daring escapade. I knew we were putting ourselves in real danger." He smiled without humor and adjusted his grip on the pistol, which seemed too large for his slender hands. "I just didn't realize *what* kind of danger."

"Young man," said Makepiece, "you're the one putting us *all* in danger. If you fire a pistol in here, you could wind up harming my daughter."

"I'm not pointing the gun at her. Now, explain to me how the brother I thought I buried in the family crypt turns out to be one of your corpse walkers."

"I will not discuss anything with you while you hold that weapon." Makepiece's voice was shaking, either from fear or anger. "If you want answers, put the pistol down."

"That's a nice looking firearm, by the way," said Jack, all breezy affability. "Single action? Shoots .32s?"

"It shoots bullets. Keep talking and I'll demonstrate." There was a sheen of sweat on Will's forehead, and his face was flushed, almost feverish looking.

"Listen to me," Lizzie began, taking a step toward him. But he flinched, the gun jerking in his hand.

"Don't touch me!" There was a thready note of panic in his voice, and for a moment, the muzzle was pointed toward her.

"Take a deep breath. You don't want to do anything you'll regret."

A nerve twitched in Will's cheek. "I won't regret it. I'd rather bury him again than have somebody else's voice coming out of his mouth." He pulled back the hammer on the pistol with an audible click.

Makepiece was the first to break the silence. "You'd kill your own brother?"

"That is not my brother. It may wear his face and body, but it's not my brother."

Makepiece turned to Lizzie. "Is he insane?"

*At least I wasn't the only one who didn't have a clue.* "There's another personality...he calls himself Jack. It may seem incredible, but it appears the donor limb has retained a cellular memory of the person it belonged to before." Out of the corner of her eye, she saw Jack frown as if he wanted to ask something, but she turned to face Will, trying to focus on his face and not the gun. "But Victor is in there, too, I swear he is. If you shoot Jack, you'll be killing your brother, as well."

"Then prove it. If you're my brother, tell me something only the two of us would know."

Jack looked at Will with Victor's face, but not with Victor's expression. There was something in the set of the eyebrows and the twist of the mouth—a hint of something volatile and violent. For a long moment, it seemed as though he would say nothing, and then, almost reluctantly, he said, "I used to read to you."

*Was he making this up?* Looking at Jack's face, Lizzie wasn't certain. He didn't seem like he was lying, but if he was telling the truth... Could the two personalities have access to each other's thoughts and feelings?

Will made it clear that he harbored no doubts. "Liar." The gun was shaking in his grip now. "You were always away at school."

Jack shrugged with elaborate unconcern as he said, "Maybe you were too young to remember it."

"Doesn't count, then. Tell me something else." Will swiped at his brow with his free arm. Sweat was running into his eyes.

"I can't just pull something out of my ar…hat," said Jack, his face reddening as he glanced over at Lizzie. "I don't remember all that much."

"Because you're not my brother."

"Fine, have it your way. But I did read to you. Some stupid children's book about a rabbit with a pocket watch and a girl named Alex?"

Will's expression flickered with uncertainty. "Do you mean…Alice?"

"Sure, whatever," said Jack, but it was clear to Lizzie that his nonchalance was an act, and that underneath, he was as troubled as Will by these memories. He and Victor were connected, and perhaps growing more so over time. "Now, would you put down that bloomin' peashooter? That thing's got a hair trigger. Longer you wave it about, the better the chance some poor cove gets a bullet in his chest."

"Shut up." Will shook his head as if to clear it. His gun hand was wavering now, and he brought up his other arm to steady it. "How do you know anything about this gun? My brother barely touched them. You're trying to trick me."

"It's not a trick. Your brother is in there," said Lizzie at the same moment that Jack rolled his shoulders and said, "Right, enough of this."

It felt as though the room narrowed until it contained nothing but Will and Jack. Time seemed to slow, giving Lizzie plenty of opportunity to watch as Jack swung up his gauntleted arm and Will raised the pistol. Her vision tunneled down further, focusing on Will's trigger finger and, because it was all happening so slowly, she had plenty of time to move in front of Victor, blocking him with her body.

She wasn't being brave. She was being practical. She *knew* Will would never shoot at her, and that was why the loud bang took her completely by surprise. It sounded like fireworks going off right next to her left ear, and then there was a puff of black smoke, the sulfurous stench of gunpowder and a ringing silence. In that frozen moment, she had all the time she needed to understand that the gun must have gone off. Just as that thought sank in, she became conscious of a burning sensation in her arm, and then the whole room tilted.

"Elizabeth!"

Now she was looking up into Jack's eyes…Victor's eyes— she wasn't sure whose eyes they were anymore, because they looked frightened, and she had never seen either man look frightened before. *Did you get shot?* She thought it, but for some reason, her mouth wasn't working right.

"Oh, my God," said Justine. "Look at all the blood!"

*Blood? Where?* Lizzie couldn't see any blood. She shivered, suddenly cold, and realized that she was lying in something wet. She felt as if she were in a tunnel, with muffled voices all speaking at once above her.

"Elizabeth," said Victor, gathering her into his arms. At least, she thought it was Victor. It was a new Victor—not the wary prisoner taking her measure, not the bemused laboratory assistant listening to her rant, and not the confident medical student telling her where to go. This Victor looked deeply shaken as he pressed down on her right arm, making her groan. "Oh, Elizabeth. Why did you step in front of me?"

What a ridiculous question. "He was going to shoot you," she said. It came out sounding breathy and girlish, more like Justine than like her usual voice.

"The bleeding isn't slowing," said Will. "Why isn't the bleeding slowing?"

"You might have nicked an artery." Victor moved his hand so that he was pressing higher up on her arm, underneath the armpit. The brachial artery. She liked the way he used the term "nick" instead of "hit." Good bedside manner, that. You don't want to panic the patient, because panic makes the heart pound, which pumps even more blood. "Is the pressure working?" If it didn't, he was going to have to apply a tourniquet, which could compromise the limb.

"Don't worry. I'm going to take care of you."

That was good, she thought muzzily. No one had taken care of her in years and years. She smiled at him and the lights began to dim, graying out Victor's features.

"Damn it, she's losing consciousness," he said. "Direct pressure, Will! I need to get that corset off!"

"Oh, God," said Will. "I've killed her." And then, abruptly, sound and light were both extinguished, and dark silence came down like a curtain.

# 33

HELP. ELIZABETH NEEDED HELP, AND WILL WAS barely able to keep pressure on Elizabeth's wound. Victor looked up and saw Makepiece watching him. Without hesitation, but with full awareness of what he was doing, he said, "You have to help her."

"I'm not a medical doctor," said Makepiece. "I have no idea what to do to save Miss Lavenza. But you do, Victor." There was a calculating look in his eye. "You are Victor now, aren't you?" He stroked his beard contemplatively. "I've known for some time that you had regained some higher cognitive functioning, but I had no idea that you had two personalities coexisting in one body."

Victor looked down at Elizabeth. They didn't have time for this. They needed to find out how much damage that bullet might have done, bouncing around inside her. "What do you want from me?"

The bushy eyebrows lifted. "Why, I want you to take charge, Victor. I want you to remember who and what you were. I want you to drive out that other personality and save Miss Lavenza."

That was what Victor wanted, as well, but could he do it? No time for doubt now. He needed to disinfect his hands. His *hand*. Clearly, his left appendage would be no help. Could he even perform a surgery one-handed? He recalled an old boast, from his other life: *I can do this with one hand tied behind my back.* God was paying him back for his old hubris. Elizabeth was so pale now, her freckles stark against her white face. She didn't look like herself, and the sight chilled him.

*No. That's the other side thinking. I'm going to need a bit of my old arrogance now,* he realized. Victor took a deep breath and made himself look only at the site of the wound.

*She's a patient. See her as a patient.*

"We need a table," he said sharply, turning to Makepiece. "In the other room. I'll clear it off."

"Wait. I also need a sheet or a blanket, something to help us lift her up without jostling her."

"In the wardrobe over there," said Justine. "Oh, dear God, is she going to be all right?"

"Yes," said Victor, because any other outcome was unthinkable.

"I've got a blanket here," Will said, his voice so choked he sounded twelve again.

Victor looked up for a moment, directly into his brother's eyes. Damnation. He recognized that whipped puppy look from childhood. He needed to get Will steady again, so he could keep it together enough to help Elizabeth...or to take over the surgery, if necessary. "Good man. We're going to tilt her as gently as possible...keep her neck and spine aligned... yes."

"I've got the table clear," said Makepiece, as they brought

Elizabeth through the bookcase opening and out into the other room.

"Daddy, please, let me out of here," Justine was calling. "I want to help."

Makepiece ignored her. There was a thoughtful look on his face as he said, "How bad is it?"

"Get me scissors so we can find out." He held out his hand without looking, and Makepiece slapped something into his palm. Victor cut through the cotton shirtwaist blouse, which was already tacky with blood, uncovering the front-lacing corset. He tried to saw through the laces with the scissors, but the thickness of the crisscrossed fabric made it impossible.

"Will! Help me loosen these."

His brother had turned away, either out of squeamishness or to preserve Elizabeth's modesty. As if she would care, under the circumstances.

Now Will was pulling ineffectually at the laces, which had become slippery with blood still flowing from her arm.

"I can't do it!" he said. "Can't we cut them or something?"

Maybe it would work this time—the laces were a little looser now. On his second attempt, however, the scissors snapped apart, the point slicing into his hand. "Damn it. I need something stronger…a hacksaw. Do you have one?"

"No," said Makepiece. "But you've *got* something stronger, Victor." He pointed to Victor's gauntleted left arm, where metal had been fused with another man's flesh and grafted onto his own body. For a stunned second, he realized that he had been so busy tending to Elizabeth that he had forgotten just what he was.

But would the hand obey his commands? He had never tried to use the limb before, only to stop it from acting on its own. Frowning, he concentrated on raising the brass-reinforced fingers to the neck of the corset. *This is your arm*, he told himself, but the arm didn't *feel* as though he had any control over it. He might as well have been seven years old again, attempting to wiggle his ears the way Henry could.

"Victor, I think she's…she's not breathing!"

Will's voice broke through the paralysis gripping him. Suddenly, Victor's hands were moving, anchoring themselves in the top of the corset and ripping it apart. He was dimly aware of his brother's whispered prayer as he bent his head to Elizabeth's chest. With a shuddering gasp, she dragged in a breath of air, then another.

"Thank God!"

"Less praying and more pressure, Will. I'm going to need to perform a surgical ligation to stop the bleeding. Makepiece, I need carbolic solution to disinfect the wound site, a scalpel, sutures and surgical sponges."

"Can you save her arm?" Makepiece sounded genuinely concerned. Perhaps he did care for Elizabeth, after all. She would need the use of both her arms to be a doctor.

Victor hesitated. *Can I do this?* The old Victor could have done this operation in the dark, but he was no longer the brash young man who had doubted everything except himself. What if he became frightened and the other one—Jack—took over? It had already happened once, when he woke from his dream of Queen Victoria to find Makepiece staring at him. In the space of an instant, he had felt something shift, and suddenly it was Jack's voice coming out of his mouth, Jack's will moving his body.

"Victor?" Makepiece's voice brought him out of his fog. "Can you help her?"

"Yes." Victor became aware of the wheezing sound of the mechanical lung in the other room, and thought about the girl in the other room, a frail bird trapped in a metal cage. *If Elizabeth dies, Makepiece must be thinking that his daughter would get a chance at a real life.*

*I may not trust myself,* he thought, looking at Makepiece, *but I trust you still less.*

Out loud, he said, "Will. I'm going to need you to assist." His brother was staring at the blood on the floor, shaking his head. "You can do this." He paused before adding, "You *have* to do this."

His brother met his eyes. "I'm here…Victor."

Victor held out his right hand, palm up. "Scalpel." The instrument was laid in his hand, and he closed his fingers around it. He made the mistake of looking down at Elizabeth's face and saw that her hair had come loose, falling over her shoulders the way it had in his dream. He paused, scalpel hovering an inch above her upper arm. This was nothing like operating in the surgical theater, with an anonymous patient and Grimbald's firm instructions to guide him. This was deeply, disturbingly personal, and the idea of slicing into Elizabeth's flesh felt obscene, but she was still bleeding, even with Will putting pressure on the wound, and he had to do this, and he had to it now.

*Help me,* he thought, not sure if he was appealing to God or some other, baser source of power. All at once, he felt a cold, hard battle readiness slide through him, steadying his hand and his nerves. He remembered this feeling, and how it always came over him right before the shooting started.

Without allowing himself to pause and question either the gift or the memory, Victor made the first incision.

# 34

LIZZIE WOKE UP WITH A DRY THROAT AND A throbbing pain in her right arm. She was in a bed, but it wasn't her own. In the gentle golden glow of gaslight, she could see that the duvet covering her was an unfamiliar dark green. There was a man's jacket and hat on a coatrack in the corner, and a masculine form slumped in a chair to her right.

*Victor.*

"Where am I?" It came out as a croak.

"We carried you into Makepiece's study." Victor had un-buttoned the high collar of his shirt and rolled up the sleeves, and his hair was tousled, as if he'd been running his hands through it. "The couch isn't quite as soft as a bed, but we didn't want to move you too much." He reached for her wrist and took her pulse, pulling back the lacy white sleeve of her nightgown. No, not *her* nightgown. She was wearing some-body else's lace-embroidered linen gown...with seed pearls at the cuffs and neckline. "This isn't mine."

"It's Justine's." He took her left hand and turned it over, pressing his fingers to her wrist.

"Thank her for me." She found herself staring first at the strong column of Victor's neck, revealed by the open shirt, then down at his fingers where they touched her pulse.

"You can thank her yourself when she wakes. I think she's desperate for company, especially of the feminine sort."

"First time anyone's called me that." She winced; it hurt to swallow.

"Throat sore? I have water, but first you need to sit up." He placed his arm firmly under her back, lifting her higher. She was embarrassed to feel the cool dampness of the fabric against his warm arm; she had perspired through the borrowed nightgown. *Maybe he won't notice.* He put the glass to her lips and she drank, trying not to think about the fact that she was completely naked under the nightgown. Could he see the shape of her uncorseted breasts through all that lace? Then she thought of a more pressing question.

"I don't suppose it was Justine who removed my clothes and helped me on with this gown?"

Victor looked uncomfortable as he put the glass on a side table and helped her lie back down. "You know, as doctors, one must learn to cultivate a certain professional detachment…"

"Oh, dear God!" She moved her right arm without thinking, and all other considerations were washed away in a flash flood of pain.

When the agony had calmed down to a dull throb, she saw that Victor was holding out two white tablets in his right palm, and the glass of water in his left.

"For the pain."

"Thanks." The throbbing in her shoulder felt as though someone was clubbing her rhythmically, but she focused on getting the pills on the back of her tongue and then held out her hand for the glass of water.

He made a move as if to help her sit up, and she glared at him until he backed off. She managed to lift her head and neck long enough to get the pills down, and then lay back down. It took a little while, but the pain began to recede. She drifted with it, remembering how the tide looked as it pulled back out to sea, exposing sand dollars on the beach.

"Feeling better?"

She was surprised to discover Victor still there, sitting beside her. "Mmm," she said. "What did you give me?" It had to have been some pretty excellent salicylin.

"Morphine."

Her eyes widened. "Oh."

"You were shot and had surgery. You needed it." He placed the back of his hand on her forehead and then on the back of her neck. "I don't think you're running a fever, but I'd like to be certain." He removed a glass thermometer from its wooden case.

"That had better be for my mouth."

His mouth quirked in a smile, which he quickly suppressed. "Yes, the thermometer is intended for oral use."

"No need to sound so stuffy about it. Since you obviously feel no compunctions about taking off my clothes, how am I to know what other liberties you might take with my person?"

"There was no one else, saving Will and Makepiece! I had no choice."

"Fine. It was clearly some onerous duty, thrust upon you by fate."

"I didn't say that."

"So you *did* enjoy it."

He took a deep breath, then released it. "I didn't say that,

either." He pressed his lips together and held out the thermometer. "Now, I need to take your temperature."

"Have you seen a lot of naked women?"

He shook the glass thermometer with a few sharp flicks of
his wrist. "I'm not responding to this line of inquiry, Elizabeth."

"I take that as an affirmative."

Checking the mercury level one last time, he gave no sign
he had heard her. "Place this under your tongue and try not
to bite down on the thermometer."

"I know how thu uthe a thermother!"

"And don't speak."

Now it was her turn to be selectively deaf. "How thu I
look naketh?"

"I wasn't looking at you as a naked woman, Elizabeth. I
was focused on ligating your brachial artery."

"Oh." She felt oddly deflated. "Han I at leasht heep ha
hulled ash a huvenih?"

"I have no idea what you're saying. Wait another moment
till I take out the thermometer." He put his hand back on
her forehead, and then, to her happy astonishment, his thumb
stroked the hair at her brow. That, she thought, was not medi-
cally necessary. Which meant it was definitely a caress. An
affectionate caress.

"That should do it." He pulled out the thermometer and
checked it. "Ninety-eight point four. Normal. No fever. Now,
what were you asking me?" He held up a palm as if to hold
off an attack. "If it pertains to nakedness or enjoyment, I refuse to respond."

She raised her eyebrows.

"Reply. I refuse to reply."

"I said, 'can I keep the bullet as a souvenir?'"

He looked a bit rueful as he said, "Afraid you'll have to—it's still in there. Removing it would just have torn up the muscle more."

"Huh." She caught the smell of medicinal alcohol as he disinfected the thermometer and put it away. "Why is it that in all the stories I've ever read the intrepid adventurer always has to dig out the bullet with nothing more than a pocket-knife and a bottle of whiskey?"

"Are there tales of the Wild West? And do they also involve people yanking arrows out of their sides and then throwing them at the enemy?"

She grinned up at him. "You read penny dreadfuls too, huh?"

"You mean that tripe about Deadwood Dick and Calamity Jane?" He flashed her a quick grin then said with a straight face, "Absolutely not. Now, are you thirsty?" She nodded and he refilled her glass from a pitcher. She lifted her head to drink just as she'd done last time, but this time she seemed to have lost some hand-eye coordination and the glass tipped.

"Oh, darn it!" The entire front of her nightgown was clinging damply to her skin. She looked up to find Victor staring at her. "What?"

He made a funny sound in the back of his throat, a sort of choking laugh.

"What's so funny?" She was smiling, ready to share in the joke, but then he wasn't laughing anymore. She looked down at herself and saw the reason: the white linen had gone transparent.

"We need—" his voice thickened, and he had to clear his throat "—we need to change you into something dry."

"All right."

She expected him to turn his head, but instead, he put one

hand on the tiny seed pearl buttons that that held the front of the nightgown together. *Of course,* she realized. *There's no way I can do this on my own, not with my wounded arm.* He hesitated, glancing at her face, then began unbuttoning the gown with surprising dexterity, given the size of his fingers.

She didn't try to stop him.

He peeled the nightgown back from her shoulders, carefully averting his gaze as he removed her left hand from the sleeve. She watched his face for any sign of a reaction as he maneuvered around her to work her injured shoulder free of the gown without jostling it. His eyes met hers, then, helplessly, as though against his will, his gaze dropped for an instant. "I… Sorry." He turned his back to her. "I don't know where Justine keeps another nightgown, so…" *Of course,* Lizzie thought, using her good hand to pull the blanket up so it covered her breasts. Justine was in the next room. The rhythmic, mechanical sound of the girl's iron lung had become background noise, but now that she was paying attention she could hear it again, a constant reminder that they were not truly alone. No wonder he looked so uncomfortable.

*Nice to think he might have kissed me, if we didn't have company.*

Except that Victor appeared to have changed his mind, because he was unbuttoning his black waistcoat, still keeping his back to her. Her mouth went dry as he threw the waistcoat over a chair and went to work on the buttons of his shirt.

"Victor?"

He peeled the white cotton shirt back, revealing the broad sweep of his shoulders. He must have decided that Justine's presence wasn't that much of a deterrent, after all. She would have to tell him that there was no way she could allow him to… He was pulling the shirttails out of the waist of his trousers now, and then he shucked the shirt entirely and she was looking at his naked back. She sucked in a breath, thinking of the charts she'd memorized showing the window formed just below the shoulder, where the trapezius, deltoid and latisimus dorsi muscles intersect. Funny, how none of the medical texts had described the beauty in the play of muscles beneath a man's skin.

Victor ended the moment by reaching behind him without turning around. "Here." His tone was curt, even annoyed. "Put this on."

*Not seduction, then.* Torn between disappointment and relief, she took the shirt from his hand. Why did everyone make it sound as though young men were always looking to indulge their carnal appetites? As far as she could tell, she was the one with all the appetite. Looking down at the shirt, she realized she had to slip her arm out of the nightgown first. She angled her right elbow, then sucked in a sharp breath as a white hot pain lanced through her shoulder.

"You all right?" He was beside her in an instant, checking for bleeding. "Good, nothing's opened up."

She looked up at his bare chest, and her mouth fell open.

"Why are you looking at me like that?" For a brief moment his right hand came up, self-consciously covering the electrodes at his neck—she hadn't noticed them until he tried to conceal them, too taken with his broad, muscular chest. The brass plate covering his left pectoral only drew attention to the perfection of his form. "You've seen me this way before, remember?"

Of course she remembered. But that might as well have been two different people, so much had changed between them since then. She hadn't even noticed that he was handsome beneath his bruising, that first time. Now…she felt she wanted to just stare at him for hours, watching the way his passing moods registered on his features.

Right now, for example, he looked annoyed.

"Well, we don't have time for maidenly modesty. I have to help you change into this."

"All right." Her heart was beating so quickly she couldn't find the breath to explain that she wasn't feeling modest at all.

"I'm not angry. Don't move your arm, I'm going to bunch this up and lift it over your elbow." He lifted her good left arm out of the covers first, then pulled her arm through the shirt-sleeve. His bare chest was right in front of her face, masculine nipple on one side, brass metal implant on the other. She could smell him, a pleasantly musky, masculine scent. "Now, let me see…" Suddenly, his eyes met hers again, and she saw that what she had taken for an impassive doctor face was really something else entirely. Everything in her body tightened.

"Victor."

"No. Do not say my name like that. Elizabeth…"

She put her good hand on the warm skin of his chest, right over the hard swell of his pectoral, and then he was kissing her, just like before but better, because this time her bare skin was pressed up against the naked warmth of his chest.

He made an anguished sound, and this time it was the hand gauntleted in metal that pulled his right hand away. His chest was rising and falling in great heaves, as if he'd just finished a race. Or a fight.

"Victor? Are you all right?"

"No, lass," he said with a rueful grin. "I'm not."

"Jack?" She searched his face for clues. "Say something, so I know who you are." Through the floating ease of the morphine, she thought about the fact that they were both naked from the waist up, a sleeping chaperone just one room away.

"Can't you tell?" His mouth was so close to hers, all she needed to do was reach up to close the distance.

"Kiss me again." She could tell them apart by their kisses. She lifted her chin, and he cupped her jaw in his hand.

"If I kiss you again, I'm afraid I won't stop."

"So don't stop."

He gave a ragged laugh. "If only you knew what you're asking."

"I do know. I'm a medical student, Jack."

He dragged in a deep breath. "No. Sorry. Not Jack."

She twined her fingers through his hair, which was so much silkier than her own. "Why are you sorry you're not Jack?" She leaned in to whisper in his ear. "You're the one I like best."

"You do?"

She nodded, leaning back. "I also like Jack, though. I think if you were a little more Jack, you'd kiss me again."

Even in the dark, she could see his eyes change. "If I were a little more Jack, I'd do more than kiss you. And you're innocent, and you're injured, and you're talking under the influence of the poppy."

She examined that for a loophole, no easy task when her mind kept skipping over the planes and ridges of his remarkable chest. "Can I just smell you?"

"What?" He pulled back, clearly appalled. "Dear Lord, I hope not."

"No, no, I *want* to smell you. I want to put my nose right there..." She pointed to the depression between his pectoral muscles and then winced as the movement pulled at her arm.

"Easy there." He was all Victor again as he checked her shoulder and then swiftly buttoned his shirt up to her throat before tucking the blankets even more firmly around her breasts. "I can't make you a respectable offer of marriage, Elizabeth, and so this can go no further. But if I could...and if you weren't under the influence of an opiate...I would kiss you from the top of your head to the soles of your feet."

Startled by his casual mention of marriage, it took her a moment to work her way through the end of his sentence. "Oh," she said. Suddenly she felt very sleepy. She was trying to think of what to say next and drifting away when she felt the brush of lips against her forehead.

# 35

A SMALL BELL CHIMED JUST ABOVE VICTOR'S head, startling him. It was the sort of bell that was used to summon a servant back at home; he supposed he was the servant here.

Checking to make sure that Elizabeth was still asleep, he retrieved his waistcoat from the chair and his jacket from the coatrack. He was still buttoning the waistcoat as he opened the connecting door to Justine's room. The girl looked even frailer than he recalled, with only her blond head visible at the front of the enormous metal machine that did the work of her atrophied lungs. "Are you all right? Do you need anything?"

"Just someone to talk to. Sorry to trouble you, but I lie here all day...sometimes I can't sleep."

"No trouble at all, if you can forgive the appalling state of me? I just donated my shirt to Miss Lavenza."

Justine dimpled. "I think we can move past the usual formalities. After all, I'm an invalid and you're nearly a doctor."

He pulled up a chair and sat down beside her. "But you're not in any discomfort?"

"Oh, no, not me. Is Miss Lavenza all right? I thought I heard her cry out at one point."

"Yes, well, she's asleep now." There was a plate with some slightly browned slices of apple and some cheddar on a side table. He wondered if it might be rude to ask if he might eat a slice.

Justine nodded at the plate, though Victor hadn't said a word. "Help yourself, if you like. I'm afraid I never eat very much, so it will all go to waste otherwise."

"Thanks."

He was just biting into the apple when she said, "You're in love with her, aren't you?"

He choked a little, then managed to swallow the bit of apple and sputter out, "I beg your pardon?" *How much had she heard?*

"I'm so sorry! I know I should have let you know I was awake." Her voice sounded thoughtful. "It's just that nothing interesting ever happens in my life." She met his eyes. "Are you very upset with me?"

*Yes.* "Of course not." He took a bite of cheese, more for distraction than from appetite. Good Lord, he'd come within a hairsbreadth of ravishing a wounded, drugged girl while another invalid listened in. *Wish I could blame this one on Jack.*

"Then don't look so grim! I assure you this evening has been the most diverting one in recent memory." Her voice, with its odd, breathless cadence, was so at odds with her words that it took Victor a moment to comprehend her meaning.

A suspicion formed.

"Since we are suspending propriety…just how old are you, Miss Makepiece?"

"Justine, please." There was a hint of mirth in her voice. "And I am seventeen."

So she was the same age as Will and Elizabeth and the other

first years. No wonder she was so restless that she would eavesdrop on strangers. "The fact that you are not in actuality a child does not excuse my behavior."

"No, but the fact that you love her does." Her huge pale eyes never left his face.

He debated how honest to be with a young woman so sheltered from life that she probably thought love was something out of the Arthurian tales. "I am very fond of Miss Lavenza," he allowed.

"That would explain the impulse to kiss her from head to toe, I suppose."

"Miss Makepiece…"

"I'm an invalid, not an imbecile. I know all about the difference between lust and love—at least, everything one can learn from Shakespeare. Unexpurgated Shakespeare."

He had to laugh at that. "That is, as I recall, a good deal."

She gave a gasping laugh, and then they were both silent for a moment. There was a crackle from the fireplace, and then Justine said, very softly, "Tell me, what is it like?"

"What's what like?" He pulled the chair closer. A thought occurred, and he hoped she wasn't asking him about what he had said to Elizabeth.

"Being a Bio-Mechanical, of course. Do you still feel like *you*? Most of the time, I mean, when you *are* you and not the other one."

That wasn't the question he had been bracing for, and it took him a moment to come up with an answer. "I don't really remember what I'm supposed to feel like. I have memories from before, but I'm not entirely sure they feel like my memories."

"Do they feel like something you read in a book? That's what my old memories feel like. Actually, the memories I have of books feel more real than my memories of walking around like a normal person." Her gaze turned inward for a moment, and then she added, "It was so long ago, I can't really recall what legs ought to feel like."

"There are worse fates," he said, his voice grim.

"You mean becoming like you? That doesn't seem so terrible. I've been trapped in that iron lung most of my life, so I don't really have very many memories worth keeping."

Victor couldn't quite conceal his reaction. "You don't know what you're asking."

"Don't I?" She was amused, as if he were the naive one.

"No," he said simply, "you don't. You may not be able to walk, but at least you know who you are. Your mind is free, if not your body. My mind is like an occupied city. What I think, what I feel… I can't trust myself."

"Would you trade places with me, then? Spend your life sealed up in here?"

It was on the tip of his tongue to say yes, he would, but then he thought of how powerless she was to even breathe on her own, and he hesitated. "I don't know."

"Liar." She said it without rancor. "You do know. So you are not the man you were. The men you were," she corrected herself. "Yet you are not dead. You have but suffered a sea change."

*Into something rich and strange*, he thought, the Shakespeare quote floating into his mind from one of his lives. "You think it would be that easy to accept that kind of change? You lack a body. I lack a soul."

She rolled her eyes. "Forgive me, but aren't you supposed to be a scientist? What is a soul, in any case? If it's some sort of essential spark of the divine, then I know plenty of people who seem to lack it."

At that moment, Victor's stomach gave a very audible grumble. "I beg your pardon."

Justine laughed almost soundlessly. "Nonsense, that's the perfect response to my nattering on about souls. Are you still hungry?"

"I suppose I am. Or else just exhausted." He tried to remember the last time he had eaten something besides the two bites of cheddar and apple. It had been a long and difficult night, and he was suddenly so tired that all he could think of was how he might acquire a rasher of ham and a pint of something foamy before collapsing.

"I seem to have worn you out—and myself, as well." Her tone was light, but she had gone even paler than usual, he realized.

"Should I try to find your father?"

She closed her eyes. Suddenly, she looked less like a child than she did an old woman, pared down to sharp bones and sharper insights. Just when he was about to go looking for Makepiece, she began talking as if nothing had happened. "I'm more interested in history than science, myself. Scientists tend to be so blinkered in their vision."

"That seems a bit harsh."

"Is it? You spend all your time working on one piece of the puzzle, while historians take a look at the whole mosaic. Take this school, for example. All this effort to produce a disposable soldier for the empire. Did you ever ask yourself why there was such an urgent need?"

He paused, one hand on the cool metal of her prison. "To save the lives of young men, I suppose. Isn't that urgent enough?"

She shook her head, the only part of her body she could move. "Yet new and improved weapons never really save lives, do they, Mr. Frankenstein? From the longbow to the revolver, each technological improvement makes the weapon deadlier."

He was so weary, he was only half paying attention to her words. "I suppose you're right."

"So why make England's armies deadlier? What reason could there possibly be?"

"War," he said, the realization coming to him in a cold rush that chased away fatigue and hunger both. "They're preparing for war." This time, when he met her eyes, he stopped seeing a lonely blond waif desperate for company. Instead, he saw the sharp intelligence of a prisoner who set her mind to roam widely in all the places her body could not follow.

"Not a distant war of choice in the Republic of South Africa, fought over mineral rights," said Justine. "Something closer to home."

"A war with the kaiser." The German emperor was as famous for his boasting and his threats as he was for his handlebar mustache and the military uniforms he wore to disguise his withered left arm. His mother was Queen Victoria's daughter, and her longing for all things English had been twisted in her son into a frustrated sense of inferiority.

Moulsdale and Grimbald wanted the kind of war that England hadn't fought in nearly a hundred years. They wanted a war the British people could rally around, with the kaiser cast as another Napoleon. And with a Bio-Mechanical queen under their control, there was no one to stop them.

Christ! No wonder the other personality, Jack, had taken over. Victor had woken up in the laboratory to his worst nightmare: the body of the dead queen, laid out beside him, reminding him of the secret that had gotten him killed in the first place...and Makepiece, watching him, waiting for him to give himself away.

In all the chaos of Elizabeth's injury, he hadn't thought about it, but now he could think of nothing else. The queen was dead, replaced by a Bio-Mechanical controlled by Ingold's administration.

Victor stood up, suddenly light-headed. This was the secret they had killed him to protect. Yet there was still a missing piece...and just like that, the memory came back.

He had gone to speak with Grimbald and discovered a loose woman in his mentor's private study, young but clown-like with her rouged cheeks, kohled eyes and scarlet lips. Her hair had been a lovely light brown, falling loose over her dirty velvet dress, but she'd smelled of urine and other bodily fluids, combined with the medicinal odor of cheap gin. "'Lavender's blue, dilly, dilly,'" she'd warbled at him, "'lavender's green, when I am king, dilly dilly, you shall be queen.'"

He'd left her there, singing herself to an inebriated sleep with nursery songs, even though he knew that Grimbald was too fastidious and disciplined to bring that sort of soiled dove to his private rooms for carnal purposes. Still, he hadn't really understood until Grimbald summoned him to the operating theater in the dead of night. "What we are about to do," Grimbald had told him, "must remain confined to this room." Then he had drawn back the sheet and revealed the face of the corpse they were going to turn into a Bio-Mechanical.

It was the queen. Instead of passing the crown to her son, Prince Edward, the deans of Ingold intended to reanimate the queen's corpse.

And then they had brought in a second gurney. "This one is remarkably fresh," said Grimbald, pulling back the sheet, "so we can expect to have excellent results."

It was the poor young prostitute who had sung "Lavender's

Blue" to him just the other night, her mind addled by gin or opium or syphillis—or a combination of all three.

He had assisted Grimbald in a daze, and then, afterward, he had done the only thing he could think of—he had gone to his oldest friend, Henry. Funny how he had never even imagined for a moment that Henry might betray him. Even now, a year and a lifetime later, that seemed the most un-believable part of all.

Mind racing, Victor thought of the fact that the Queen of England and all its colonies was actually a Bio-Mechanical, and under Moulsdale's control. Then Victor thought of Eliza-beth, lying in the next room. *They may decide she knows too much, simply because she spent time with me.* And then there was Will, his little brother.

"Miss Makepiece, I beg of you, do not tell your father what we discussed." He got to his feet, fear chasing away his fatigue. As soon he could rouse Elizabeth, they would make their way to London. He had no idea how they would gain access to the Prince of Wales once they were there, but there would be time to figure that out later.

"You still don't understand, do you?" She sounded almost impatient.

His hand was on the doorknob when comprehension dawned. He turned the knob, just to confirm what he al-ready knew.

The door was locked.

He was as much a prisoner as Justine.

# 36

IGOR LUMBERED INTO THE ROOM, LABORI-
ously pushing a wheeled cart loaded with metal domed plates.
One of the cart's wheels was turned the wrong way, and
squeaked across the floor like a tortured mouse. Aldini pat-
tered along, either lured by the sound or by the aroma of
cooked eggs and bacon escaping from the covered plates.

"Good morning, Igor." Lizzie sat up as best she could. Igor
didn't acknowledge the greeting, but Aldini gave a little mewl
and jumped onto her bed.

Victor, who had been sleeping on the chair beside her bed,
sat up, stretching his spine. "What time is it?"

"I'm not sure. Morning, I think." It was hard to be sure,
in the windowless room. Why didn't Makepiece keep a clock
here? It felt a bit as though time were being made to stand
still here, perhaps so the girl in the spirophore wouldn't be
reminded of the passing hours that never brought any change
to her restricted existence.

*Until now. My getting shot is probably the high point of her life so far*, thought Lizzie. She knew it was unkind, but there was something about that frail flower of a girl she couldn't like.

"I must have fallen asleep. I didn't intend to." Victor rubbed the shadow of stubble on his chin. The gaslights had been turned low, and now Igor shuffled from fixture to fixture, turning the knobs until the last of the night's shadows were dispelled and the room was filled with soft golden light.

"You must have needed the rest." Down by her ankles, the cat prowled back and forth, looking for a way under the blanket. Victor winced as he got up from the chair; he must have slept in an uncomfortable position. "How are you feeling?"

"Not too badly, all things considered." She nodded at the cat, who was kneading the covers with her sharp little claws and purring like a well-primed engine. "Aldini, I adore you, but I think you need to get off." Already, she could feel the pain returning, like an orchestra warming up. Right now, the throb in her shoulder was just a bow drawn slowly across a violin's strings and a few high sharp trills of a flute. If the cat kept walking on her, though, the pain would launch into a full blown rendition of Tchaikovsky's "1812 Overture."

"Come on, girl. Down with you." Victor reached out for the cat, and Aldini flattened her ears and hissed. "Ah, I forgot, you don't trust me anymore." He looked wistfully at the cat, but then, with one of those mercurial feline shifts in mood, the cat batted at the big hand and then threw herself onto her back.

Lizzie smiled up at Victor. "I think she likes you."

An expression of happy surprise crossed his aquiline features, making him look almost boyish, but then Igor clattered a fork and Aldini jumped off the bed to cower under the bed. Victor frowned and glanced at Igor, who was uncovering the food plates, then back at the door.

"Victor? Where are you going?"

"Just checking on something." He turned the doorknob, then looked nonplussed when it swung open, admitting Makepiece.

"Thank you, my boy. Don't forget to shut it—it lets in such a draft."

Victor looked at the open door, then back at Makepiece. "I thought I might just take Miss Lavenza back up to her room now."

"Don't be absurd. She's just had surgery! You can't move her yet." Makepiece gestured to Igor, who was placing a tray over Lizzie's lap. "Come, sit and eat. Besides, I suspect you're feeling a bit under the weather at the moment, no? Fatigued, light-headed, experiencing some aches and pains in your joints?" Opening a medicine cabinet, Makepiece extracted a hypodermic needle and a small glass vial. "What with all the excitement last night, we forgot to give you your infusion of ichor." He inserted the needle into the vial of luminescent green fluid and slowly raised the plunger.

Victor stood by the open door for a moment, his eyes never leaving the syringe. Then, very quietly, he closed the door and walked back to the chair where he had spent the night, as grim as if he had just received a death sentence.

Lizzie realized that she hadn't thought about Victor as a Bio-Mechanical in ages. She wondered if Makepiece was using this little demonstration to remind them both that he was reliant on the school for his very existence. He couldn't just *leave* Ingold.

Makepiece primed the syringe, and a drop of green fluid appeared at the tip. "Your sleeve, Victor?"

Victor rolled up his sleeve. His face was set in hard lines, a muscle jumping in his jaw.

Once the shot was administered, Makepiece nodded at Igor, who carefully handed Lizzie a tray of food.

"Thank you, Igor."

She lifted the cover on her plate and saw rashers of streaky bacon, a small mound of fried kidneys and onions, a pair of fried eggs and buttered toast. She had learned to tolerate kidneys, since anything prepared with liberal lashings of Worcestershire sauce tasted mostly of Worcestershire sauce, but her stomach was still a little uneasy after the morphine, so she nibbled on a slice of dry toast.

Victor, apparently untroubled by a delicate stomach, tucked into the plate of food Igor gave him as if he hadn't eaten in weeks. He ate with perfect manners, she noticed, holding the tines of his fork curved backward in the English fashion.

"Well," said Makepiece, checking the teapot. "That seems sufficiently steeped. I trust everyone is feeling a bit better after a night's rest." He looked up at Igor. "Go fetch Justine." The Bio-Mechanical grunted and shuffled into the other room.

"So," said Victor, pushing away his plate, "how long are we going to go on with acting as though this were a social occasion?"

"I see no reason why we can't approach this as civilized folks. Care for a spot of tea?" Makepiece's voice was as calm as ever.

"I care for an explanation," said Victor, glaring at Makepiece as the scientist handed Lizzie a cup of tea.

Just then, Igor shambled in, carrying Justine in his wiry arms. The hunchbacked monster and the ethereal girl—they looked like a lurid illustration she'd once seen in her copy of *The Hunchback of Notre Dame.*

Igor laid Justine on the chaise longue as though she were made of spun glass, then arranged the blanket over her wasted legs, and she murmured something to him that made the mal-formed face break into a smile.

"That's enough, Igor." Makepiece waved off his servant. "Take away the dirty dishes." In a much softer tone, he said to his daughter, "Feeling like a bit of breakfast, my dear?"

Justine shook her head. "Just some tea, thank you." She turned to Lizzie for the first time. "How are you today, Miss Lavenza?"

It was wrong to find that breathless sweetness so irritating. Mustering a smile, Lizzie said, "Much better, thanks. And thank you for the loan of your gown."

Makepiece poured cream and sugar into a cup and then handed it to his daughter on a china saucer. He seemed more composed now, or perhaps Lizzie had been imagining his nerves before. "Here is your tea, but you really should try to eat something."

Justine smiled at him as though he were the child. "In a little while, perhaps."

"How about you, Miss Lavenza?"

"I'm afraid I couldn't."

"Victor? Ah, he seems to have fallen asleep. Well, it was a long night, I daresay."

Victor was slumped in the chair, and for a moment, she thought that he had simply succumbed to exhaustion. Then she realized that something was wrong. "Oh, my God," she said, turning to Makepiece. "The injection—did you drug him? Is he...is he dead?"

"No, no, merely asleep. A necessary precaution."

"What do you mean?"

Makepiece waved this away as if it were a formality. "All in good time. By the way, you haven't inquired as to the well-being of your other friend."

*He doesn't know about Aggie and Byram, then.* "Is Will all right?"

"The younger Mr. Frankenstein is currently sitting in Professor Moulsdale's study." Makepiece pulled out his pocket watch and checked it. "He is being asked to explain what he was doing in a part of the school that is off-limits to students, at any hour past lights out, when students are meant to be in their rooms."

Lizzie closed her eyes for a moment, then composed herself. "What's going to happen to him?"

"In all likelihood, he will be expelled. So long as he keeps his mouth shut."

Lizzie let out a long breath. "Thank God."

"Indeed. It all could be much worse," said Makepiece, "and would be, if Moulsdale had *you* in his hands. You see, I'm afraid my colleagues know about how close you've become with Victor, and they will assume you know his secrets. Which is why it is imperative that you remain here with us."

"But she can't remain here indefinitely, Papa." It was difficult to read Justine's pale, gaunt little death's-head of a face, but she seemed wary, as if the worst was yet to come.

Moulsdale gave his daughter a cryptic smile. "Aye, as Hamlet said, there's the rub. Miss Lavenza cannot stay here indefinitely, and she cannot leave without risking... Well, let us say that Moulsdale and Grimbald can be quite Machiavellian when it comes to protecting the school's interests."

"If I can't stay and I can't leave, what do you suggest I do, Professor?" Lizzie was proud of how matter-of-fact she sounded, asking the question. There had to be a way out of this, and if she kept calm, she would find it.

"There is a solution. A good one, I believe, though it may sound a bit radical at first." Makepiece's smile was so warmly paternal that she felt the knot of tension in her stomach relax. "And the best part is, it will help you as much as it helps my Justine."

"Papa, no." Justine was shaking her head, as if trying to forestall some terrible announcement.

"What is it?" Lizzie looked to Justine, but the girl just looked back at her, eyes red-rimmed and weepy. "Professor. What do I need to do?"

"You just need to trust me, my dear girl. Igor and I can handle all the rest." As if this were the cue, Igor wheeled in a cart carrying a full set of surgical tools, including a bottle of chloroform and a mask.

The hard thud of her heart was like a fist knocking in her chest, and her vision narrowed until all she could see were the gleaming surgical instruments arranged on the tray. She knew that this was the work of her sympathetic nervous system, but her body was miles ahead of her brain, and she couldn't fit the pieces together in any way that made sense. She made herself speak. "I don't understand, Professor. What is the bone saw for?" It was ebony handled, of a size used for major amputations. "My arm is fine. There's no sign of infection."

"You know," said Makepiece, as if continuing some other, older conversation, "Justine always said she wanted me to perform the Bio-Mechanical process on her, but I refused. For years I insisted that I would perfect the formula that would allow her to regenerate her own limbs. But now my girl is a woman, and her life is passing her by."

She heard the shuffle and scrape of Igor's footsteps.

"Well done, Igor." Makepiece took the Galvanic Reanimator's brass helmet from his assistant's hands and contemplated it for a moment as if it were a work of art. "All that has changed, however, thanks to you." Makepiece pulled back his sleeves and began attaching the helmet to the leads of the etheric magnetometer. "Because of you, I know how to preserve her mind during the Bio-Mechanical procedure."

There had to be something she could say to pull him back. "I don't understand. I thought you admired me. I thought... I was your student, you said. How can you just tell me that you're going to kill me for parts?"

"No, no, my dear Miss Lavenza...Elizabeth, if I may." Makepiece appeared genuinely distressed as he took a glass bottle that glowed green with ichor and attached it to a length of rubber tubing. "You don't understand. It is because I esteem you so highly that I can do this. Look how Jack lives on in Victor. You will be like two sisters. My Justine always wanted a sister. She will be the dominant personality, of course, because I have been strengthening her mind with your ingenious device." He indicated the etheric magnetometer, now attached to the brass helmet. "Best to give her one last treatment, I think, before we begin."

*He's insane.* She had always thought that insane people were violent, raving and irrational, but now she could see that insanity could be a subtle illness. It could touch one part of the mind and leave the rest intact. It could cause a trusted friend to look you calmly in the eye and tell you with perfect courtesy that he was going to murder you.

"Papa," said Justine, her voice clogged with tears as Igor began to buckle the helmet's leather straps around her head. "Please, don't do this."

"Silly goose, this is what you always wanted." Makepiece approached his daughter with his surgically gloved hands held up in front of him, palms forward.

"Not like this." Justine managed to look pretty even while crying. "Not by robbing this girl of her life!"

"My sweet child, I wouldn't do this if Miss Lavenza weren't already doomed. If Moulsdale and Grimbald find her first, they'll use her to fix the queen. Either way, she's as good as dead."

He nodded at Igor, who moved over to the head of the bed. "Bring her into the laboratory."

"What? No!" Lizzie scrambled off the bed, jarring her injured arm and sending a sharp bolt of pain lancing through her whole right side. For a moment she just stood there uncertainly, barefoot and barelegged on the cold wood floor, as Igor shuffled toward her.

"Professor Makepiece," she begged as Igor grabbed her wrist in his rough, callused hand, "please don't do this! You were my father's friend!"

But all Makepiece did was pick the bone saw up from the floor and examine the blade. "Put her on the operating table," he said. "And use the restraints."

# 37

A ROLL OF GAUZE BANDAGES WRAPPED AROUND Lizzie's chest and lower abdomen was all that kept her from being completely naked on the bed. Justine, she saw, was covered only by a sheet, but then, her poor legs needed no restraints. She wondered if the other girl was as cold as she was; the heat from the radiators did not reach the middle of the room, and her arms and legs were covered with goose-flesh. From time to time, she gave an uncontrollable shudder.

The metal helmet of the large magnetometer had already been placed on Justine's head, and the smell of carbolic acid filled the small room. Makepiece was talking softly—to Justine, presumably—as he fiddled with the controls on the box, which was large enough to serve as a chair or a small table.

Victor was still slouched in a chair, unconscious. She closed her eyes, trying to hold back the tears that kept trickling down her face.

"Father, please, it's not too late to stop." Justine's whisper seemed oddly amplified. "You can still stop all of this."

Makepiece smiled down at his daughter. "But why would I want to?"

"Because if you kill her to remake me, then you and I will both be transformed into monsters."

*I think I like her after all,* thought Lizzie. *Though not enough to give up my life for hers.*

"Brace yourself."

There was a crackling sound as her magnetometer was turned on to its highest setting, and then Justine went rigid, her whole frail body racked with spasms as she made a sound of anguish so impossibly loud that it seemed to echo inside Lizzie's head. For a moment, everyone froze. *That's it,* she thought. *He'll have to stop now. There's no way he'll put his daughter through that kind of agony.* Then she saw Makepiece's face as he approached her. He was actually smiling, so fixated on his goal that nothing could move him.

"Your daughter—is she all right?"

"Of course, my dear," said Makepiece, calmly inserting a chloroform-soaked gauze sheet into a small steel basket. "Justine can endure a few moments of pain, knowing that a cure is finally at hand."

"Please, please, don't do this." She didn't want to beg. She wanted to be brave and strong and silent, but this was Makepiece, and maybe pleading would move him.

"There, there," he said, bending over her, suddenly paternal and soothing. "It's the anticipation that's the worst part, and that's almost all over now."

"You're wrong," she said. "The worst part is dying."

He sighed. "You're distraught. But just think: the improvements you helped me make to the Galvanic Reanimator are going to preserve your intelligence and even some of your memories. Isn't that a fitting memorial to your talents?"

"But I don't want a memorial!" She moved her head frantically from side to side, looking around the room for some kind of help. "Igor, please, don't let him do this to me! Victor, wake up, please help me!"

"Igor," said Makepiece, and now his voice was devoid of any emotion. "Hold her."

She felt strong hands clamping down on her head. *Will I even know who I am when I open my eyes again?* she wondered. *Will it be all Justine, or will there be anything left of me at all?*

"Try to take deep, even breaths," said Makepiece, fitting the mask over her face.

She tried to hold her breath, but in the end she had to inhale, and the overripe-fruit smell of the chemicals burned the inside of her nostrils. It would be just like going to sleep, except she would never wake up. Well, it was probably easier to go this way than to be shot. Yet she kept expecting a last-minute reprieve to come from somewhere. It was human nature, her father used to say, to hold out hope until the very end.

And then, just as her thoughts began to ripple and swirl from the cloying sweetness of the fumes, she heard a voice over her left shoulder, and suddenly there was reason to hope.

"Sorry to interrupt you, Doc, but I think you're going to have to let her go."

It was Jack! Somehow, he must have fought off the effects of the sedative.

"Igor, restrain him." Makepiece continued to hold the mask over her nose and mouth, squeezing the rubber balloon.

She had an absurd thought, as she looked up at Makepiece's face: *his nose hairs blend in with his mustache.* She giggled, hardly knowing why.

"Sorry," Jack was saying, gesturing with the scalpel in

a way that made it seem unmistakably like a weapon. "I really can't wait. Terribly impatient, me. It's a character flaw."

"Igor," snapped Makepiece, "handle this."

Igor, standing beside Justine, made a little grunting squeal of distress.

Jack grinned, as if this were all a lark. "Remove the mask, Professor, or I'll remove your thumb."

"Igor! What's wrong with you?" Suddenly, the mask was gone and she could breathe again. As her muddled thoughts cleared a little, she saw that Makepiece was snapping at Igor, who remained stubbornly by Justine's side, grunting to himself like a frightened animal.

"Stop that, I tell you! I gave you a command, you cretin!"

Igor grunted again and, this time, Makepiece turned to his daughter and said, "Justine, will you reason with… Justine? Justine?" The pale girl made no response, and Makepiece hurried over to her side. "Dear God, she's not breathing!" Raising his head, he looked desperately around the room. "My daughter… Victor, please, I need your help…"

Jack shook his head. "You got rid of Victor, remember?"

"Bring him back! Can't you see she's dying?"

The word seemed to galvanize Igor. Lizzie saw him lunge sideways at Jack, taking him by surprise, and then there was a scuffle and crash, the sound of something scraping across the floor, a door slamming shut. She couldn't see what happened next, but after a moment, Makepiece said, "Well done, Igor. You dumped him outside? Good, good. Well done. And now we will help Justine." Then the mask was placed over Lizzie's face again, and she couldn't tell whether her eyes were open or closed anymore, because there was a metronome made of light in front of her, ticking back and forth, back and forth, keeping time with her heartbeats, and then…no light and sound at all.

★ ★ ★

"You have to wake up! Wake up!"

The voice was Justine's.

"Miss Lavenza. Elizabeth!" The girl's voice was strong and insistent, not breathless at all.

Lizzie opened her eyes. "Why is everything so foggy?"

"There's an angry mob of villagers carrying torches and pitchforks just outside the front doors of the school. They've already set fire to the main hall, and now they're torching the laboratory. This whole place is made of old wood, and once it's alight, it will burn up fast. Can you sit up?"

"No." She blinked, trying to clear her vision, but the haze remained. She looked at her left wrist and saw that the restraint had been unbuckled. Her right wrist was free as well, and for some reason, her arm was not supported by a sling. "Yes. Maybe." She rolled over on her left side, which made her cough. "Where is everyone?"

"Never mind. We have to move quickly."

"I'm trying." She couldn't go anywhere wearing nothing but a few strategically placed bits of gauze, so she looked around till she saw a lab coat and managed to put it on, awkwardly buttoning it with her left arm. She coughed again, then realized that her vision was growing more clouded. "Justine... I think there's smoke in the room." Now she could smell it, too, and taste its harsh tang in the back of her throat.

"I know."

Lizzie shuffled over to the girl where she lay on the table, feeling no more nimble than Igor, and tripped. She fell hard, jarring her injured right arm.

"You all right? Elizabeth?"

Lizzie couldn't respond at first, as shock waves of pain raced up her shoulder. After a stunned moment, she realized what she was lying on: a body. She scrambled up and saw that it was Professor Makepiece, his brown eyes staring sightlessly over the rims of his spectacles. There was no sign of any wound, but she didn't need to check his pulse to tell that he was dead.

There was a shuffling sound behind her, and she gave a sharp, instinctive scream, and heard an answering sound—a grunting squeal. "Igor," she said, recognizing the sound before she spotted him hunched in a corner beside Justine's bed.

"You have to hurry now," said Justine. "Can't breathe…"

She managed to get herself up without touching Makepiece, and used the table to maneuver over to Justine. There were singed wires on the Galvanic Reanimator's helmet, which still covered the girl's head. The coppery tang of blood in Lizzie's mouth mingled with the bitter taste of smoke. "Are you all right? What happened?"

"My father's heart failed him. In more ways than one."

Lizzie tried to feel a pang of regret for the professor's passing, but all she could think was that his death had saved her life. "I am sorry for your loss," she managed.

"You don't have time to be sorry."

She was right; the air in the room felt uncomfortably hot, as if it they were standing near an open furnace. Lizzie tugged at the helmet with her left hand. "I can't budge it."

"Igor." Justine's voice was sharp. "Help her."

Igor lurched over and succeeded in yanking off the helmet. Lizzie looked into the girl's face. "Are you all right?"

Makepiece's daughter struggled for breath. *I might be, if we stop wasting time.*

Lizzie stared at her. "Justine…" She must be hallucinating from the smoke, but still…she could have sworn that Makepiece's daughter hadn't moved her lips. "How did you…?"

Justine turned her head. *Igor, you'll have to carry me out.* Igor moved as if galvanized, hoisting the slender girl into his arms, Lizzie moved as quickly as she could toward the door. She yanked her hand away before it came into full contact with the doorknob. Burning hot.

*Under the rag rug,* said Justine's voice in her mind. *The trap-door.*

Of course.

Lizzie pulled back the frayed kilim rug, revealing the trap-door beneath. *Please,* she prayed, for once in my life, *let me remember the right way.* She stumbled on the last step and fell, sprawling, onto the hard ground. The darkness pressed in on her, the cold, packed earth smell of the passageway reminding her of a grave. For a moment, she just remained there, thinking, *Maybe it's a nightmare.*

*You're all right. Get up.*

"You're not as nice as you like people to think you are," said Lizzie, getting to her feet.

*True. But then, who is?*

# 38

LIZZIE EMERGED FROM THE TUNNEL AND JUST stood for a moment, shivering as she watched fire consume the Ingold Academy of Medicine. Two of the four main buildings were already fully engulfed, and students were still spilling out of the other structures, crying and shouting out their friends' names.

It was all happening with astonishing speed, the bright orange flames rippling in the high arched windows of one building before leaping with a crackle to appear, weaving and darting, through the windows of its neighbor. There was a scuffle, and she turned to see Igor climbing out of the tunnel, his bent head covered with a fine dusting of soot and ash as he tried to protect the limp girl in his arms.

Alarmed, Lizzie checked the girl's pulse at the side of her throat. Still alive. Justine's eyelids fluttered.

*And with a brand-new talent, it seems.*

Before Lizzie could consider the implications, there was a sharp crack as fire claimed the upper floors of the School of

Surgery. In the next instant, the slate roof collapsed in on itself. Next, the fire dismantled the wooden additions of previous generations—beamed Tudor halls and elegant Georgian rooms and all the ingenious mechanical improvements of the present age—hundreds of years of incarnations, crumbling in a puff of smoke like a conjurer's trick. Soon all that would be left were the ancient stones of the abbey itself, the old bones of the original structure.

*Victor*, she thought. Had Igor killed him, or left him outside to die? Then she thought of Will and Byram and Aggie, possibly unconscious or dying in the fire. She buried her face in her hands.

"Miss Lavenza."

She turned, shocked to see Professor Grimbald emerging from the tunnel. His mustache was singed, and there was a patch of raw pink skin on his cheek where he had been burned. His army greatcoat had been flung over a pair of navy pajamas, which should have made him appear ridiculous. It did not. He was holding something in his arms—a body, draped in a blanket. For one, stomach-wrenching moment, she thought it might be Victor, but no, the shape was far too small.

"Miss Lavenza, can you help me? We need to get up the hill to help the others."

"Help you?" She gave a laugh that teetered on hysteria. "I can't even help myself."

Grimbald glanced at Igor, taking in the unconscious girl in his arms, then looked at Lizzie properly for the first time, taking in the tangled hair falling down her back, her bare legs visible beneath Victor's shirt.

"Take my coat." He shifted the body in his arms, managing to shrug himself out of the wool cape so he could hand it to her. "You need it more than I."

She draped the garment around her left shoulder, then used her left hand to draw the fabric over her injured right arm, sucking in a breath when the movement jarred the wound. His cloak smelled reassuringly of pipe tobacco and bay rum, and she thought for a moment of her father.

"Why are you being kind to me? I thought you just wanted me dead, so you could use me for spare parts."

He looked genuinely shocked. "What in the name of heaven made you think that?"

*Stop*, said the voice of reason. *Don't say anymore.* But she couldn't seem to stop herself. "Professor Makepiece told me everything. About how you murdered Victor. About the queen."

His nostrils flared above his mustache, but he gave no other sign of emotion. "I never meant to hurt Victor. I loved that boy like my own son. As for you, girl…I may not think you belong here, but I would sacrifice my own life before letting someone take yours. I'm a soldier, Miss Lavenza, not a killer."

She thought about her friends, trapped in the burning building. She should have gone back for them. She should at least have tried.

Grimbald's sharp eyes missed nothing. "You once told me you were as fit as any man to be a student here. Were you wrong?"

Her spine stiffened. "No."

"You don't sound very certain."

"No," she said more firmly, "I wasn't wrong."

"You've been injured."

"Yes." For some reason, his blunt assessment brought tears to her eyes.

"You've been injured, but you fought your way out of there."

"Yes." She blinked away the tears.

"Stop that sniveling. You're a soldier, Lavenza. A soldier and a surgeon. You're going to push down your own pain, and you're going to do what needs to be done."

"Yes, sir."

A hint of humor touched his steel-blue gaze. "And you're going to take all those things I said about women not being suited to medicine, and you're going to shove them down my throat. Am I right?"

That made her smile. "Yes, sir."

"I'm trusting you managed to find your way to a cadaver despite my admonitions."

"I…"

"Good." He turned, hefting the body in his hands a little higher. "There are wounded up there who need you." His hands and wrists, she now saw, were blistered from the fire, yet he was still managing to carry the blanket-covered body. She wondered whose corpse it was to matter to him so much.

As she followed Grimbald up the hill, she realized that he must have been hurt more badly than she'd realized. He was limping, and his bare feet were red and blistered, like his hands. Despite the additional strain on his arms, he was also holding the body away from him, which made her suspect that the burns did not stop at his ankles.

"How much of you is burned, sir?"

He glanced at her sharply. "More than a quarter of my body."

She tried to remember what she knew of burns. "We should probably disinfect the affected area, sir."

"We have more pressing concerns." He nodded toward the chaos of villagers and students outside the burning buildings.

They had reached the top of the hill, and now Lizzie could

see that wounded medical students were lying side by side with Bio-Mechanicals. Shiercliffe and some of the other nurses were attempting to separate the more seriously injured burn victims, and suddenly, she saw Aggie, her familiar red hair tumbling down her back as she pleaded with the crowd.

*Thank God*, she thought, *at least Aggie's alive.*

"You're not murderers," Aggie was telling one woman. "Reason with them, Mrs. Coombes. If we formed a bucket line, we might be able to put out the flames."

"They're monsters!" The woman's voice rose to a shriek. "Unnatural mechanicals!"

Lizzie looked where the hysterical woman was pointing, and with a surge of joy she saw Victor kneeling on the ground next to another victim of the fire. Victor was bare chested under his waistcoat and jacket, and the electrodes at his neck were exposed, but all his focus was on the unconscious student. He lifted the young man's wrist, feeling for a pulse, then moved his hand to check the student's throat.

That was when she realized: it was Will lying in the grass, eyes closed, face parchment white.

"Wake up, Will," Victor was saying. "You have to wake up."

"Will!" Byram shoved Victor aside and cradled Will's head. "What have you done to him?" Then he looked up and saw Victor clearly for the first time. "Dear God. It's you."

Victor looked haunted as he said, "He saved me—pulled me out of there. When I came to, he was lying here."

"Oh, God, Will." Byram's dark head was bent over his friend and his shoulders began shaking.

*Just a few hours ago, we were in the common room, joking around,* Lizzie thought. It felt like decades had passed since then.

Will coughed and opened his eyes. "Nick." It took Lizzie

a moment to realize he meant Byram. She'd never heard him called by his first name.

Byram's face lit up with an expression she had never seen before. "Damn, but you frightened me."

Just then, there was an explosion. This time, it was the School of Medicine's roof that collapsed. The crowd of villagers gave a roar of approval, some of the men raising their pitchforks and axes. Then someone shot off a rifle, and Grimbald stepped forward.

"Cease this nonsense this moment." He pulled back the blanket from the body in his arms. "Or would you also burn your queen?"

It took a moment for the crowd to recognize the short, stout old woman in a black head veil and high-necked black gown. There was a murmur from the crowd and then a shout.

"He's killed her!"

"They've murdered the queen!"

Grimbald bent down and whispered something in the queen's ear, and her eyes opened.

A burly, bald man wearing a laborer's neckerchief sank to his knees. "She's alive," he gasped, sinking to his knees.

"She's alive!"

The phrase was repeated as the crowd began to kneel.

"The queen!"

"Speak to us!"

"Hush!"

"Quiet!"

"She's going to speak!"

Lizzie looked at Grimbald, then at the small, portly figure in his arms. The high lace collar of her gown did a fine job of concealing the electrodes at her neck, but if you knew to look for them, they were there.

"The people wish you to speak, Your Majesty," said Grimbald.

The queen blinked, and then said, in a quavering voice, "Incendiary remarks architecture."

The crowd murmured.

"What was that?"

"Something 'bout incidents."

"Did that make any sense to you?"

Whatever these people were like as individuals, right now they were a mob, edgy and alert to any possibility of threat. Just like a flock of birds or a herd of deer, it would take only a small nudge to propel them all into a new and dangerous direction.

Lizzie looked at Grimbald, and she knew that everything hinged on what she did next. She could denounce him, and the school. True, she might lose her best chance at working in the field of medicine which interested her the most. Justine would likely remain an invalid for the rest of her life. As for Victor…she did not know what would happen to him if the mob learned the truth. Yet if she spoke out, the guilty would be punished and no more innocents would be sacrificed in the name of science. All Lizzie had to do was reveal the queen for what she was: a malfunctioning Bio-Mechanical.

Or she could make a different choice.

She stepped forward. "The queen said to cease these incendiary actions. Her Majesty is not well, and has come here for treatment." Her voice rang out, too loud, too female, too American.

For a moment, no one spoke. Then there was an excited buzz of voices from the crowd, but the tone was one of wonder, not agitation.

Grimbald nodded at her. "Well done, Lavenza."

"The bluestocking crumpet gavottes colonial," said the Bio-Mechanical Queen Victoria.

The burly bald man stepped forward. "What does Her Majesty say now?"

"She says you must help to put out the flames," said Lizzie. Out of the corner of her eye, she saw Victor, shouldering his way through the crowd to get to her. "You must help the wounded."

The queen fixed her with a beady look. "Expedite wanton impertinence," she said, sounding more than a little peevish.

"Indeed, she will, Your Majesty," said Grimbald, with a small, approving smile. "In fact, she already has." Queen Victoria seemed mollified by this, and now the buckets of water were making their way to the blaze.

It wasn't going to be enough to save most of the buildings. As she looked around, hoping to see some big horses pulling a firewagon, she noticed Moulsdale for the first time, huddled under a blanket and cradling a flask of whiskey. "It's all gone," he said in a broken voice. When he raised his chin, there were tear tracks running through the soot on his round face.

"Not all of it, Ambrose," said Shiercliffe, reaching her hand out for the flask. She tossed back a long swallow, then wiped her hand on the back of her sleeve before handing back the flask. "We can rebuild. We can start over."

"I can help," Lizzie said, an idea forming so quickly she wasn't entirely sure what she was about to say next.

"You?" Moulsdale sat up straighter under his blanket, gathering something of his old dignity. "What help could *you* possibly provide?"

"Professor Makepiece is gone." She felt no emotion as she said it, but Moulsdale clearly did—he sagged again, as if her very words were deflating him. "You'll need someone who knows engineering, and I... I'm my father's daughter."

"You're not suggesting we make you head of the engineering school?" Shiercliffe's voice was sharp with sarcasm. Even with her lace veil torn and her face streaked with soot, she managed to look forbidding.

But Lizzie was not intimidated. "No," she said, still feeling the same, strange sense of battlefield calm. "I know I still have a lot to learn. But I can help out until you find a replacement."

"She's right, you know," Grimbald said, his face showing the strain of carrying the Queen in his arms. "There. Down you go." With a grunt of pain, he settled her beside Moulsdale. The Bio-Mechanical monarch regarded the head of medicine with some suspicion.

"You," she said to Moulsdale. "You are familiar with the old saying, 'He who constipates is costly'?"

"I am afraid not, Your Majesty."

"Imbecile. Do not disturb us for at least an hour." She took a deep breath and closed her eyes.

Moulsdale turned to Grimbald. "You really think we ought to trust her in Makepiece's lab?"

"Yes." Grimbald glanced at Lizzie and added, "I underestimated her before. And she's right—we need her skills."

Lizzie smiled at Grimbald, startled but pleased at the compliment. "I will do anything I can to help the school," she said, as much to Grimbald as to Moulsdale, "but there's something I want in return."

Shiercliffe and Moulsdale made nearly identical sounds of outrage, but Grimbald held up his hand. "Name it."

"I want Victor reinstated as a student in the school of surgery."

Grimbald frowned. "Miss Lavenza, I don't see how a Bio-

Mechanical—even an unusually high-functioning specimen—can possibly be capable of attending our university."

"You want to see how it's possible?" Lizzie asked, meeting his eyes with a hard stare. She let Grimbald's cape slip off her right shoulder, revealing the bandage on that arm. "Victor operated on me last night—I was shot, and he stopped the bleeding and saved my life. He is fully capable of becoming a surgeon, Professor. Either he comes back as a student, or neither of us does."

Grimbald examined Victor's work, nodding slowly. Then his gaze drifted to a point behind Lizzie, and a small, unexpected smile lifted the ends of his mustache. "I believe there's someone waiting to speak with you."

Lizzie turned.

"Elizabeth." Victor was staring at her as if he couldn't believe his eyes. "You're all right." His face was darkened with ash and soot, and a bandage, stained with red, was wrapped around his dark hair. In the flickering light, he might have been a pirate straight out of a penny dreadful tale.

Striding toward her, he said, "I thought— I feared—" He closed his eyes for a moment. "But you're all right?"

She nodded. "Justine helped me."

"There's a streak of white in your hair." He touched her right temple.

"Never mind that, how is your head?" Her hand hovered over the bandage.

"A bit dented, but not broken. How did you escape from Makepiece?"

"He died," she said. "It was his heart."

Victor grew very still. "Before he could change you?"

"Yes. I'm fine, really," Lizzie said reassuringly. "Aside from the gunshot, of course. What about you? How did you get out in time?"

Victor's smile was wry. "Jack seems to have a talent for getting out of scrapes." His hand reached up to cup her jaw, his fingertips cool against her flushed skin, and then, in front of all the world, he kissed her. It was a kiss fueled as much by grief as by passion. Yet her arms went around his neck, clinging to him. He tasted of ash and salt, and then just of himself.

"Elizabeth," he said, pulling away. His thumb brushed something from her cheek—dirt or tears, perhaps both. "I am so sorry." He kissed her again, a quick, fierce press of his mouth to hers.

With a rush of embarrassment, Lizzie realized that she had just been kissing Victor in full view of Grimbald and the other heads of school. She glanced back and was relieved to see them deep in their own discussion. "I suppose we'd better go and see who needs help," she said.

"All right." He stroked the side of her cheek with his thumb and then strode away, moving among the wounded before kneeling beside a medical student whose hands had been blackened by the fire. She stared after him for a moment, hit by a wave of fatigue that made her eyes lose focus. A sharp cry startled her back into alertness.

"This one's alive," shouted Aggie. "I need a doctor!" Lizzie looked around to see which doctor she was calling, and then realized: *she's talking to me.* Stepping carefully in her bare feet over the jagged pieces of fallen masonry and broken glass, she made her way to Aggie's patient. There were bits of paper everywhere—letters and class notes, some of them still floating almost magically as they burned into ash. *This must be what a battlefield looks like,* she thought.

"I can't stop the bleeding," said Aggie, and suddenly Lizzie realized the patient was Sabina Hillier.

"Where's it coming from?"

"Not sure… Wait. Let's get her skirts up." Aggie lifted Sabina's skirt, revealing the puncture wound high on her right calf. A tip of white bone was protruding from the young woman's stockinged leg, and even though the blood wasn't gushing out, it was bleeding steadily.

"All right, we need to apply a tourniquet." Lizzie looked around, trying to think of what to use. "How quickly can you get one of your corset laces loose?"

"This is faster." Aggie ripped a strip from her petticoat and started to tie the fabric just under the girl's knee.

"Not there," said Lizzie. "Tie it above the knee, instead. There's only one bone in the upper leg, so it will be easier to tighten it there."

Aggie started over, and Lizzie found a stick to help tighten the tourniquet. As they worked together, something cold and wet fell on her hand—rain, she thought at first, but then she looked up and realized it was snow, the first of the season. By the time they were done and she could look up again, a thin powder of white was coating the ground. "Aggie." She reached out and brushed a flake from her friend's hair. "Look. It's snowing." Her breath was misting in the cold morning air.

"Now there's a bit of luck."

Lizzie looked back at the school. There wasn't much left of the upper floors of the main building, but the Gothic arches of the medieval abbey were still standing, and even though the sun was hidden by the clouds, the pale sky was now brighter than the dying embers of the fire.

When she turned back to her patient, she found that two medical students were carrying Sabina away on a stretcher.

Aggie was moving away, too, a knowing smile on her face, and it was the smile that made Lizzie look back to find Victor, kneeling beside her. The bandage around his head was streaked with dirt now, and should be changed soon, and a purple bruise was forming under his left eye, but he looked surprisingly happy.

"Look who made it out in one piece," he said, and Lizzie saw that Makepiece's black cat was nuzzling her cheek against Victor's thigh and purring.

"I wonder how many lives she has left," said Lizzie, running her hand over the cat's fur, which was dusty but remarkably unsinged.

"I don't know, but I suspect that Aldini's probably going to outlive us all." He stood up, holding out his right hand to Lizzie. There were cuts and scrapes on his palm, and a second-degree burn mark on his wrist was already beginning to blister.

"I don't want to hurt you," she said.

He grasped her hand, pulling her up beside him. "That's supposed to be my line."

She was looking down at their entwined fingers when he placed his left hand over them, the metal cool against her skin.

"Aren't we a pair," he said.

She nodded, lost for words. Yesterday, she had been a medical student and a scientist. She had no idea what the future held for her now.

She knew one thing, though: whatever else she was, she was not alone.

# EPILOGUE

LIZZIE AND VICTOR STOOD BY THE RAIL AS THE *Sea Swallow* steamed toward London, watching as the city's wharves and warehouses came into view. It was an unseasonably mild day for January, with no sign of the dense, malodorous yellow-gray fogs that Lizzie had read about in the papers.

"Look, that's St. Paul's Cathedral," said a well-dressed woman to her young child, lifting the girl so she could see the famous dome. A boy in a flat-brimmed cap was sitting perched on the rail itself, waving at the enormous ocean liner that was just ahead of them. It all looked a bit precarious; besides the big steamship and their own boat, there were other, smaller vessels all crowding into the same narrow stretch of river.

Victor smiled down at her. "You're frowning. Are you wishing we'd taken the train in with the others?"

"Oh, not at all." Lizzie tilted her head back to look him in the eye. Unlike most of the other men, he was formally dressed in a top hat and long coat, the high, starched collar hiding the electrodes at his neck. "This is so much nicer."

"I must admit, I thought this might be a little less... crowded." They both looked out at the water, and found they were eye level with the lower decks of the larger ship. As the distance closed, they could see the name of the boat— the *Lucania*—and third-class passengers waving, from men in flat-brimmed caps to women in kerchiefs, with throngs of children running and weaving among the adults.

Suddenly, the boat's whistle blared, making Lizzie jump.

"You all right?"

She glanced back at Victor. "I keep thinking we're going to ram into each other."

"I think the captains know what they're doing. Tell me, is that the sort of ship that brought you over from New York?"

She nodded. "The *Oceanic* was a little bigger, if you can believe that."

"Hang on, we're coming up to Tower Bridge." He looked at her. "Trust me?"

"Of course. Why do you ask?"

"Because I want to do this." Putting his gloved hands on her waist, he lifted her with easy strength and settled her on the railing. In the late-afternoon light, the towers glowed a reddish gold.

"All right," she said, glancing nervously at the other passengers, "that was lovely. You can let me down now." Victor's hands were still at her waist, and he was standing so close behind her that she could feel the warmth of his body all along her back.

"Why, am I hurting your arm?"

"No, that's healing up nicely."

"Then stop wiggling. You want to see the bridge open, don't you? I thought that was the whole point of going by boat."

"Not the *whole* point."

"No," Victor agreed with a smile. "There were other considerations."

"I was a bit surprised that you agreed to this, you know. I thought you would write back telling me, no, what are you thinking, consider your reputation if we travel without Aggie and the others as chaperones…"

Victor looked away, frowning. "That's what I should have said."

"Stop that! After everything we've been through, I can't believe you're still going to act as though I'm some sort of princess and you're a hideous leper."

"I might as well be."

"Don't be ridiculous. You are Victor Frankenstein, Ingold's top student in the School of Surgery, and I'll punch anyone who says different."

"You might have to punch my father, then. And possibly my mother, as well."

"Why? Weren't they thrilled to have you back?" After the fire, Lizzie made a deal with Moulsdale and Grimbald: come up with a way to reinstate Victor as a student, and she would keep silent about the queen's condition. Victor's parents were informed that he had been in a coma, and not dead as they had originally been told. The uncomfortable question of whose body had been interred in the family crypt was not discussed, although Victor himself had his suspicions. In any event, Victor's unexpected recovery on the night of the fire was deemed a medical miracle, no doubt because miracles were not meant to be explained.

"I wouldn't say that my parents were thrilled, no. They seemed…quite pleased at first, but my mother never stopped frowning when she looked at me. She said there was something different about me now. My father was more direct. He asked if they used any of that Bio-Mechanical flimflammery on me."

Lizzie winced. "What did you say?"

"I said, 'How do you want me to respond, Father?' He told me he wanted me to reassure him that there was nothing un-natural about me." Victor's jaw clenched.

"Did you tell him the truth?"

Victor shook his head. "He didn't want the truth. At one point, I asked him what he wanted to do about the body interred in the family tomb under my name. He said he didn't care to discuss the matter. His precise words were, 'Why must you insist on dwelling on this unpleasantness?'"

"That's so..." Lizzie trailed off, shaking her head. "So there's still some stranger buried there?"

"Well, 'buried' isn't quite the right word, as it's a big marble mausoleum, but yes, I suppose so." Victor paused, then added, "Although I suspect that it might not be a stranger at all."

Lizzie frowned. "I don't understand."

Victor touched his left arm, as though he felt a sudden ache there. "I haven't run into any Bio-Mechanicals that feel... familiar. Connected."

"Oh." It had never occurred to her to wonder before, but of course—something must have happened to the rest of Jack.

He looked away. "In a way, it's sort of fitting that his remains are there. I don't hear him so much now, not as a separate voice, anyway. Either he's fading away, or...perhaps he's just become a part of me."

Lizzie had no idea what to say to that. Perhaps it should have unsettled her, the thought that the two had become one, but instead she was happy to think that Jack might not have just vanished from existence. Should she say that out loud, or would that make Victor think she preferred Jack?

"On a lighter note," he said, turning back to face her, "I think Will's getting used to having a brother again."

"I'm so glad. I thought about you a lot, you know."

"I thought about you, too."

"Really? Then why didn't you write me?" After Ingold had burned down, when most of the other students had returned home to their families, Lizzie and Sabina, the Jamaican girl, had gone to stay with Aggie in her mother's cottage. "I kept waiting for a letter."

"I know. I thought—maybe it was better to give you a chance to think things over. And then you wrote me, and I figured you had your chance. And here we are."

She cupped his jaw in her hand. "Is that your attempt at making it up to me? Woefully inadequate. You owe me letters. Long, heartfelt letters. With feelings in them."

He pressed a kiss to her palm. "You'll get them. But you might want to stop looking at me like that."

"And why is that?"

He squeezed his hands where they held her waist. "Because the bridge is opening, and if you don't look over there, you're going to miss the whole thing."

As she watched, the lower portion of Tower Bridge began to lift in the middle, creating an arch for the large steamship to pass through. It really was a marvel of engineering, and she wondered if, on one of their days off, they might be able to see how the mechanism worked.

When she turned around, she was surprised to see that Victor had been watching her, not the bridge. His expression remained pensive as he helped her back down on her feet again, and she wondered what had caused the shift in his mood. Perhaps he was thinking about his parents again. She tugged at his white cravat. "So, Mr. Frankenstein. Prepared to become a student again?"

"I hope so. I still need to pinch myself from time to time to believe that I have my old life back."

"Not quite your old life," she said, indicating the approaching city.

"True. It's going to be a lot noisier and smoggier, for one thing. A bit rougher."

"I can't imagine anything rougher than the past five months."

Victor smiled down at her, touching the streak of white at her temple. "You have a souvenir."

She adjusted the brim of her hat, tugging it down. "Don't remind me. Maybe I'll dye it."

"Don't you dare. It's very distinguished."

"Don't you mean old?"

"I meant to say it's very handsome. And yes, St. Roch's can hardly be worse than what we've already gone through. But the truth is, I don't really care where we are, as long as we'll both be studying together. And—" he hesitated, taking a deep breath "—if you'll have me, Elizabeth, I'd like us to be partners in more than medicine." Reaching into his jacket pocket, he pulled out a small jeweler's box.

She stared up at him, caught completely off guard. *"What?"*

"I'm sorry," he said, his face falling as he took her silence for hesitation. "I just realized—I wasn't thinking—it's just a promise ring, you understand. But if that seems too much of a commitment, given what I am… I will always require a supply of ichor on hand to survive, and there are other considerations…"

She stopped his words by standing on tiptoes and pressing

a kiss to his mouth. "There," she said. "I don't give a fig for what you are. And now you're thoroughly compromised, so you'd better go ahead and promise me." She held out her left hand, and he placed a tiny emerald ring on her index finger.

Out of the corner of her eye, she saw a man with pince-nez and a goatee reading a newspaper with the headline: *Queen Victoria Refuses to Meet Kaiser Wilhelm*. Tensions were rising between the two countries, but that was a problem for another day. For now, she and Will and Aggie and Byram were all going to be together again, studying in London. As soon as they were properly set up, Justine was going to get a chance at a new Bio-Mechanical body. It might seem wrong, given the terrible things that had happened a short time ago, but she was almost absurdly happy.

Tucking her hand into the crook of Victor's arm, Lizzie turned to watch a seagull as it banked and turned. A gust of wind threatened to blow her hat off, and for a moment, she felt as if she were the one flying, the whole bustling city of trolleys and horse-drawn carriages spread out beneath her. From a bird's-eye view, the *Sea Swallow* must seem like a toy boat in a pond, and the new clock tower at Westminster Palace no more than a child's sand castle. As they grew closer, the city would grow large and real and complicated, but for now, with the grace of a little distance, London felt like a marvelous playground, the reward for all the trouble they'd endured.

Resting her head against Victor's broad shoulder, she watched as the gull raced them to shore.

★ ★ ★ ★ ★

# ACKNOWLEDGMENTS

THIS BOOK HAD A VERY LONG GESTATION, SO there are many people who have helped and advised me along the way. My thanks to:

My editor, Michael Strother, for enthusiasm, faith and excellent questions. And to my other editor, Lauren Smulski, for taking me on and helping make the book better.

My agent, Jennifer Laughran, for dry humor, warm praise and patience.

My colleague, Shelly Bond, who was there at the book's very beginning, for encouraging me to make the book more political.

Brilliant artists Al Davison and Alain Mauricet, for reading early drafts and sketching the characters.

Ruthie Knox, Mary Ann Rivers, Darrah Cloud, Rachel Pollack, Liz Edelstein and Carol Goodman, for sage feedback along the way.

George Hanna and Bryan Lucier of the Steamship Historical Society of America, for arcane research assistance.

Laura Silverstein, for listening to me kvetch and moan until I had an epiphany, and then listening to me kvetch and moan all over again.

Mark Stapylton, for endless hot dinners, daft Britishisms, and the mistaken belief that everyone learned to write with a fountain pen.

Ziva Kwitney, for countless emotional and literary tune-ups.

And a special debt of gratitude to Elinor, my favorite mad scientist, for the macabre delight of watching *London Hospital* with me (*Casualty 1906, 1907* and *1909* in the UK).